* * *

His every move was so purposeful, so sure and so determined.

His body was so strong and hard and big. Everything he did, he did better than anyone else.

He had a law degree from Stanford, and a business degree from one of those snooty eastern colleges. He'd shot a charging rhino, wrestled alligators. He'd made love to the most beautiful women in the world, taken his father's millions and turned them into billions.

And once, long, long ago, he had been six years old. A little boy. A boy who woke up in the middle of the night and went into his baby brother's room.

Where he had been found the next morning, out cold on the floor, a large bloody bruise on the left side of his head.

And the baby—vanished. Forever...

* * *

CONVENIENTLY YOURS: Cast of Characters
A Bravo Family Saga

THE NINE-MONTH MARRIAGE
—Cash Bravo and Abby Heller

MARRIAGE BY NECESSITY
—Nate Bravo and Megan kane

PRACTICALLY MARRIED
—Zach Bravo and Tess DeMarley

MARRIED BY ACCIDENT
—Melinda Bravo and Cole Yuma

THE MILLIONAIRE SHE MARRIED
—Jenna Bravo and Mack McGarrity

THE M.D. SHE *HAD* TO MARRY
—Lacey Bravo and Logan Severance

THE MARRIAGE AGREEMENT
—Marsh Bravo and Tory Winningham

And watch for...

MARRIAGE: OVERBOARD
—Gwen Bravo McMillan and Rafe McMillan
(Weekly serial at www.eHarlequin.com)

THE MARRIAGE CONSPIRACY
—Dekker (Smith) Bravo and Joleen Tilly
(Coming in October only from
Silhouette Special Edition)

CHRISTINE RIMMER

THE BRAVO BILLIONAIRE

Silhouette Books

Published by Silhouette Books

America's Publisher of Contemporary Romance

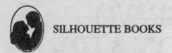

SILHOUETTE BOOKS

ISBN 0-373-48436-4

THE BRAVO BILLIONAIRE

Copyright © 2001 by Christine Rimmer

All rights reserved. Except for use in any review, the reproduction
or utilization of this work in whole or in part in any form by any
electronic, mechanical or other means, now known or hereafter
invented, including xerography, photocopying and recording, or in
any information storage or retrieval system, is forbidden without
the written permission of the editorial office, Silhouette Books,
300 East 42nd Street, New York, NY 10017 U.S.A.

All characters in this book have no existence outside the imagination of
the author and have no relation whatsoever to anyone bearing the same
name or names. They are not even distantly inspired by any individual
known or unknown to the author, and all incidents are pure invention.

This edition published by arrangement with Harlequin Books S.A.

® and TM are trademarks of Harlequin Books S.A., used under
license. Trademarks indicated with ® are registered in the United States
Patent and Trademark Office, the Canadian Trade Marks Office and in
other countries.

Visit Silhouette at www.eHarlequin.com

Printed in U.S.A.

Dear Reader,

I can hardly believe it. This book,
The Bravo Billionaire, marks the eighth in
my series of stories about the Bravo family.
The first seven books, as you may know,
appeared in the Silhouette Special Edition line.
I started out thinking I was going to write only
three Bravo books—the stories of three cousins:
Cash, Nate and Zach.

So much for what I started out thinking. Your
response to the Bravos has been so enthusiastic,
how could I help but write more Bravo tales?

With *The Bravo Billionaire,* I had a great time
creating a new branch—the L.A. branch—
of the Bravo family. They are fabulously
wealthy, and they live in a huge hilltop Bel Air
mansion called Angel's Crest. The hero, Jonas,
is the man who has everything—except love,
family and companionship. He swears he
doesn't want those things. But that's before his
mother's will forces him into close contact with
Emma Lynn Hewitt. Emma, a west Texas dog
groomer with a heart as big as her home state,
is determined to make of Jonas a kinder, gentler,
better man....

I do hope you enjoy this bigger-than-ever Bravo
tale.

All my very best,

Christine Rimmer

For Steve,
always.

Chapter 1

Jonas Bravo did not like to wait.

Make no mistake. He knew how to wait. He was actually quite good at waiting—when he considered the wait worth it, when it would mean a fat return on an iffy investment, or a plum contract in his pocket.

He *could* wait and he *had* waited. But he refused to wait unnecessarily, when waiting, as he saw it, would get him nowhere.

People who made Jonas wait unnecessarily never did it more than once. Because the famous Bravo Billionaire had ways of showing his displeasure. He could do it with a look, with a certain inner stillness—a look and a stillness that made the object of his displeasure wonder just what kinds of scary, crazy things Jonas Bravo might do if pushed too far. They all knew the stories about him, about what he and his family had been through when he was a child, and the wild things he'd done during the earlier years of his manhood. So they wondered—and they worried.

And they didn't displease him again.

Apparently, the receptionist at McAllister, Quinn and Associates, Attorneys at Law, had been warned not to make Jonas wait. Young, faultlessly groomed and predictably gorgeous, she glanced up when he got off the elevator, which opened about ten yards from her desk. Her stunning china-blue eyes went round as dinner plates as she regarded him across the expanse of parquet floor and good Oriental rugs.

She bounced to her feet. "Mr. Bravo. This way. Mr. McAllister is waiting for you." She bustled to the big elaborately carved double doors that led to the inner sanctum and quickly pulled one of the doors wide. Jonas gave her a curt nod and went through, heading down the wide wood-paneled hallway toward Ambrose McAllister's corner office.

The receptionist rushed along in his wake. "Um, Mr. Bravo. Mr. McAllister asked me to show you to the—"

Jonas froze her in her tracks with a sharp backward glance. "I can find my own way."

"Oh. Well. Of course, whatever you—"

"Thanks." He didn't have to look behind him again to know that she had returned to the reception area where she belonged. He passed a few secretaries' nooks. Ambrose's minions looked up, muttered swift, respectful, *Hello, Mr. Bravo*s and went back to what they were supposed to be doing.

Ambrose's door opened just before Jonas reached it. The lawyer who had handled the personal legal affairs of the Los Angeles Bravos for over three decades didn't miss a beat.

"Jonas. Here you are." Ambrose took Jonas's hand

and shook it. Though he was well into his seventies now, Ambrose McAllister's handshake remained firm and his bearing proud. "So good to see you." Silver brows drew together in a perfectly orchestrated expression of concern—*real* concern, in this case, Jonas knew. Ambrose honestly cared for the members of the Bravo family and had become something of a family friend over the years. But he *was* a lawyer, and a damn good one. Good lawyers knew how to manufacture appropriate expressions on demand.

"How *are* you?" Ambrose asked.

"Fine."

Ambrose shook his head sadly. "I know I already said this at the funeral, but Blythe *is* missed. Greatly."

Jonas dipped his head in acknowledgement of the lawyer's sympathetic words. Since the death of his mother, Blythe Hamilton Bravo, seven days before, Jonas had heard a lot of condolences and he'd done a lot of nodding in acknowledgement.

"And how is that beautiful little sister of yours?"

"Mandy's doing well."

Jonas's sister, Amanda, had been adopted by his mother two years ago. At the time of the adoption, Jonas had been furious at Blythe. The way he saw it then, she had no business taking on an infant at an age when most women were well into their grandmothering years.

But Jonas's fury had not lasted. How could it? Mandy was…special. She had the knack for melting even the hardest of hearts. Jonas still wasn't sure how she'd done it, but somehow, the sprite had managed to break down even his considerable defenses. Within a month of the baby's coming into their lives, Jonas had accepted his fate. He loved his little sister and he would do anything for her.

Ambrose leaned closer and spoke more confidentially. "You know, don't you, that if there is *anything* I can do, not only as your family's attorney, but as a—"

"I do know, Ambrose. And I appreciate your thoughtfulness."

"Damn it." Ambrose lowered his voice even further. "She was too young. Only sixty…" Blythe had died of a particularly virulent form of leukemia. It had struck suddenly and killed her within two months of the original diagnosis. "I know it must be difficult, for both you and the child."

"Honestly Ambrose, we're managing."

The lines of concern between the silver brows deepened—and then relaxed. "Well. I'm glad to hear it." Ambrose clapped Jonas on the arm and let go of his hand. "Let's move on to the West Conference Room, shall we? We'll be more comfortable there."

It was not Jonas's intention to become comfortable. "Ambrose. What's this about?"

Instead of answering, Ambrose said mildly, "Right this way." He herded Jonas around the corner and down another wide hallway. Jonas allowed himself to be led, though he disliked having his questions evaded almost as much as he disliked being made to wait.

And this was not the first time Ambrose had refused to give him answers on this subject. Last Friday, when the lawyer had called to set up this meeting, he would only say that it concerned Blythe's will. Before her death, Blythe had asked Ambrose to invite Jonas to his offices. Certain issues required discussion.

"What issues?" Jonas had demanded.

"Monday, Jonas. My office. Two o'clock?"

Jonas had tried to get the lawyer to simply come out to the house or drop in at Bravo, Incorporated. Ambrose had held firm. He'd said that Blythe had felt that a neutral setting would be better for everyone.

"Why a neutral setting?"

"I'll explain it all on Monday."

"Ambrose. Who the hell is *everyone?*"

But Ambrose wouldn't say. "Please forgive me, Jonas. You'll have all the information you need on Monday. At my office."

Jonas had let the lawyer off the hook. After all, the man was only doing his job, following his client's wishes—the client being Jonas's exasperating mother, in this case. Who could say what Blythe Bravo had gotten up to in those last grim weeks before her death?

"All right, Ambrose. Monday. Two in the afternoon." He'd ended the call.

So now it was Monday. It was 2:04 p.m.

And some answers had better be forthcoming.

"Here we are," Ambrose said cheerfully, stopping before another pair of carved double doors. A bronze plaque on the wall to the left of the doors read, West Conference. Ambrose slid adroitly around Jonas and opened one of the doors. "After you."

Jonas didn't see the kennel keeper until he'd stepped over the threshold.

She was sitting all the way down at the end of the table, in one of the twelve high-backed cordovan leather swivel chairs, her back to the west wall, which consisted of one huge pane of glare-treated glass. Beyond the glass lay Century City in all its smoggy splendor, high-rises shimmering beneath the August sun.

The kennel keeper, whose name was Emma Lynn Hewitt, wore a snug-fitting jacket the color of orange sherbet. If she had a shirt on under the jacket, Jonas couldn't see it. He could, however, see a tempting swell of cleavage. Her silky pale blond hair curled, soft and shiny and unrestrained, around her very pretty face. It wasn't long, that hair, only chin-length, but still, it always managed to look just a little mussed, a little wild. Though the conference table blocked his view, he knew without having to look that her tight, short skirt would be as orange as her jacket. And that her shoes would have very high heels and open toes.

By all rights, Emma Lynn Hewitt *should* have looked cheap. But somehow, she didn't. Somehow, she managed to look…sweet. Sweet and way too damn sexy. She also came across as if she meant business. He didn't know how she did that, though he suspected it had to be in the way she held herself—chin high, slim shoulders back.

Just another of Blythe's strays, he reminded himself, a little nobody from a bend-in-the-road town in Texas. As it had turned out, his mother's investment in the woman's dog grooming and boarding enterprise had been a profitable one, so he couldn't fault the perky Texan on that count. Still, he had always disliked her.

Though he effortlessly schooled his face to betray nothing, Jonas noted a certain raw feeling in his gut— as if someone had taken a cheese grater to it. He was thinking the obvious: What in hell is she doing here? But he didn't speak the question aloud. It would have been bad strategy, was too likely to betray his dismay. The Bravo Billionaire, as any dedicated tabloid reader would avidly tell you, did not experience feeble emotions like dismay.

There was a blue folder in front of the kennel keeper. And one in front of each of the two chairs to her left and to her right. Her folder was open. She'd apparently been reading the contents while she waited for him and for Ambrose. Judging by the strange, rather stricken look on her face, what she had read must have surprised—even shocked—her.

The cheese grater sawed another layer off the lining of Jonas's stomach. He realized he no longer felt the urge to ask what she was doing here.

No. All at once, he didn't even want to know.

Ambrose said, "Jonas. You've met Ms. Hewitt?"

"I have."

The woman started to stand, then appeared to think better of the move and kept her pretty little butt in the chair. She swallowed. And nodded.

He nodded back.

"Have a seat." Ambrose had him on the move again, ushering him down the long table toward the chair—and the folder—to the right of Emma Hewitt.

Jonas sat. Ambrose crossed behind the kennel keeper and took the chair to her left.

Once settled in his chair, Ambrose opened the folder on the table in front of him and then reached in his breast pocket and pulled out a pair of half glasses. "Ahem. Jonas." He put on the glasses. "Before she died, your mother made a few changes to her will. She asked that I call you and Ms. Hewitt in together to discuss them."

Jonas sat very still.

Peering over the tops of his glasses, Ambrose gestured at Jonas's folder, which Jonas had not yet allowed himself to touch. "If you'll just read the sections I've highlighted, I'm sure Blythe's wishes will be made clear to you. And of course, I'll be right here to answer any questions you might have."

"I see," said Jonas.

The kennel keeper said nothing. She was a splash of hot orange in his side vision.

"Please," Ambrose urged. "Have a look."

What damn choice did he have? Jonas opened the folder and began to read.

A quick scan of the highlighted passages and he had the picture.

Once he understood his mother's insane intention, he closed the folder and said, very quietly, "All right. I've read it."

"Good." Ambrose glanced at the dog groomer. "Ms. Hewitt? Have you looked through your copy?"

She nodded.

"Well," said Ambrose. "As I said, please feel free to ask any—"

"Wait a minute," said Jonas. Ambrose waited. "I think we need to make certain we're all in agreement as to exactly what it says here."

Ambrose announced, "An excellent idea." Then he fell silent—as if he expected Jonas to explain the will that he had prepared.

Not a chance. Jonas said nothing. And the dog groomer from Texas kept her mouth shut, as well.

Ambrose realized the task had fallen to him. "Well," he said. "Ahem. As you can both see, the issue here is custody—the custody of the child, Amanda Eloise Bravo."

Ambrose laid it all out for them.

"The will now requires that you, Jonas, must marry Ms. Hewitt here—and cohabit with her at a location of her choosing—for one year. During that year, you and Ms. Hewitt are to have joint physical and legal custody of your adopted sister. At the end of that year, should either you or Ms. Hewitt choose to divorce, then full custody of Amanda will be yours, Jonas. However, if you fail to marry Ms. Hewitt within three weeks of your mother's death—and to *remain* married to her for one full year—then custody goes to Ms. Hewitt.''

Ambrose paused to remove his reading glasses. He took a snowy white handkerchief from his breast pocket and began wiping the lenses of the glasses. He did all this while looking at Jonas, a look that managed to be both regretful and unwavering. ''And should you try to contest the will, all legal expenses incurred by Ms. Hewitt in fighting your suit will be paid by your mother's estate.''

Ambrose put his handkerchief back in his pocket. He folded his glasses and set them on top of his folder. ''That's about it,'' he said with a grim smile.

Jonas stared at the lawyer. He kept his face composed, but he was thinking that he would really enjoy breaking something. Yes. He'd very much like to rip something in two.

Blythe's death had caused him far more pain than he would ever admit. And the pain—which he knew to be grief—had taken him completely by surprise. He was thirty-six years old, after all, and had believed himself immune to grief since well before his tenth birthday. Apparently, he had believed wrong. Because deep in his most secret heart, he missed his harebrained mother terribly.

And somehow, the fact that he'd ended up missing her so damn much made this ridiculous alteration to her will all the more infuriating. She'd set this whole thing up and then managed to die without dropping him so much as a hint as to what he was in for.

''I do have a question,'' said Jonas.

Ambrose lifted those silver eyebrows.

Jonas hit him with it. ''Did my mother honestly imag-

ine that paying Ms. Hewitt's legal expenses would keep
me from taking this issue to court?''

Ambrose put on his most solemn expression. ''I can't
say what your mother imagined. But I hope you realize
that the will before you is perfectly legal and binding.
If you fail to marry Ms. Hewitt within the next two
weeks, you could very well lose custody of your sister.''

''I *could.* But I won't.''

Ambrose looked suddenly weary. ''Jonas. Who can
ever be truly certain of any outcome when it comes to
the vagaries of our legal system? I'm only saying that if
you fail to abide by the terms your mother has set out
here, the possibility is quite good that when the matter
comes before a judge, Mandy will go to Ms. Hewitt.''

Jonas waved an impatient hand. ''Look, Ambrose. We
both know that my mother spent a number of years in
one of L.A.'s finest psychiatric hospitals. I could put up
a valid argument for mental incompetence.''

Ambrose's expression had become downright reproachful. ''You could, but I think you know that that
kind of an argument would be unlikely to hold up under
scrutiny. Your mother's clinical depression occurred
three decades ago. Two of the doctors who attended her
then are still living. At your mother's request, I con-
tacted both of them and each assured me he would be
willing to testify that she completely recovered from her
condition. And she never relapsed. She was…eccentric,
perhaps. But she was also in full command of her fac-
ulties when she set out these changes to her will.''

Jonas gave the lawyer his coldest stare. ''I suppose
you'll attest to that.''

Ambrose did not waver. ''I certainly will. Jonas, I
promise you, I did discuss this at length with Blythe.''

''Did you make any effort to talk her out of it?''

"As a matter of fact, I did. But she wouldn't be swayed. She insisted that she wanted these changes in the will. She said she honestly felt they were for the best—for Mandy. And for you."

Jonas said nothing for a full count of ten. When he did speak, he was pleased to find that none of the rage shimmering through him could be heard in his voice. "All right. So you're saying you believe these changes are going to stand up in court."

"Yes."

"And my mother's estate provides the funds so that Ms. Hewitt here can make certain they do."

"Exactly," said the lawyer, still regretful—and still firm. "Jonas, I'm sorry, but I've said it before and I'll say it once more. If you fail to marry Ms. Hewitt, your sister could very well end up in her custody."

Jonas allowed the corners of his mouth to lift in a humorless smile. "That is, assuming Ms. Hewitt is *willing* to become Mandy's guardian."

"Well, yes," the lawyer allowed, looking slightly uncomfortable at that suggestion. "And I did point that out to Blythe. If Ms. Hewitt is unwilling, then these changes become meaningless."

If Ms. Hewitt is unwilling…

The words seemed to ricochet tauntingly in Jonas's brain.

Of course, Ms. Hewitt was willing. His mother wouldn't have done this without Ms. Hewitt's consent and active participation—would she?

She did it without mine, he thought, and then shoved the idea into the back of his consciousness.

Miss Hewitt *was* willing. She had to be. She'd seen her chance to catch herself a rich husband and she'd jumped at it.

Jonas turned his head just enough to give the woman in orange a withering stare. She stared right back, defiant, but a little too pale—as if she were every bit as surprised by this news as he.

Fat chance. The bitch probably dreamed up the whole insane scheme and kept after his mother on her damn deathbed until she agreed to it.

Blythe had always wanted the one son she had left to marry and give her a few grandchildren to spoil. But Jonas had made it poignantly clear to her that he never would. A man's family, he had learned at a very young age, provided big opportunities for incalculable loss.

No, thank you. He ran his own life and he answered to no one and he couldn't lose what he didn't have. And he was…content. He liked his life just as it was and saw no reason to change it.

But evidently, his mother had decided to give him a reason.

She'd known his one weakness, the weakness she herself had created by adopting the sprite. His weakness was Mandy. And Blythe had used Mandy—just as this dog groomer from Texas had used *her*.

"Ambrose," Jonas said. "Thank you for answering my questions. Now, I have a few things to say to Ms. Hewitt. Leave us."

Ambrose hesitated. Jonas knew why. The lawyer thought it unwise to leave the little Texan alone with him right then. After all, one could never be sure what the Bravo Billionaire might do when provoked.

In the past, when he'd been younger and less disciplined and his people did not do what he asked them to do, Jonas sometimes threw things. Expensive, very breakable things always worked best. Things that shattered satisfyingly on impact. Once, he'd thrown a Ming vase through a stained-glass window. And on another occasion, he'd tossed a Tiffany bowl at a marble fireplace. He had also, during what he thought of as his Great White Hunter phase—a short phase, really, though the scandal sheets liked to make much of it—stood his ground to bring down a charging rhinoceros. Beyond the rhino, the rumor mill had it that he'd wrestled alligators and won, and that he'd gone at a grizzly bear with only a hunting knife for a weapon.

He never denied such rumors. Why should he? Being considered fearless and unpredictable had always worked in his favor.

"Ambrose," he said, making a warning of the name.

The lawyer shifted nervously in his chair and turned his worried gaze on the dog groomer. "Er, Ms. Hewitt. Perhaps *you* have some questions?"

And, right then, for the first time since Jonas had entered the room, the dog groomer spoke.

"It's all right, Mr. McAllister." Her voice was a honey-eyed Texas drawl. It crept along Jonas's nerve endings, setting off little flares of annoying heat right below the surface of his skin. He found himself staring at the tiny mole, low down on her right cheek, midway between her pert nose and her soft lips.

"You go on now," she said. "I'll talk to Mr. Bravo alone."

Chapter 2

Emma Lynn Hewitt could see that the lawyer was worried for her. And maybe he had good reason to be. It was probably plain crazy for her to volunteer to be alone with Blythe's scary, overbearing son right then.

But come on. What could the man *do* to her, really? If looks could kill, she'd have keeled over stone dead when he walked in the room and spotted her sitting there.

He was probably going to say some ugly things. He might even throw something—that big crystal water pitcher on the credenza over there, or maybe even a swivel chair or two. She had heard he sometimes threw things. But to the best of her recollection, she hadn't heard that he threw things at *people*.

No. She didn't believe he would do anything to physically hurt her. He would just use words to try to beat her into submission. Well, sticks and stones, as her aunt Cass used to tell her all the time. Words, even the mean, hard words of Blythe's big, scary son, could not hurt her unless she allowed them to.

This was *not* her fault, whatever Jonas Bravo chose to believe.

The lawyer coughed. "Ms. Hewitt. Are you certain about this?"

Emma reached out and gave the lawyer's sleeve a nice little pat. "I'll be just fine. Don't you worry 'bout me."

"Well. If you're positive..."

She beamed him a giant-sized smile. "I am."

Mr. McAllister picked up his glasses and stood. Emma watched the tall, kind-faced lawyer walk down the length of the big conference table and go out through the double doors. It was a lot easier looking at the lawyer than at the man who sat beside her with tension radiating off him like steam.

As soon as the door swung shut behind the lawyer, Blythe's son spoke in that arresting voice of his, which was soft and deep and just a little bit rough, like velvet when you rub it against the grain.

"This is your doing, isn't it?"

Emma sucked in a big breath through her nose. One of her best groomers and dearest friends, Deirdre Laventhol, was real big on yoga. In yoga, you always breathed through your nose.

It was supposed to be calming.

Emma slowly let the breath back out the same way she'd sucked it in. It didn't help much. She still felt angry and confused and a little bit afraid of the man who was so determined to blame her for something she had not done. Her heart was beating too fast. Just racing away in there. And her hands felt clammy. She had to resist the urge to rub them on her skirt.

Oh, Blythe, she thought miserably, *why* did you do

this? I told you I plain don't like him. And he never liked me. I *told* you that.

But Blythe hadn't listened. She was like that sometimes, once she got an idea in her head.

Emma would say, "I don't like him and he doesn't like me, either. He always gives me that narrow-eyed suspicious look, like he's waiting for me to grab the silver and run—or to cheat you out of every last penny you own."

And Blythe would say, "You're wrong, Em. You don't understand him. Naturally he's hostile with you. He doesn't want to admit the attraction. But you're the woman for him. And he's just right for you." And then Emma would groan and order her friend to forget that idea. Blythe would always drop the subject about then, which left Emma assuming that her friend had gotten the message.

To assume, Aunt Cass used to say, *makes an* ass *out of* u *and* me, *too…*

Emma made herself look at him again. It wasn't that he was so *hard* to look at. He was a big, muscular man in a high-dollar suit with a burning look in eyes that sometimes looked blue—and sometimes looked black as the darkest part of the night.

Not handsome. No. His features were too blunt, too…basic for that. Not handsome, but *masculine*. Emma had always thought that the air kind of vibrated with male energy whenever Jonas Bravo was around— even when he wasn't ready to chew nails like he was now.

Women were supposed to be drawn to him "like moths to a dangerous flame." Yep, she'd actually read that about him somewhere. Blythe had told her that his "playboy phase" had come to an end around the time he turned thirty. But during it, he'd dated the most beautiful and charming women in the world. Famous actresses. The stunning youngest daughter of one the nation's oldest and wealthiest families. Not to mention a long string of starlets and showgirls from both the good old U.S. of A. and abroad.

Blythe had often mentioned oh so casually to Emma that in the past few years, Jonas had hardly dated at all. Blythe had said she considered that a good sign. She thought he was ready for the real thing, for the love of his life.

In fact, looking back now, it seemed to Emma that Blythe was constantly bringing up Jonas whenever she and her friend spent time together. It seemed, looking back, that she should have been warned that Blythe might do something crazy like this—something bizarre and extreme, something just next door to desperate, to try to get her and Jonas hooked up.

But then, Aunt Cass'd had a saying for that, too—the one about hindsight always being twenty-twenty.

"Don't give me that wide-eyed innocent look," the Bravo Billionaire growled. "Admit it. You set this up."

Emma folded her clammy hands in front of her, yanked her shoulders up tall and looked him dead in the eye. Think bold, she told herself silently. Think one hundred percent completely unconcerned about the mean things this awful man is saying to you.

"Didn't you?" he taunted.

She answered truthfully—as if the truth was going to do her a bit of good with this wild man. "I most certainly did not. I didn't know a thing about it until I walked in here today."

One side of his mouth curled lazily into a sneer. "Fine. Then get out of the way."

Now, what did that mean? She was not *in* his way. If he wanted to leave, he could get right up and go. "Pardon me?"

"Get out of the way. Refuse to marry me and decline to assume custody of my sister. If you won't marry me and you won't take Mandy, either, there's no problem. She'll go to me."

The wild man had a point. Nothing said she *had* to go along with Blythe's crazy scheme. Mr. McAllister had said the same thing a few minutes ago, hadn't he?

If Ms. Hewitt is unwilling, then these changes become meaningless....

Emma could just...do what Jonas Bravo wanted her to do. Get out of the way. Mandy would go to him and— well, wasn't that the right thing, anyway?

Emma opened her mouth to tell him she'd do what he wanted: step aside. Make no claim on Mandy.

But the words got caught in her throat.

A little over five years ago, right after her aunt Cass died, Emma had first come to L.A. She'd brought nothing but a few cheap clothes, a battered Ford four-door, a degree from a two-year business college in Odessa and a burning will to succeed, to make a mark upon the world. She'd taken a job at a famous deli/restaurant on Fairfax—just until she could figure out what kind of business she intended to make her mark in.

She'd met Blythe Bravo the second morning on the job, when Blythe had dropped in good and early for a black coffee and a plain bagel to go. It was immediate, the feeling of connection between them. It didn't matter that, on the surface, they had nothing in common. Emma had looked in Blythe's eyes and known that things were going to be all right, that she didn't have to be secretly terrified anymore. She had lost her dear aunt Cass and she was starting all over. But she had found a rare friend. That gave her confidence, made her certain that she really *was* going to make it in L.A.

"When can you take a break?" Blythe had asked the third time she walked into the deli and found Emma behind the register. "We'll do lunch."

After that, they met two or three times a week—for lunch, to take in a movie, sometimes just for coffee and serious girl talk. Within a month, Emma was telling Blythe her idea of creating a special kind of "pet retreat." And Blythe was offering to be her backer....

Emma owed Blythe so much. She did want a chance to repay her—not only for giving Emma her start, but also for holding out her hand in true and binding friendship.

Some people—like the man who was trying to push her around right now—would say that Emma came from nothing. Her daddy and her mama had both been dead by the time she was five. She'd been raised by a goodhearted, sun worshipping, platitude-loving aunt in a double-wide in a dinky, dusty west Texas town called Alta Lobo.

So yes. Some folks might say she was a nobody from nowhere.

But in Alta Lobo, in her aunt Cass's double-wide, Emma had learned a number of important lessons. One of them was that if you can possibly give a friend what she wants, you do it.

Emma longed to do just that, to grant her dear friend's dying wish.

But, oh, Blythe, she thought miserably. Oh, Blythe, why *this*? *Anything* but this, to get myself hitched up to this awful man.

Emma was not sure she could bring herself to do it—even for the very best friend she had ever known.

The awful man in question was still watching her through those blue-black angry eyes, waiting for her to give in and say she'd do what he demanded.

Well, she wouldn't do what he demanded.

Not right yet, anyway.

He would just have to wait a little longer, because she needed time to think.

Emma slid the strap of her bright orange purse high onto her shoulder. She closed the folder on her copy of Blythe's will and tucked the folder under her arm.

Jonas said, "Where do you think you're going?"

"Out of here."

"Oh, no you don't. Not yet."

Emma pushed back the big leather swivel chair and stood. "This is a lot to think about. I'm not makin' any snap decisions, Mr. Bravo. I need a little time."

He looked at her as if he'd like to pick her up and toss her through that big window behind her. And probably all he'd do was smile in satisfaction when she hit the pavement ten stories below. "Time, Ms. Hewitt, is the thing we don't have much of. You've got to marry me in the next two weeks—or you've got to prove to my satisfaction that you do not intend to try to claim custody of my sister."

"Excuse me," Emma Lynn Hewitt replied. "I do *not* have to marry you. And I do *not* have to prove a single thing. I have to decide whether or not I can bear to grant my dearest friend's dyin' wish. And if I decide I just can't make myself do that, since to do it I'd have to marry up with you, *then* I have to figure out whether or not I want to fight you for custody of sweet little Mandy. Those are the things that I *have* to do and they are *all* that I have to do. And in order to do them, *I need some time.*"

She turned for the door, thinking as she headed for it that maybe refusing to marry him would be the best way to go. She could refuse—and then fight to get Mandy put in her care. Maybe that would satisfy her obligation to her friend. After all, the little sweetheart would certainly have a better chance at a happy, normal life with her than she ever would with Jonas Bravo.

"I'll see you in hell before I let you have Mandy," the billionaire said before she got out the door.

Emma paused, turned to face him again and gave him her sweetest, brightest smile. "I'm sure you know just where you're headed, Mr. Bravo. But whether I'll be there to meet you remains to be seen."

"We are not finished here."

"Oh, yes we are. I told you. I need a little time to think."

"How much time?"

"A few days. Then I'll get back to you."

He started to stand. She didn't stay to watch him come at her.

She darted through the door, yanked it closed behind her and headed for the exit as fast as her three-inch heels would carry her.

Chapter 3

Jonas dropped back to his chair as soon as the blonde in the orange suit bolted from the room. There was nothing to be gained by following her right then, nothing left, at that moment, to use on her save physical force. And contrary to what a lot of people believed, Jonas Bravo never used physical force. He only let them think that he might.

A few days, she had said. She would get back to him in *a few days.*

What the hell, Jonas wondered, was *a few days?* Two? Three? Four?

He felt caged. Caught. Bested.

Made to wait.

He sat alone in the conference room for several minutes, giving his frustration a chance to abate, at least minimally. Eventually it occurred to him that Ambrose would be ducking back in shortly, just to check and make sure he hadn't torn the little dog groomer limb from limb.

Since Jonas felt zero inclination to deal with Ambrose again right then, he left the lawyer's offices and went to Bravo, Incorporated, which was housed in the Bravo Building, a towering forty-story structure of pale granite and dark glass in downtown L.A.

He had a meeting at three with the project manager of a certain upscale shopping center that was due to open in six weeks. It was a project in which he'd made a significant investment of Bravo, Incorporated funds.

The meeting lasted two hours. When it was over, Jonas hardly remembered a thing that had been said. He kept thinking about the kennel keeper, about that word, *few,* about what she had really meant when she said it.

About how damn long she intended to make him wait.

After the meeting, there were calls to make and papers to sign. He spent an hour and a half closeted with one of his assistants, going over correspondence and contracts he needed prepared.

By seven, he had had enough.

He was supposed to meet the CEO of a certain Internet startup group for dinner at L'Orangerie. But he knew it would be pointless. Right then, he couldn't have cared less if every decent tech stocks opportunity out there passed him right by. He had his secretary call and reschedule the appointment for Thursday night.

After all, Thursday was three days away. He'd have his answer from the dog groomer by then—wouldn't he? Weren't three days *a few?* He flexed his thick, powerful fingers, thinking how pleasant it would be to wrap them around Emma Lynn Hewitt's neck and begin to squeeze.

Before he left his office, he downloaded the file on the Hewitt woman into his laptop. There might be something in it he had missed, something he could use to get her to start seeing things his way and to do so as quickly as possible.

Jonas kept files on all of his mother's various causes and charities, as well as on her friends and acquaintances. In spite of what had happened thirty years ago, when she'd lost a son and a husband within months of each other and spent four years in psychiatric care as a result, Blythe Bravo had ended up a trusting soul. She was also a person who felt a responsibility to leave the world a better place than she'd found it. Jonas felt no such responsibility. And he made it a point not to trust anyone until they had proven they were worthy of trust.

He'd had the Hewitt woman investigated five years ago, when she'd first popped up in his mother's life. Once he'd read the report provided by his investigators, he'd come to the conclusion that, while she rubbed him the wrong way personally, Emma Lynn Hewitt was probably harmless.

Harmless. He scowled as he thought the word.

And he felt bested again.

By a blonde with big breasts and inappropriate shoes.

On the way home, in the quiet back seat of the limo, he studied the file. He was still going over it when he reached Angel's Crest, the hilltop Mediterranean-style house in Bel Air where Bravos had lived for three generations. Jonas owned a number of houses and apartments, among them a hunting lodge in Idaho, a small villa in the south of France and a penthouse on Fifth Avenue. But he considered Angel's Crest his home.

Palmer, who ran the house, greeted him at the door. "Good evening, sir."

Jonas nodded. "Palmer." He handed the butler his

briefcase and the laptop. "Put these in the study, will you?"

"Certainly."

He told Palmer that he'd have a light meal in the small dining room in one hour and then he climbed the curving iron staircase to the second floor.

He visited his sister in the nursery. As usual lately, she babbled nonstop. It was all two-year-old talk, that phase of language development consisting in the main of instructions and demands.

"Jonah"—she always called him Jonah, he assumed because the "s" at the end of his name was as yet beyond her—"come here," and "Jonah, sit there," and "I like this story. Read it to me."

He felt better. Soothed. Just to see her round, smiling face, her mop of dark curls and those big brown eyes. To know that she was safe. Always, he would keep her safe. He employed round-the-clock security at Angel's Crest. What had happened to his brother would never happen to the sprite.

She did say, "Jonah, I want Mama," looking up at him solemnly, with absolute trust—and a sadness that tore at his heart.

He took her on his lap and explained for—what was it? The tenth time? The eleventh?—that Mama had been very sick and had to go away and would not be coming back.

Claudia, the nanny, reappeared at eight-thirty with a shy smile and a questioning look.

"Bath time," he told Mandy. "Be good for Claudia."

With a minimum of fuss, Mandy allowed him to say good-night.

He stopped in his private suite of rooms for a quick shower and a change of clothes, then he went on down to the smaller of the house's two dining rooms, where Palmer served him his meal. He ate, reminding himself not to dwell on how damn huge and quiet even the small dining room seemed without Blythe's easy laughter and teasing chatter to liven things up a little.

The food, as always, was excellent. He told Palmer to be sure to give the cook his compliments.

It was after ten when Jonas retreated to his study, a comfortable room of tall, well-filled walnut bookcases, arching leaded-glass windows, intricate crown moldings and big, inviting chairs upholstered in green and blood-red velvet. He sat at his inlaid mahogany desk, opened the laptop and dug into the file on Emma Hewitt again.

What he read didn't tell him any more than he already knew. She was an orphan from Texas with two years in a nowhere college under her belt. At the time he'd had her followed she had been twenty-one, working the morning shift at the restaurant where she'd met his mother and keeping a stray cat and an iguana in her studio apartment, unbeknownst to the landlord. There had been no boyfriend at the time, though Jonas thought he remembered Blythe telling him there had been some-one last year—or was it the year before?

And if there had been someone, was that someone still around? Jonas shrugged. Since he didn't have a clue what the woman planned to do about Blythe's will, he supposed, at this point, that the possibility of a boyfriend was pretty much a nonissue.

The file—or, technically, the series of files—contained a number of pictures snapped on the sly by one of the detectives he'd hired. There she was in her little white blouse and short black skirt, grinning at a customer, her order pad poised, pen ready to roll. And there she was at some Hollywood nightspot, with what looked like a strawberry daiquiri in front of her and a wide, happy smile on her face. And at Venice Beach, wearing cutoff shorts, a skimpy little nothing of a top and inline skates, being pulled along by a high stepping, beautifully groomed pair of Afghan hounds. In that picture, he couldn't help but notice, her legs looked especially long, her breasts particularly high and full.

Jonas sat back for a minute and rubbed at his eyes. Full breasts and long legs, he reminded himself, were not the issue here.

He looked at the screen again, began bringing up the pictures one by one, noting as he did so that the love of animals came through good and clear. The cat and the iguana. The Afghan hounds. A shot taken in a pet store, with a parakeet on her head and a mynah bird on her shoulder, one at what looked like Griffith Park with someone's tiny Chihuahua balanced on her outstretched hand.

Jonas stared off in the direction of the limestone mantel, thinking of Bob and Ted, the pair of miniature Yorkshire terriers his mother had owned. Though as a general rule, Jonas had no liking for small dogs, Bob and Ted had surprised him. They were smart and obedient and not particularly prone to yipping. And they'd been fiercely dedicated to their mistress.

Not too long ago, Bob and Ted had moved in with Emma Hewitt. Blythe, in the hospital then for what would be her final stay, had told Jonas she wanted the woman to have the dogs. He hadn't objected. He'd figured that the kennel keeper was an appropriate choice to inherit the Yorkies. At that point he hadn't known that the Yorkies weren't everything his mother intended for Emma Lynn Hewitt to inherit.

Jonas scrolled through the personal information file.

The phone numbers had not been updated. There was the number of the deli where she'd worked five years ago, and the number of that studio apartment in East Hollywood where she'd lived when she first came to Los Angeles.

He had the current numbers somewhere, didn't he? The business number, at least, should be easy enough to find in the phone book or online.

But he knew where he would be certain to find them both.

He got his palm planner from his briefcase, left the study and went upstairs again, this time to his mother's suite. In her white, pink and gold sitting room, which Blythe had recently redone in grand Louis XVI style, he picked up the phone. As he'd expected, she had the kennel keeper on autodial. There were three numbers: home, mobile and business.

Jonas wasn't about to talk to the Hewitt woman on his mother's phone in his mother's rooms with his mother's things around him, reminding him all too poignantly of what he'd told his little sister earlier that evening: that Blythe was not coming back.

He found a white leather address book in a drawer beneath the phone and got the numbers from it, entering all three in the palm planner. Then he returned to his study.

He sat down at his desk again, picked up the phone and glanced at the serpentine clock on the mantel. It was nearing eleven. He called the home number.

She answered on the third ring. "Hello?" He heard fuzziness in her voice, a slight slurring, as if he'd wakened her. An image flashed through his mind: the kennel keeper in bed, wearing something skimpy and eyeflayingly bright, the Yorkies snuggled in close, one on either side of her.

He blinked to clear the image. "How long is 'a few days'?" he asked in a gentle and reasonable tone.

Evidently, the sound of his voice was enough to banish sleep, because she said his name—his *given* name—flatly, all traces of fuzziness gone. "Jonas."

"How long is 'a few days'?"

He heard her take in a breath and sigh as she let it out.

He began again. "I asked how—"

"I heard you." She heaved another sigh. "I'm sorry. I just don't know yet. I have to think this over. I have to...consider what all this will mean."

"What's to consider?"

"Plenty. I know you don't believe me, but this was a pretty big shock to me, too."

He tapped his palm planner lightly on the desktop. And then he set it down and stared at it, not really seeing it, reluctantly coming to grips with the fact that he *did* believe her. He'd seen the look of sick astonishment on her face when he'd entered that conference room and she looked up from the new will. He'd wanted to think she was in on his mother's scheme. But now he'd had some time to mull it over, he supposed he had to admit that that angle just didn't add up.

If she'd been in on it, why would she be giving him the runaround now?

She wouldn't—unless she was hoping he'd make her an offer.

Fine. An offer, then. "How much do you want?"

She didn't say anything.

So he went ahead and started laying it out for her.

"Sign an agreement giving up all claim to my sister and I'll pay you—"

"Don't even tell me."

"Why not?"

"Because I can't take any money from you."

"Of course you can take money from me."

"No, I cannot."

"Why?"

"Blythe was my *friend.* I can't take money to betray my friend."

"This is no betrayal."

"To me it would be. I'm sorry. I won't take your money."

"It seems to me, Ms. Hewitt, that if there *has* been any betrayal in this situation, it's already occurred."

"Pardon me?"

"The way I see it, my mother betrayed all of us. You. Me. And Mandy, too."

"Your mama did not betray anybody." There was indignation in her voice now. Indignation with a Texas twang.

Jonas rubbed the bridge of his nose. He was getting a headache between his eyes. "All right. Perhaps I've used the wrong word. How about *tricked?* Is that better? Or maybe just plain old screwed."

"Blythe Bravo did not—"

"She screwed us, Ms. Hewitt. Or at least, she screwed *me.* And my sister."

"That is not true. Your mama absolutely without a doubt wanted only the best for you. And for your sister."

"The best. That would be *you?*"

There was silence on the line again. Finally, the dog groomer said softly, "Well, I guess your mama thought so, now didn't she?"

Jonas picked up his palm planner and then set it down. He looked at the spines of the books on a shelf about ten feet from where he sat—all gold-tooled leather, beautifully bound. A number of harsh remarks were passing through his brain, things to the effect that he did not consider a woman who'd been raised in a trailer in some place called Alta Lobo, Texas, to be the best thing for him.

He wisely did not let those remarks get out of his mouth.

"So what do we do now, Ms. Hewitt?"

"Well, I don't know yet."

"Ms. Hewitt, you *are* trying my patience."

"You know, I got that. I got that loud and clear."

"I could make you a very rich woman."

"Well, that is real nice. But no thanks. I mean it. I truly do. I will call you, as soon as I can make up my mind what to do."

Right then, he heard one short, sharp bark. "Oh, sweetie," she said. For a minute, he thought she was talking to him. But then she *did* talk to him, and he realized the difference. "That was Ted. He says hi."

Damn her. She had the dogs. She wasn't getting him or his sister.

"You have yourself a nice night now," she said.

"Ms. Hewitt—"

"'Bye..." The line went dead.

Jonas pulled the phone from his ear and stared at the thing. She had hung up on him.

Nobody hung up on him.

Except, apparently, for Emma Lynn Hewitt.

He called again the next night. She told him that no, she had not made up her mind yet.

He hung up on *her* that time, because he knew if he didn't that he would end up raising his voice. Jonas Bravo was not a man who ever needed to raise his voice.

After that, he gave up on phone calls. For two entire days he did nothing about the problem, though it seemed to him that the whole time a clock ticked away relentlessly inside his head, counting down the seconds, the minutes, the hours, moving him closer to the date by which he had to be married to Emma Lynn Hewitt—or possibly lose Mandy.

By the time those two days had passed, it was Thursday night, ten days since Blythe's death, eleven days before the deadline set out in the will. And three days since the meeting at McAllister, Quinn and Associates.

Three days. If that wasn't a damn *few,* he didn't know what was.

And he'd come up with another angle, another offer he could make her.

Friday, he spent almost three hours closeted with his top corporate attorneys, getting the whole thing in order, lining out exactly what he was willing to do and how it would be accomplished. One of his secretaries typed the thing up.

By then, it was after four. He put the finished prospectus in his briefcase and called for the limousine. A half an hour later, his driver pulled up in front of Emma Hewitt's place of business in Beverly Hills. The driver got out and opened Jonas's door for him.

Jonas paused on the sidewalk to reluctantly approve the clean, simple lines of the building. The large plaque on the wall by the big glass door gave the establishment's name: PetRitz. And a brief description of the services provided: Grooming, Boarding, Animal Care. Not a billboard or a tacky picture of a pink poodle in sight.

He gave Ms. Hewitt no credit for this clear display of good taste. In Beverly Hills, tackiness was not permitted, at least not when it came to places of business. No billboards, no neon, no cheesy advertising art of any kind.

Jonas knew that it was his mother's money and influence that had landed the dog groomer in such a prime location. And it was Blythe's connections with wealthy animal owners all over the Southland that had brought the Hewitt woman a huge clientele right from the first.

But he also realized that it was the Hewitt woman herself who had somehow managed to keep all those fickle, demanding, big-spending pet lovers coming back. From the day it opened its doors, PetRitz had been a success. Everyone who was *anyone* took their precious pedigreed pooches to Emma Lynn Hewitt's exclusive pet salon.

And Jonas had been standing on the sidewalk long enough.

He strode up to the glass door and went inside, where he was instantly bombarded with color and sound.

The waiting room boasted hibiscus-pink walls, lots of big, soft chairs and a skylight overhead that let in plenty of light. There were plants everywhere, palms and huge, trailing coleus, ficus trees, giant ferns and big-leaved begonias. Among the greenery, there were several fish tanks in which bright-colored tropical fish darted about and a couple of huge terrariums where large reptiles basked under glowing heat lamps. A few customers were waiting, sitting in the fat chairs, looking prosperous and contented, thumbing through copies of *Pet Life* and *People*. Their animals waited with them. A dignified Irish setter, patient on a leash. A Burmese cat hissing in a carrier. A parrot that kept whistling and asking, "What's the matter, pretty baby?"

Music was playing. The Dixie Chicks, he thought. Which figured.

And he could also hear bird sounds—not including the parrot. Piped in or real? Had to be recorded. He didn't see any birds perched among the greenery.

There was a reception counter opposite the door. Behind it, at a computer, sat a plus-sized young woman with hair the same color as the counter: jet-black. The young woman wore a smock the same screaming pink as the walls.

Jonas crossed the room and stood right in front of her. She punched up something on the keyboard, scowled at the screen, then looked up at him, ditching the scowl for a welcoming smile. "Hi there. Need some help?" She wore a rhinestone in her nose, three studs in her left ear and four in her right. On her ample pink bosom rode a black lacquer name tag with pink metallic lettering. Pixie, it read.

"Well, Pixie. I'd like to speak with Emma Lynn."

The black brows inched closer together on the wide forehead. "Wadeaminute. I know who you are. Blythe's son. The one they call the Bravo Billionaire."

"Call me Jonas. Please."

Pixie beamed in pleasure. "All right. I'll do that. Jonas."

"May I speak with Emma Lynn?"

Pixie heaved a huge sigh and her rather close-set eyes grew scarily moist. "I'm so sorry—about Blythe. She was the greatest."

"Yes. There was no one quite like her. Now...would you get me Emma Lynn?"

"Oh. Yeah, sure." Pixie got up from her chair and went to a black door on her side of the counter. "I'll tell her you're here. Won't be a sec."

Pixie was gone for more than a sec.

Approximately two minutes after she disappeared, another woman in a pink smock came through the black door and took Pixie's place behind the counter. Jonas continued to wait, moving to the side every time a client approached to pick up a pet or drop one off.

It occurred to him after he'd been standing there for about five minutes, listening to twittering birds and the Dixie Chicks and then after the Dixie Chicks, to Sheryl Crow, that he felt like a salesman. Someone in pet supplies, briefcase in hand, waiting for the owner to come out and grant him a few minutes of her precious time.

Waiting.

His least favorite activity.

And he'd been doing it a lot lately. Way too much.

Because Emma Lynn Hewitt wouldn't make up her damn mind.

There was another black door on his side of the counter, on the same wall as the one behind it. A third woman in a pink smock came out of that door twice to take pets from the people at the counter. It didn't take a Mensa candidate to figure out that the two doors led to the same hallway.

When the second hand on the big wall clock behind the counter had gone around for the seventh time since Pixie had left him, Jonas decided he'd had enough. He turned around and went through the door on his side of the counter.

"Uh. Excuse me," the woman behind the counter called after him. "You can't go back there...."

He ignored her and pushed the door shut behind him.

He was in a long, pink hallway, with three black doors on either side, and one at each end. Sheryl Crow and the birds continued to serenade him.

He stepped across the hall and pushed open a door. It was some kind of lounge, with counters and a refrigerator, a coffeemaker, a couple of couches against the wall, a round table and several chairs. Yet another pink-smocked woman sat at the table sipping coffee and reading a paperback novel. She looked up and frowned at him.

"Excuse me," he said, and pulled the door shut again.

He tried the door next to it.

An office, with a desk and a big pink swivel chair. Lots of plants, just as in the reception room. Pictures on the bookcases—one of his mother, his sister and the Yorkies out by the pool at Angel's Crest.

Her office, he thought. But where the hell was she? He ducked out of that room and shut that door, too.

Before he could open another one, Pixie emerged from the door at the far end of the hall.

She frowned at him reproachfully. "Jonas. I *said* I'd be right back."

He walked toward her. "Where is she, Pixie?"

Pixie stopped looking reproachful and started looking nervous. She backed up against the door she'd just come through. "Uh. I'm sorry. Right now, she can't be disturbed."

"She can't."

"No."

Jonas halted about two feet from where Pixie stood blocking the door at the end of the hall. "Why not?"

"She, uh, she's working with an especially sensitive client at the moment. She told me to tell you she'll be getting in touch with you real soon."

"Real soon?"

"That's right."

Jonas flexed his fingers around the handle of his briefcase. "Pixie."

"Uh. Yeah?"

"I want you to move away from that door."

Pixie's plump chin quivered and the rhinestone in her nose seemed to be blinking at him. "No, I can't do that."

"Yes, you can. And I think you should." He took the three steps that were necessary to bring him right up close to her.

She looked at him and he looked at her.

"I'm not a very nice man, Pixie. Do you understand?"

Slowly, she nodded.

"Get out of my way."

Pixie maintained the stare-down for another ten seconds. That was all she could take. Then, with a small moan, she sidled to the right.

"Thank you." Jonas opened the door.

Beyond it, the walls were cobalt blue with white trim and the floor was black-and-white linoleum, a classic checkerboard pattern. A pink-smocked Emma Lynn Hewitt stood by a metal-topped table with some sort of adjustable pole attached to it, a noose at the end of the pole. On the table, below the dangling noose, sat a dog. A very small dog—perhaps seven inches tall and six pounds, max. The dog had long, soft-looking caramel-colored fur and bright, slightly bulging eyes.

Jonas registered these details in the first second or two after he entered the room, right before the dog attacked him.

Chapter 4

The dog leapt at him, yapping.

Emma Lynn Hewitt came after it, emitting firm and totally ineffective commands. "Hitchcock, stay! Hitchcock, sit!"

Jonas lifted his briefcase, positioning it as a makeshift shield. The little dog slammed against it and dropped to the floor, where it lay stunned for perhaps a count of three.

And then it was up again, grabbing onto the end of Jonas's left trouser leg with its sharp, white teeth.

"Oh, please don't kick him," begged Emma.

The dog growled and wriggled and ripped at his pant leg. Jonas stood absolutely still. "Then I'd suggest you get him away from me. Now."

"Hitch. Here, Hitch…"

The dog paused, blinked, and then picked up where it had left off, nails clicking fiercely on the linoleum as it yanked backwards, making a rag of the fine lightweight wool.

Emma knelt. "Hitchcock. Front."

The dog froze. Growled.

"Front, Hitch. Front."

The dog gave another growl, then let go.

She scooped the animal into her arms, stood, and backed up. "Good boy. Such a very, very good boy." The dog whined and licked her chin. She glanced at Jonas. So did the dog, which immediately started growling again. "Wait outside in the hall. I'll be right there."

Jonas advised, "Don't disappoint me, Emma."

"I won't. I promise. I'll be right out."

He turned for the door.

"Send Pixie in," she said, as he opened the door.

Since Pixie was standing on the other side wearing the guilty expression of someone caught eavesdropping, there was no need to relay the message. Pixie went in as soon as he got out.

For once, the dog groomer didn't make him wait.

In under a minute, she came out of the blue room, closing the door and then slumping against it, pale head bowed. She was wearing leopard-skin patterned pants beneath the pink smock, the kind that fit like a second skin and came to just below her knees. There were black platform thongs on her feet. Her toenails were metallic gold. Right then, she reminded him of a very young, very vulnerable Marilyn Monroe.

"I *am* sorry," she said, still looking down. "Hitch hates the noose, so I don't use it. After a little conversation and a lot of praise, he's usually real good for me. But you surprised him, bursting in the room like that. Pomeranians don't like surprises."

"No kidding."

One of the pink-smocked women—this one skinny as a rail with short, spiky red hair—came out of a door at the opposite end of the hall, leading a fine-looking collie on a leash. The woman paused. "Em? You okay?"

Emma looked over, forced a smile. "I'm fine, Deirdre."

Deirdre took the collie through the door to the waiting room.

Emma turned her gaze on him then, her expression wistful. "Don't tell me. Let me guess. Armani, right?"

He realized she was referring to his tattered trousers. "Vincent Nicolosi."

"Who?"

"Never mind."

"Someone so exclusive, I've never heard of him, huh?"

He shrugged.

"You just send me the bill, all right?"

As far as Jonas was concerned, they'd talked enough about his trousers. "I have something important to discuss with you."

"Jonas, I really don't have time right now to—"

He was already striding back down the hall. He stopped at the door that led to the office room. "In here."

"Jonas, I can't—"

"In here. Now."

Amazingly, she did what he'd told her to do, platform thongs clipping smartly as she came toward him. She opened the door. "After you."

He went in.

She followed, gestured at the two pink Naugahyde chairs opposite the desk. "Have a seat."

He didn't sit. He laid his briefcase on her desk, opened

it, and took out the prospectus. "Here." He held it out to her.

"What's that?"

"A plan I've put together."

She folded her arms below those ripe-looking breasts. "What kind of a plan?"

"A damn good one." Since she wouldn't take it, he dropped the prospectus on the desk. "We're going to expand this business of yours. You'll open five new PetRitz locations—in Santa Barbara, San Francisco, Dallas, Philadelphia and New York City. One a year, starting next year. I will take all the risks, and put up all the money. The majority of the profit from this venture will be yours."

"It will?"

"Yes."

"And what exactly do I have to *do* to get so lucky?"

"You'll contribute your time. Lots of it. And also your...expertise."

"I heard that." Her eyes were moss green, or maybe hazel. They kept changing color. And they seemed to be twinkling with humor right then. That little mole above her lip tucked itself into the shadow of her cheek as she grinned.

"Heard what?" he demanded.

"The way you hesitated before you said 'expertise,' like you didn't really mean it."

"I assure you. I did mean it."

She tipped her head to the side. "Sure you did. And a Texas summer never gets all that hot."

"Emma, I am very well aware that you've done a fine job here. PetRitz, by any standard, is a success. And my mother realized an excellent profit on her investment."

"You bet she did."

"So now, I'm going to help you expand."

She kept her arms wrapped around her. "In exchange for what?"

"In exchange for—"

She put up a hand. "No. Don't tell me. Let me guess." She fluttered her eyelashes, which were curly and dark around those almost-green eyes. "I know. You want me to agree to give up any claim to Mandy."

He sought the most diplomatic way to say yes.

Before he found it, she prompted, "Am I right?"

"Emma—"

"Just answer the question."

"All right. Yes. You'll give up all claim to custody of Mandy."

"No."

He glared at her. "Just read the damn thing, will you?"

"I'm not going to give up my claim to custody of your sister. Or at least, if I *do,* it's not gonna be because you have paid me off. Oh, Jonas." She raked both hands back through that white-gold hair and she groaned at the ceiling. "Haven't we been through this already, more than once?"

"No. This is all new. This is a great opportunity for you to build on what you've got here."

"Well, fine. It's a great opportunity and I'm passin' it up—considering that to take it would mean I'd have to turn my back on the dyin' wish of the second most wonderful woman I have ever known."

He must have frowned.

Because she explained, "The first most wonderful bein' my aunt Cass. You know all about my aunt Cass, now, don't you? Blythe told me how you sicced your detectives on all of her friends. How you keep *files* on folks, how you never, ever trust anyone.''

"Excuse me. There *are* people whom I trust.''

"Oh, sure. Maybe. After you've had your detectives on them, keepin' track of their every move for ten or twenty years.''

He felt that urge again, to wrap his hands around her pretty neck and squeeze. He spoke more quietly than ever. "You have no idea the kind of precautions a man in my position has to take.''

"You don't *have* to take precautions, Jonas. You just *do*. I mean, all those *guards* you have out there at that mansion of yours...''

He did not have *guards*. Not exactly. He employed a skilled and discreet security force to patrol the grounds at Angel's Crest.

The woman was smirking. "Bel Air is a gated community, with security guards checking out anybody who tries to get in. And then you've got that big stone fence around your property. And did I mention that *other* locked gate smack in the middle of that high stone fence, that gate with the camera that zooms in on anyone who rings to be let in? And is that all? Oh, no. There is more. Because you've also got those guys straight out of *Men in Black* sneakin' around in the jacaranda trees, talkin' to each other on their walkie-talkies. I mean, pardon me, Jonas, but you are kind of paranoid.''

"No." He spoke with extreme patience. "I am not paranoid. I am careful.''

"You are *too* careful. And I keep thinkin' that, no matter how much you love Mandy—and I do know that you love her, Jonas—but no matter how much you care for her, she can't help but be affected by the way you are, by the way you keep people away from you, the way you are so afraid to trust anybody.''

"I am not afraid.'' He spoke more forcefully than he meant to.

She actually had the temerity to roll those just-about-green eyes.

Clearly, they were getting nowhere. He said, very quietly, "I want you to take a good, long look at that offer.'' He turned to leave.

She spoke to his back. "Jonas, this is pointless. I am not goin' to—''

"I'll call you tonight.'' He shut the door on her before she could finish whatever it was she had started to say.

He called her at midnight. She answered the phone on the first ring. "What?''

"Did you read it?''

"I did. All the way through to the part about how I give up all claim to custody of Mandy. And then I stopped reading.''

"Why?''

"Because I'm not takin' this offer—which I already told you this afternoon. If you'd only bothered to listen, you could have saved yourself a phone call tonight.''

At that moment, Jonas realized he was truly and completely fed up with this woman. So fed up that he said exactly what he was thinking. "I could ruin you, Emma Lynn Hewitt.''

She gasped. He found the small, shocked sound inordinately satisfying. "I guess that was a threat, huh?''

"Let's call it a warning.''

"Call it what you want. It won't work.'' There was steel beneath the twang. "A person's got to stand for somethin' or she'll fall for anything. My aunt Cass used to say that.''

Terrific. Now she was going to beat him over the head with clever little sayings from country-western songs. ''I could care less what your aunt Cass used to say.''

''Well, all right. Then listen to this. This is what *I* say. *You are not bullyin' me into doing things your way.*''

The problem, Jonas realized then, was that she meant exactly what she said. Damn her.

This couldn't be happening to him. But it was.

Everyone had a price—except, apparently, Emma Lynn Hewitt. For Emma Lynn Hewitt, no amount would be high enough.

He *could* break her, financially, and she knew it. Yet even the threat of losing everything she'd worked for wouldn't make her give in and see things his way. The woman had *values*. And she was determined to stick by them. She would come to her own decision, in her own time. And whatever that decision was, he was going to have to live with it.

''Oh, Jonas.'' Her tone, all at once, had become insultingly gentle. ''I do understand why you are how you are. Blythe told me all about it. And it's no secret anyway. I know it was all over the newspapers back then. Such an awful, terrible thing. I am so sorry, that ugly things like that can happen, that sometimes evil never gets made right. And Blythe, well, you probably know that she blamed herself. She said that her breakdown took her away from you just when you needed her most.''

Jonas put the phone below his chin and sat back in his chair. He looked up at the intricately carved crown moldings overhead.

Emma Hewitt blathered on. "When she was better, she tried to reach out to you. But she said, by then, you'd spent so much time feelin' all alone that you were used to it. You wouldn't open up to her. You wouldn't open up to anyone, you wouldn't—"

Jonas had heard enough. Very quietly, while she was still talking, he hung up the phone.

After that, Jonas waited. He had finally understood that he had no other choice. He did not call Emma Hewitt or try in any way to contact her again.

Three more days went by. During that time, he found he was coming to grips with the fact that there would be a long court battle.

So be it. Possession was nine-tenths of the law. Mandy lived with him and she would continue to live with him. He could have his lawyers stall and negotiate for years. By the time Emma Hewitt won custody—if, in the end, she *did* win—Mandy would be all grown-up and running her own life, anyway.

By Monday, one week before the deadline set out in Blythe's will, Jonas had become certain that he would not hear from the Hewitt woman until the deadline had passed and her lawyer got in touch with his lawyer to begin the custody suit.

That night, she came to him at Angel's Crest.

Chapter 5

It was eleven-thirty at night and it was raining when Palmer got the call from the gatehouse. The butler found Jonas at his desk in the study.

"Ms. Emma Lynn Hewitt at the main gate, sir."

Jonas shut the lid on his laptop, aware suddenly of the feel of his own blood, the hot surge of it through his veins. "Tell them I'm expecting her and let security know she's on the way up."

"Of course."

"Show her in here when she gets to the house."

"I'll do just that, sir."

Palmer left him.

Jonas got up and went to the bank of windows nearest the desk. He stared out at the night, at the lacy shadows of the jacarandas moving in the wind and the waving branches of the palms. The hard warm August rain pinged against the leaded-glass panes, glittering as it slithered down.

The study was at the front of the house. After a time, he saw her headlights cut the night. The lights slid past the window where he stood and stopped not far from the front portico. They went dark.

Jonas didn't move. He waited, standing absolutely still.

Soon enough, he heard the door behind him open. "Ms. Hewitt," Palmer announced.

Jonas turned.

She stood in the doorway, Palmer close behind her. She wore an ordinary gray raincoat thrown over a curve-hugging shirt of some sort of elasticized lace. The shirt didn't quite meet the waist of her clinging white bell-bottomed pants. His glance moved down. She wore rain-wet platform sandals on her feet. There was purple polish—polish the same color as the tight lace shirt—on her toes.

"Hello, Jonas."

He met her gaze. Her eyes were very green right then. And troubled. Raindrops glittered in her pale hair.

"Thank you, Palmer," Jonas said.

The butler left them.

"I want to see Mandy," Emma Lynn said.

"She's asleep."

"I'm not going to wake her up. I just…I have to see her."

"Why?"

"I meant what I told you, Jonas. I *have* been making up my mind."

"Fine. Why is it necessary for you to see my sister?"

She seemed at a loss for a reason, only looked at him, an urgent kind of look, through those troubled green eyes.

He left the window and approached her. Her eyes widened as he got close, as if she feared his nearness. But she didn't step back.

He went past her. "This way."

Emma followed Jonas out to the entry hall, with its ebony-inlaid walnut floor and its coffered and arched cathedral ceiling rising three stories high. The grand foyer, Blythe had always called it.

Jonas began to climb the curving staircase. Emma fell in step behind him.

Mandy's rooms were on the second floor. Jonas went past the dark playroom and entered the bedroom. Lightning flashed once, bright and hard, outside. For a split second, the yellow and blue walls stenciled with dragonflies and dancing frogs were cast into sharp relief.

Then the room plunged into shadow again. The rain drummed away outside, a low sort of sighing sound.

Mandy had graduated from her crib to a big white four-poster several months ago. She lay in the center of the roomy bed, on her side, the quilted yellow and green comforter covering her to her waist, both hands tucked beneath her plump chin. Her thick, silky curls looked very dark against the yellow pillow.

Emma tiptoed to the bed and stood looking down, painfully aware of Jonas, so silent and watchful, in the shadows behind her.

Mandy yawned, then let out a small, contented sigh. She rolled to her back, flopping her arms up and out, so that her hands lay palms-up on the pillow at either side of her head. Her little fists tightened, then went lax again.

As Emma stared at those small, perfect hands, it almost seemed she could hear Blythe's voice in her mind....

"Am I crazy, Em? Am I totally irresponsible, to want a baby so much at this time in my life?"

"No, you are not crazy. Not crazy at all."

It had been a Saturday. The Saturday after Thanksgiving. They'd been Christmas shopping. And they'd stopped in at a Mexican restaurant on Melrose for lunch.

Blythe had leaned toward Emma across their table, her face earnest, her voice low. "I want...I guess I want a chance to do right by a child, to help someone grow up and to do a good job of it. I wasn't there, when it mattered, for Jonas." She sat back, her eyes suddenly far away and dark with pain. "And with my other baby, I never even had a chance."

Emma was the one leaning closer then. "Blythe, don't do this to yourself. What happened was not your fault. Not in any way."

But Blythe shook her head. "I could have been stronger. I *should* have been stronger. Jonas needed me then. And I failed him terribly."

Emma had said what Aunt Cass would have said. "You can't live in yesterday. You can only live right now." Then she'd added what she really thought. "And right now, today, you would make a wonderful mother."

"Oh, do you think so?"

"You bet."

Blythe looked so young at that moment, sitting back in the booth, a soft smile on her face—but then, she had always looked years younger than her real age. And she'd been blessed with lots of energy. Until the illness that claimed her so suddenly, she was a person who just brimmed with life.

Emma asked, "But *could* you? I mean, aren't there laws about how old you can be?"

Blythe picked up her water glass and raised it, as if

in a toast. "Money and influence do have their uses."
She set the glass down without drinking from it. "However, there is no getting around the problem of Jonas.
He would be furious."

Emma dipped a chip in salsa and popped it into her
mouth. "Well, fine. Let him be furious. It is not his
decision."

"But if anything happened to me in the next few
years, he could end up being the baby's guardian."

"Blythe. Nothin' is going to happen to you."

"I'm sure you're right. But if something *did* happen,
you and I both know that Jonas is not emotionally
equipped to bring up a child. He would need help,
Emma."

Emma crunched another chip. "Now, come on. You
weren't listenin' to me, were you? I said that nothin' is
going to happen to—"

"*Would* you be there? That is what I'm asking you,
Emma. It's a great deal to ask, and I know it. But it's
very important to me. To think that I could count on you
to help out, to give Jonas a little…guidance, if something happened to me."

On the bed, Mandy sighed again and turned her darling little face toward the far wall. Emma stared at the
curve of her beautiful cheek.

Would you be there?

Emma had looked across the booth at her friend and
said, "Yes. You know that I would. If it ever comes to
that—which it will not—I will be there to help out."

Emma had said yes. Yes, after all, is what a person
should always try to say to a friend. It had been a promise. A promise she'd been foolishly certain that she
would never have to keep…

Emma turned from the sleeping child. Jonas was wait-

ing for her in the shadows. She nodded. He gestured for
her to go ahead of him. She did, as far as the upstairs
hall. Then he took the lead again. They went back the
way they'd come, down the curving stairway, through
the grand foyer, along another hallway to the room the
butler had called the study, with its beautiful rugs, inviting velvet-covered chairs and pretty jewel-paned windows.

Jonas shut the door. "Take off your coat. Have a
seat."

"No. I won't stay long."

He stared at her, a probing, knowing look that caused
her stomach to go all jittery. She shivered.

One corner of his mouth lifted the tiniest bit in the
Jonas Bravo version of a smile. "You *are* nervous."

Why deny it? "You bet I am."

"Why? What's going on?"

Lord, give me strength, Emma thought.

She wrapped her raincoat closer around herself,
yanked her shoulders back and announced, "All right,
Jonas. I'm willin' to do what Blythe wanted me to do.
I will marry you. For one year."

Chapter 6

Jonas found, surprisingly, that he was relieved. It wasn't the best decision she could have made. He would have liked it a lot better if she'd simply agreed to stay the hell out of his and Mandy's lives.

But it could have been worse. At least this way, in a year when they divorced, there would be no doubt that Mandy would stay with him.

"No more stalling," he said. "We'll get married right away."

Those eyes, moss green at that moment, widened. She didn't speak, but she did nod.

Fine. He'd take that nod as a yes. "And another thing..."

She frowned. "What?"

Jonas did not consider Emma Lynn a gold digger. She might have platinum hair and a wardrobe straight out of a Victoria's Secret catalogue, but in the past week, the woman had shown herself to be burdened with an excess of integrity.

Still, a man in his position couldn't be too careful. "I'll expect you to sign a prenuptial agreement. I'll settle a few million on you, but that's all you'll get out of me."

She stiffened. And her soft red mouth became a firm line. "I don't need a few million from you, Jonas Bravo. You make out those papers to say I get nothin'—and you get nothin' of *my* fortune, either."

He couldn't help it. He laughed. As the sound escaped him, he realized it was something he didn't do all that often. He composed himself, asked, quite seriously, "What fortune is that, Emma Lynn?"

She had that cute little turned-up nose of hers aimed at the ceiling. "The fortune I'll *earn* soon enough, you watch me."

He *was* watching. And he was thinking that she did possess a certain spunky charm. She had just succeeded in amusing him. And that was a rare thing. Women so seldom amused him anymore.

Maybe he'd become jaded. There had, after all, been an excess of women in his life during his mid-to-late twenties. All of them had been beautiful and bright and so clever. But sooner or later, they all wanted more than he wanted to give them. He would move on.

The endings of affairs tended to be unpleasant—all those tears and impassioned recriminations. Gradually, he'd come to the conclusion that the great sex at the beginning of a romance just wasn't enough to make up for all the big emotional scenes at the end. So he had dated less and less until, in the past two or three years, he found that he wasn't dating at all.

But he had to admit that sometimes he missed having

a woman in his life. He missed the feel of a soft, warm body beneath him in bed. He missed kissing. Yes, he really had liked kissing. He liked the taste of women, the sweetness of their mouths beyond the soft boundary of their lips.

Emma Lynn, he couldn't help but notice, had a very pretty mouth, not too wide, but with full lips. Her mouth was slightly open at the moment. He could see her nice white teeth, which were just the slightest bit overlapping in front—not perfect.

Strange. He liked that.

He also was finding that he'd begun to like that mole above her lip on the right side, the way it slid into shadow when she smiled.

He moved a step closer to her, took in a careful breath.

Yes. A fresh, sweet, scent. Like roses—roses wet with morning dew.

It probably wouldn't be entirely unpleasant to have her in bed. In fact, having sex with his *wife*... that could be an interesting diversion. He doubted the attraction would last the entire year, but why not make the most of it while it did?

He wanted to touch her, to reach out and run his finger along her cheek.

Had he ever touched her? He didn't believe so. He didn't believe he'd ever so much as taken her hand.

That was odd, wasn't it? It had been five years since his mother had first introduced them. He remembered that introduction clearly. He had heard them, the two of them, laughing together in the living room off the grand foyer. Or perhaps laughing wasn't the word for it. They were giggling, like a pair of teenage girls sharing secrets. He'd decided to investigate.

He'd pushed open the tall double doors. And there

was his mother in her Chanel and pearls, sitting on one of the striped silk sofas with a way-too-sexy blonde. The blonde wore a very red, very revealing pair of shorts and a skimpy halter top.

His mother had glanced over at him in the doorway. "Jonas, come in. You must meet Emma Lynn…"

He had not come in. He had nodded a curt greeting and bowed from the room, pulling the doors shut as he went.

After that, there'd been no real occasion to touch Emma Lynn. No reason he would want to. She irritated him, and she'd never seemed particularly fond of him, either.

Well, now he was going to marry her—for a limited time, anyway. And he'd decided he'd probably take her to bed. He did want to touch her now. So he would. He reached out his hand.

Emma gulped.

Omigoodness. Jonas was going to touch her. Now why in the world would he go and do that?

She knew she should say something, move back, flinch away.

But she didn't. She remained absolutely still as his big, square hand brushed at her hair, slid along her cheek—and then dropped away.

They were standing just inside the door of his study. And now neither of them was moving. Emma felt that she *couldn't* move, couldn't think. Could hardly even breathe.

Jonas Bravo had *touched* her.

And now, he was looking at her so strangely. The very air felt changed. Charged. It seemed to vibrate with the tension between them—a whole new kind of tension. The sexual kind.

Emma's silly throat had gone bone-dry. She gulped again.

What was this? She did not need this—to get all hot and bothered over Blythe's big old bully of a son.

Okay, they were getting married. But there wasn't going to be any funny stuff, no there was not. Blythe's will hadn't said a thing about the two of them sleeping together. Emma was going to open him up and teach him a little about giving and caring.

But sex? Uh-uh. There was no need for that and they were not going to go there.

"Um. It's getting late, isn't it? I'd better be headin' out."

Jonas allowed himself a second smile—this one more obvious than the first.

Yes, he was thinking. There it was, beneath the irritation. Attraction. *Mutual* attraction. Interesting.

And she was completely bewildered by it. Not prepared for it, *fighting* it, even.

Jonas felt better by the second.

The way he saw it, Emma Lynn Hewitt's confusion provided a clear opportunity. It represented his chance to get the upper hand with her. And if there was one thing that Jonas Bravo understood, it was the importance of getting and keeping the upper hand.

He moved in closer. Her eyes got wider. "When?" he asked softly.

She actually licked those pretty full lips. "Um... what?"

"The wedding. When?"

She only stared at him, her gaze sliding from his mouth, to his eyes, then back to his mouth.

Imagine that. Emma Lynn Hewitt had nothing to say.

He answered the question for her. "I'll tell you when.

Tomorrow. First thing. We'll fly to Vegas. We can be back in L.A. by tomorrow night.''

"Tomorrow?" She looked more bewildered by the second. She also looked aroused. Jonas decided he liked her that way. Aroused and bewildered. And at a loss for words.

"Tomorrow," he repeated. "I have some important meetings on Wednesday. I'll need to be back in town for those."

"Oh. Important meetings. Of course."

Jonas found himself debating the pros and cons of a kiss. He did want to taste her—but no. Waiting would be better. Tomorrow night, he'd be kissing his wife.

The idea sent a bolt of heat through him. All at once, he was rock-hard.

Yes. It *could* be amusing, to be married for a year.

Marriage wasn't for him. He never would have willingly agreed to such a thing. But since his dotty mother had fixed it so he *had* to marry, well, at least he'd be marrying a woman who, he might as well admit it now, had begun to intrigue him.

She was so deliciously contradictory. The high moral standards, the do-it-to-me shoes...

And it *was* only temporary. Might as well make the best of it.

"I'll pick you up at your house," he said. "Be packed and ready. Say, ten o'clock?"

"Ten. Tomorrow morning? I don't...it's all so fast..." She was hedging suddenly, backing toward the door.

Perhaps, he decided, a kiss was in order, after all.

"Emma Lynn."

"What?"

"Stand still."

She froze—but her mouth kept going. "I...I have to go. Really. I can't—"

"Soon." He closed the space she'd put between them.

She looked up at him, her eyes jewel-green now, soft lips slightly parted. "Uh. No. I think I should go now."

He bent his head, brought his mouth to a distance of one inch from hers. "Now?"

"Now..."

He hardly had to move at all, just that inch—and he had her mouth. She gasped, and then she stiffened.

He remained absolutely still, mouth to mouth with her, waiting.

Until she sighed. Her breath was sweet, as if she'd been eating apples. And the dewy-rose scent of her was all around him.

Slowly, so as not to startle her, he took her shoulders and very gently pushed the raincoat away. It collapsed to the floor.

She made a small, urgent sound in her throat, a word that didn't quite take form. A protest, a plea? He couldn't have said.

And he didn't care. Her mouth parted a tiny bit more. He slipped his tongue inside and pulled her body in to his.

Chapter 7

The kiss went on for a long, long time.

Somewhere in the back of Emma's mind, a voice that sounded very much like her aunt Cass scolded her roundly, telling her to stop this foolishness, to stop it right now.

But Emma was not listening to the wise voice of her dead aunt. She was too busy kissing Jonas back, moaning and sighing, rubbing her shameless self against him, running her hands over his huge hard shoulders, along his big neck and up into his thick brown hair.

My goodness, the man knew how to use that tongue of his. And she didn't mean for talking, no she did not. And his hands were every bit as busy as *her* hands, sliding all along her rib cage, and around to her back, then cupping her bottom and yanking her in even closer to him.

He was on her like paint. And she was loving it—loving the feel of those big hands on her skin when he pushed up the puckered lace of her shirt and caressed what he uncovered.

Her breasts were just aching for him to hurry up and get there. And she was, well, she was getting very damp, real humid down south, everything opening and softening, hungry and ready.

He was ready, too. She could feel him, down at the base of her belly—hard, wanting her. Just like she wanted him.

This couldn't be happening. With Jonas Bravo, of all people. They didn't even *like* each other.

Did they?

She moaned. He moaned. His tongue did naughty things to her tongue and his hands, like her hands, would not be still.

Until he grasped her shoulders.

And, very gently, pushed her away.

Her eyes popped open. He was holding her at arm's length, those incredible hands of his firm on her shoulders. She stared at him. His lips looked bruised. She didn't even want to think about what her lips must look like. They had kissed so hard and long, they'd probably injured themselves.

"Time to go home, Emma Lynn," he said tenderly.

"Home," she repeated, in the voice of a woman hypnotized.

He smoothed her hair and tugged on the hem of her shirt, which had gotten all bunched up beneath her bra. Then he knelt and scooped up her coat. "Turn around."

She obeyed, still feeling as if she'd been sucked in to some kind of trance. Her body felt all quivery, and her brain felt way too slow, as if someone had filled her head with big, soft handfuls of fluffy cotton balls.

"Give me your arm," he said, that rough-velvet voice

of his driving her crazy, making her wish she could just turn around and throw herself on him, just climb him like a tree.

But some shred of dignity must have remained to her. She did not act on her wish. She did what he told her to do. She gave him her arm. He put it into the sleeve of her coat.

"Now the other arm."

She gave him that one, too. He guided the coat up and settled it onto her shoulders.

"There," he said, and touched her, at the nape of her neck. She shivered. He made a low, knowing sound in his throat, and he rubbed his finger up and down along the back of her neck, causing heated little goose bumps to rise, making her shiver all over again.

She let her head drop forward, giving him easier access, and she couldn't stop the tiny moan that pushed its way out of her throat.

He bent closer, laying both hands on her shoulders again. She could feel the size of him, the heat of him at her back. She held her breath. And then his lips were there, on the nape of her neck, so soft and warm and exactly what she longed for.

She moaned again, louder than before.

And he responded by pulling her back against his body. His arms banded around her.

"Jonas," she whispered, letting her head fall back, into the crook of his shoulder.

He cupped her breasts, testing their weight and fullness. She moaned some more, in pure delight. Oh, it felt so good. So right. To want him. For him to want her.

Then he went still.

Emma didn't move, either. Better not to. Better to just...wait, for a moment. Until they could let each other go. All at once, she was aware of the rain again, the low, constant sound of it, like a whisper and a roar at once, against the windowpanes.

His hands fell away. He stepped to the side, reached for the door. She moved out of the way so that he could open it.

Then he took her hand and wrapped her fingers around his arm. "I'll walk you out." He moved toward the door and she went right along with him, her body thrumming, her mind a big fuzzy wad of cotton balls.

The hallways at Angel's Crest were very wide, plenty of room for two people to walk side by side. He led her out to the grand foyer and opened the huge studded mahogany door, letting in the scent and sound of the rain.

He pulled her out beneath the massive front portico with its row of stone pillars and its mosaic-tile floor, turning briefly to shut the big door, then guiding her on, to the top of the wide steps leading down to the front drive. The warm rain was a soft flood, dripping off the portico roof in silky, glittering sheets.

"Is your car open?"

She nodded.

"Come on, then."

They ran together, down the steps. They were drenched by the time they reached her red SUV.

He yanked open the door for her. "Get in."

She stepped up behind the wheel. Her key was in the pocket of her coat. She felt for it, found it, put it in the ignition.

Jonas was still standing there, his hand on her open door, watching her. Rain ran down his face, off the end of his big, blunt nose and along the cleft in his square chin. His beautiful dress shirt clung to his body, outlining the heavy muscles in his shoulders and his arms.

She felt weak inside, looking at him.

And then he leaned toward her and caught her mouth again, hard and hungrily. She tasted the rain, which felt cool on his lips. He opened his mouth, sucking. She sucked right back.

But only for a moment.

As quickly as he'd kissed her, he was pulling away. "Tomorrow morning. Ten o'clock," he said. "Be ready."

"I…" She got out the one word and nothing more, because she'd completely forgotten whatever she'd started out to say.

Jonas didn't seem to mind. He shut her door, waved at her and then stood there, rain pouring down on him, staring in her side window at her, looking slightly put out.

She realized he was waiting for her to start the car and drive away.

Well, all right. Good idea.

She turned the key, put the vehicle in gear and drove around the big open space in front of the mansion, until she was pointed toward the long drive down the hill, between the double row of palm trees. Jonas remained there, in the rain, watching her. She couldn't resist repeated glances in her rearview mirror. He stayed right where she'd left him, staring after her.

He should go in, get out of the rain. But he didn't. And she got so absorbed in checking on him that she almost drove smack dab into a palm tree.

That did it. She kept her eyes on the drive ahead from then on.

At home, which was half of a roomy duplex in North Hollywood, with three bedrooms and a tiny patch of patio in back, the Yorkies were waiting, their little bodies shaking with joy, even yipping once or twice, to welcome her back. She knelt and picked them up, first Bob and then Ted, letting them swipe their doggy kisses on her cheeks and telling them how very glad she was to see them again.

"Oh, you little sweeties. It has been a whole *hour*...."

Festus, the black-and-white cat who had shown up at her door the first week she came to L.A. and lived with her ever since, sat back in the open arch that led to the kitchen. He was much too dignified to beg for attention. Once she'd greeted the Yorkies, Emma went to him. He allowed her to stroke his head and scratch him behind the ears.

Emma hung her coat in the closet by the front door. The Yorkies pranced behind her down the hall as she went to her bedroom to pack for her wedding trip.

Her wedding trip...

Good Lord in heaven. Was this really happening? Had she actually agreed to marry Jonas Bravo? Tomorrow. In Las Vegas.

The idea of it stole all the breath right out of her body. She sat down on the edge of her bed with its cute white iron frame and comforting white chenille spread. The Yorkies jumped up to sit beside her.

What had he said? That he had important meetings on Wednesday, so they'd be back by tomorrow night. It would be a short trip, not a lot of time for seeing the sights.

But even though they weren't staying the night, she'd need to pack a few things, make a few arrangements. She picked up the phone on the bedside table and called Deirdre Laventhol.

Deirdre answered on the fourth ring. "Wha...huh?"

"It's me."

Deirdre groaned. "It's also after midnight, in case you didn't notice."

"Sorry. Something has come up. I have to be gone all day tomorrow and I'm not sure when exactly I'll be back. I want to bring Festus and the Yorkies over to the shop first thing. Would you keep an eye on them for me, and take them home with you when you close up?"

"What? You don't want to board them?"

"That's real funny."

It was a running joke at PetRitz. The grooming end of the business was doing just great, but no one—especially not rich Beverly Hills matrons—wanted to board their pets if they could avoid it. They let their servants watch their animals or they hired pet-sitters. So the roomy accommodations at PetRitz rarely saw use. Instead, Emma sometimes took pets home with her, and her employees picked up extra cash staying in big, beautiful houses, caring for the animals while the owners were away. Emma had plans, within the coming year, to discontinue the boarding service.

"What is going on?" demanded Deirdre.

"Will you do it?"

"Yeah, sure."

"Thanks. I owe you one. And now, I have to—"

"Uh-uh. No way. You woke me up. You got me to baby-sit Festus and the Yorkies. Now, you tell me what's up."

"It's too crazy. I can't get in to it now."

"You said you owed me. I'm collecting. Tell."

"But it's just too—"

"Em. I mean it. Speak."

Emma fell back across the bed. Bob whined and tried

to lick her face. Ted jumped on her stomach, tipped his head to the side and perked up his ears.

"I'm waiting."

"All right." She patted Ted on the head and ordered Bob to sit, which he did, instantly.

"What do you mean, sit?"

"I was talking to Bob."

"Sure you were. Well?"

Emma went ahead and said it. "I'm gettin' married."

Deirdre let out a yelp. "What? Who to? And hey, how come I'm not invited?"

"Oh, calm down. It's only temporary."

"Huh, what?"

Emma rolled to her stomach and toed off her platform sandals. They dropped to the rose-patterned needlepoint rug by the bed. "Deirdre, it's a weird thing. You hear what I'm sayin'?"

"Tell me more."

Deirdre was a good friend. Almost as good a friend as Blythe had been. For a while, after Emma moved out of that first East Hollywood studio apartment and before she bought her house, she and Deirdre had shared a place in West Hollywood. Deirdre was the illegitimate daughter of a Las Vegas showgirl and a famous movie director. Her mother had died a number of years ago. Her father gave her money now and then but didn't want her intruding too much in his life. Deirdre was tough on the outside and a cream puff on the inside. And she could always be trusted to keep whatever you told her to herself.

Emma told her everything—pretty much, anyway. Starting out with what Deirdre already knew: that Jonas Bravo was a cold, distant man who could stand to open up a little. Emma went on to explain what Blythe's will

had asked of her and how she'd decided to honor the
dying wish of her friend. She left out the part about how
she and Jonas had gone at each other hot and heavy less
than an hour ago, how if he hadn't stopped it, they'd
probably be rolling around naked on the floor of his
study right about now.

"You're right," said Deirdre when Emma was done.
"This is seriously weird. Are you sure that you know
what you're doing?"

"Nope. But I'm doin' it anyway. She was my true
friend, Deirdre. And I can't turn away from what she
has asked of me."

"I liked Blythe. A lot. But she was asking for *trouble,*
in my humble opinion."

"I'm doin' it, Deirdre."

"All right. I hear you. I'll watch the animals."

After she said goodbye to her friend, Emma tried to
pack.

But what was there to pack, if they'd be back before
bedtime? She ended up throwing a few things in her
overnighter, tucking a couple of dresses into a garment
bag and telling herself that it would be enough.

Once the packing was done, she took the Yorkies for
a short walk, discovering as she stepped out into the
night again that the rain had stopped. Finally, well after
one in the morning, she brushed her teeth and washed
her face and climbed into her white iron bed. The Yorkies cuddled in close and Festus curled up at her feet.

Of course, she couldn't sleep. Her life had been turned
upside down. She was marrying Jonas Bravo—even if it
wasn't a *real* marriage.

And Jonas had kissed her.

Well, *more* than kissed her.

And she had not uttered one little syllable of protest.

Because she had liked it. She had liked it way, way too much.

In his bedroom at Angel's Crest, Jonas wasn't sleeping either. But not sleeping was nothing new to him. He had a slight problem with insomnia. So that night, after he'd made all the arrangements for the trip the next day, he lay in his big bed, with his hands laced behind his head. He stared into the darkness and he thought of how amusing Emma Hewitt had turned out to be. And now, for a time, he would be married to her.

Pleasantly aroused, he smiled into the darkness. He was in control of this little situation now.

And he intended to stay in control.

By the next morning, Emma had come to a few important conclusions. She had thoroughly evaluated her own actions of the night before. And she had decided that she was not very happy with herself—or with Jonas Bravo.

Yes, all right. They were getting married. But only for Mandy's sake, only in order that Emma could help Jonas to open up, to learn to trust the basic goodness in other people a little. There was nothing in Blythe's will about the two of them crawling all over each other.

And to be tough and truthful, well, Jonas hadn't done a thing that she hadn't wanted him to do. She supposed she had to face the facts here. The Bravo Billionaire had gotten to her. She was only a human woman. It wasn't easy to stand firm against all that testosterone, those big hard muscles and that steely will.

Plus, he knew how to kiss. Oh, did he ever know how to kiss....

No. Now, that was not good. She was not going to

think about his kisses. She was going to keep foremost
in her mind that her job in this marriage was to help
him become the kind of man who would be a loving,
giving guardian to Mandy. The torrid love affair angle
was out.

She would not be sleeping in Jonas Bravo's bed. And
if he thought that she would, he was in for a surprise.

Emma had one white suit, and she wore it the next
day to be married in. The suit fit nice and snug and the
skirt was short and tight. Beneath the jacket, she wore a
little nothing of a camisole and on her feet she wore
T-strap dress sandals, with little gold buckles at the ankle
and sleek three-inch heels.

Jonas arrived right on time, at ten on the nose. Emma
had already taken the dogs and Festus to PetRitz and
made sure Deirdre had her cell phone number in case
some emergency cropped up.

Emma's duplex was a reverse floor plan, with the ga-
rage in the front, the living area facing the back patio,
and a long walkway down the side of the building leading up to the door. She loved the house, mostly because
it belonged to her. She'd gotten a great deal on it just
last year. But the inconvenient layout meant that she
couldn't watch for Jonas's arrival without standing out
in the driveway—which, of course, she did not do.

She knew that he usually rode around in a long black
limousine and she half expected him to send his driver in
to fetch her. But when she answered the door, there he
was, dressed so beautifully in a lightweight suit that had
no doubt been made by hand for some incredible price.

"Ready?"

She met those midnight eyes. It was not easy. She
felt…embarrassed, after the way she had behaved last

night. Embarrassed and way too attracted. He looked so good and solid and *big*. And he was staring at her like he wouldn't mind taking right up where they'd left off, with her moaning his name and his hands where they shouldn't be.

"Yes," she said, "I'm ready," at the same time ordering her silly heart to stop knocking like a sledgehammer inside her chest. She had her small suitcase, the garment bag and her purse right there by the door. She bent to pick them all up.

He took the suitcase and garment bag away from her. "I'm sure this will do for tonight," he said. "Tomorrow, we'll have to see about moving whatever else you want to bring with you to Angel's Crest."

She stopped halfway through the door. "I'm moving? To Angel's Crest?"

He looked at her, a patient, level, very knowing look. "Emma. The terms of the will are that we have to live together. You remember that."

"Well, I know, but I—"

"By the way, where are the dogs?"

Emma hardly heard the question. She was too busy dealing with the idea that she'd have to move to Angel's Crest—not that his assumption about where they'd live had really surprised her. Naturally he'd take it for granted that they would live at his mansion. And it did make sense, she supposed. She could hardly expect the Bravo Billionaire and his little sister to move into her North Hollywood duplex with her—could she?

But still, they should have discussed it last night. Heck. There were probably a lot of things they should have discussed last night. But instead, they'd started kissing and that been the end of all the things they should have done.

"Emma. The dogs?"

"Hmm? Oh. A friend is watching them. And Jonas, I think we have to talk a little about—"

"You'll bring them with you, to Angel's Crest. And that stray cat, I suppose. Even the damn iguana is fine with me."

She just felt so...agitated. And there was a yearning, inside her, to move closer to him, to put her hand on him, against his broad chest or on his shoulder, anywhere, she wasn't particular. She just wanted to touch him, to feel the warmth of him against the palm of her hand.

What were they talking about?

Oh. The dogs and Festus and Homer. He'd said she could bring them all to Angel's Crest. "Homer lives at PetRitz now. He has a nice big terrarium in the waiting room. Didn't you notice it the other day when you were there?"

"Homer. That would be the iguana?"

"That's right."

"I probably saw it. I saw several terrariums."

"Well, he was there."

He shrugged. "Bring the dogs and the cat, then—and right now, lock the door and let's go."

"Yes," she said, wishing she didn't feel so dizzy and distracted. "And wait a minute. How did you know about Homer and my cat?"

He just looked at her.

She figured it out. "Oh. Right. It's all in my *file*, isn't it?"

"Emma. We have to get going."

"All right. I know. I'll just...set the burglar alarm." She rarely set it, but since she wasn't sure when she'd be back, she decided it might be a good idea this time. The control pad was right by the door. She stepped back inside and punched the combination to arm the thing. Then she locked the door and turned to Jonas, who was waiting, looking a little impatient, several steps down the walk.

"I'm coming, I'm coming…"

He strode off and she hurried to keep up.

The driver was standing by the side of the limo. He opened the door for them. Jonas handed over Emma's suitcase and garment bag, and stepped aside so that she could get in first.

Emma flashed the driver a grin. "Thank you."

The driver tipped his hat. Emma slid across the soft leather seat to the far side. Jonas got in, too. The driver closed the door and then detoured around the back of the big car to stow Emma's luggage in the trunk.

The driver had climbed in behind the wheel way up in front beyond the glass partition and started up the engine before it occurred to Emma that something very important was missing.

She turned to Jonas. "Where's Mandy?"

He gave her a puzzled sort of frown. "At home where she belongs."

"We're stopping at the mansion then? To pick her up?"

He looked at her as if she'd just suggested he blow up a bank. "No."

"She's *not* coming with us?"

"Of course she's not."

"Why not?"

He let out a long, put-upon breath of air. "Emma, I have no intention of dragging my two-year-old sister to Vegas and back. It's an insane suggestion. We'll be home tonight. She won't even know we were gone."

"That's not the point."

"Of course it is."

"Will you kindly stop saying 'of course,' like something is right just because it's what *you* think? We are doing this for her sake. And by golly, she is going to be there."

"She is two years old."

"Yes. She is. And she's comin' with us."

"No, Emma. She's not."

They glared at each other. The big car rolled away from the curb.

Emma said, "Stop the car."

Either the partition that separated the front seat from the back was soundproof, or the driver had ignored her. The car rolled on, down to the end of her cul de sac, around and back the other way.

Emma spoke directly to Jonas. "Stop the car. Now."

His eyes shifted away, then back. The nerves-of-steel Bravo Billionaire had gotten the message. Emma Lynn Hewitt meant business.

"Damn it, Emma," he said in a voice right next door to a whisper. "I've made no arrangements in terms of security. It's not safe."

Suddenly, she *hurt* for him, for what she knew he had suffered as such a young child—for what he'd lost and what he couldn't seem to help fearing he just might lose again.

She spoke gently. "It *is* safe. She'll be with us. We'll never let her out of our sight."

Jonas turned away.

The car had left Emma's street behind. They were headed for the freeway. Emma said, "Tell the driver to pull over, Jonas. Tell him to do it now."

He looked at her again, a look as cold as a dead rattlesnake. He did not tell the driver to stop.

She hated to do it to him, to say the forbidden word. But at that point she didn't see that she had much of a choice. "I would think, Jonas Bravo, that you of all people would never stoop to…kidnapping."

Jonas said nothing. He kept on looking at her, his face expressionless.

Emma said it again. "Stop the car."

He pushed a button built into the armrest on his right. "Larry. Pull over."

The car slid in near the curb and stopped.

Emma asked, "Has she been out of that mansion once since Blythe died?"

He took his sweet time replying. Finally, he said, "At this point in her life, everything my sister could possibly need is right there, at Angel's Crest."

"So. She hasn't left the mansion since Blythe passed away."

He granted her the tiniest, most disinterested of shrugs.

She told him, "That little girl is not going to spend her whole life on a hill in Bel Air. Starting today, she's gettin' out now and then."

He muttered, very softly, "Damn you, Emma Hewitt."

And she laid it right out for him. "I'm sorry, but I am not going to budge on this one. We are driving back to Angel's Crest now, and we are picking up that little girl. Because as far as I'm concerned, Jonas Bravo, if we don't, we are lookin' at a deal-breaker here."

His eyebrows rose and he gave her another absolutely icy look. "Oh, are we?"

"That's right. No Mandy, no marriage."

Chapter 8

Mandy babbled all the way to the airport and then conked out during the flight. The private jet, which was done up like somebody's living room—a living room with all the furniture bolted to the floor—was pretty quiet after that.

The two bodyguards Jonas had insisted must go with them didn't have a lot to say. And Mandy's nanny, Claudia, was very sweet and very shy. She sat over in a corner, thumbing through a magazine, looking up and muttering something prayerful in Spanish every time the jet hit a little turbulence.

Jonas, wrapped in a silence both brooding and grim, sat in a big leather chair by a window and looked out at the high, white clouds rearing up below them and the limitless blue sky above. Emma left him alone. She sat in another leather chair on the other side of the plane and she looked out her own window and told herself that her bridegroom would lighten up eventually.

When they touched down at McCarran International, a car was waiting to take them straight to one of the new hotels on the strip, where glass sculptures adorned the lobby ceiling and exotic plants grew everywhere. They were shown to a five-room suite with a view of a man-made lake several floors below.

Ambrose McAllister was waiting for them in the suite. He had the marriage license with him and he also had the prenuptial agreement all ready for signing.

Emma sat down and read the agreement. It gave her five million dollars, should the marriage end, and made it clear that she agreed she would receive nothing more.

Emma said—to Mr. McAllister, since Jonas wasn't speaking to her—"I don't want a red cent when this is over. I told Jonas that."

The attorney explained that the law contained within it certain assumptions of fairness. If she didn't take the five million, she would be in a position to sue for even more, as it could be construed as unfair that she got nothing when the marriage ended.

"Mr. McAllister. I am not suing anybody. I make my own money and I don't want any of his."

Jonas, who'd been standing at the window staring out at the Las Vegas skyline and the mountains beyond, turned around and glared at her. "Oh for God's sake, Emma. Will you sign the damn thing and let's get on with this?"

Emma thought, well what do you know? It can talk. She glared right back at him. "I told you—"

"Sign it," he said again, then added bleakly, "Please."

The "please" kind of did it. She said, without heat this time, "Is it so hard for you to take a person at her word?"

"This isn't about taking you at your word. As Ambrose just told you, it's about fairness. When this is over, you will know that you were fairly treated. We'll avoid resentments, which can become damned expensive."

"Fairness," she echoed.

"Yes."

"And this is really what you want, for me to sign this?"

"Yes, Emma. It is."

"Sign right here." Mr. McAllister was holding out a gold pen.

Shaking her head, Emma took the pen. In one year, she would be a multimillionaire. Imagine that. It didn't seem real. She wished she could feel a little better about the whole thing. But then she glanced over at the far side of the room, where Mandy sat on her nanny's lap, chattering away.

For Mandy's sake, she thought, and she signed with a flourish.

A few minutes after Emma had signed the agreement, there was a knock at the door. One of the bodyguards let in a tall man in a gray suit. A justice of the peace.

Emma turned to Jonas, who had stopped looking out the window and stepped forward to shake the justice's hand. "We're getting married right here, in the hotel room?"

He actually answered her, but what he said was so nasty, she almost wished he hadn't. "Is that going to be another deal-breaker for you?"

She smiled—very sweetly, she thought. "No, not at all. I'm ready. Let's do it."

So Emma and Jonas stood before the justice of the peace, who began to recite the wedding vows. He barely got started when Mandy cried, "Me, too!"

Jonas turned to the little one. She ran to him and held out her arms.

He scooped her up and they faced the man in the gray suit once again. Jonas and Emma repeated their vows, one and then the other. Mandy caught on and when it was Emma's turn, she giggled and sang out her own bright and happy, "I do."

The man in the gray suit said, "Do you have the ring?"

And Jonas pulled one from his pocket. Emma stared at it in wonder. Somehow, the man had managed to go out and get her a ring? Amazing. But on second thought, she supposed that a billionaire didn't have a lot of trouble getting anything he wanted on real short notice.

He took her hand and slipped the ring on her finger, all in a very matter-of-fact manner, without once glancing up into her eyes. It was a whole lot of ring, a huge diamond solitaire set high in a platinum band.

Mandy cried out in delight, "Ooh, pretty!" and reached for the glittering stone. Jonas caught the little hand and kissed it, and nodded at the justice of the peace. "Go on."

At the end, when the justice said, "You may kiss the bride," Emma half expected Jonas to mutter, "No thanks." But he said nothing. He turned away and set his little sister down.

Mandy laughed. "Kiss, Jonah. Kiss." She held up her little mouth and he gave her a peck.

Then she went straight to Emma. "Kiss?"

So Emma bent and gave Mandy a quick, fond kiss of her own.

"Thank you," said Mandy.

"You are most welcome."

Mandy giggled again and toddled off, calling for her nanny. "Claudia, gimme a kiss!"

Emma watched her, thinking that at least so far, the little sweetheart didn't seem to have been damaged much at all by her big brother's overbearing protectiveness.

"Emma."

Her breath caught in her throat. She turned her head and looked at him. In his eyes, behind his anger at her for forcing him to bring Mandy along, she saw last night. Vivid as a needful cry, the memory of it echoed through her. All of a sudden, she was all tangled up in yearning. Her body was hungry, her mind thick and slow.

He took her arm. Heat sizzled where he touched her, little arrows of arousal shooting all through her, confusing her, ruining the sweet clarity she had found for a while there, while she fought to get Mandy the right to be here, while he demonstrated his cold fury with the fact that she had won.

Maybe if she just didn't look at him...

She jerked her gaze downward, focused desperately on the second button of his fine silk shirt. But he only put a finger beneath her chin and guided her face up to his.

He said her name again—in a whisper, that time.

And she whispered back, "Jonas..."

And then he was kissing her. His tongue was inside her mouth and she was glad to have it there. She sighed as he pulled her close and deepened the kiss even more.

The bodyguards and Mr. McAllister, the justice of the peace and the nanny and Mandy—all of them were watching. And Emma didn't care in the least. Jonas was kissing her.

And she did not want him ever to stop.

* * *

Once he felt his new bride's total compliance, Jonas pulled away.

He did it gently, and with some regret, unable to keep from thinking that this suite he had taken for the afternoon included a perfectly acceptable master bedroom. He could get rid of Ambrose and the justice of the peace and lead Emma to bed right here and now. Claudia would see to Mandy, and his men would go about their business doing what he paid them to do, making sure those in his care were safe.

He did feel a certain urgency, to have her. For a number of reasons. First and foremost, she excited him. He'd accepted that fact now. He wanted her, quite powerfully.

Beyond that, it had been a long time since he'd taken a woman to bed. He *had* missed the pleasure sex brought him, as well as the release. Now that he'd found a specific woman he wanted, his recent abstinence seemed to be working against him, making him more eager, more hungry for the act than was probably wise.

Also, he'd done a little more thinking since last night. By the terms of his mother's will, he had to be married to Emma for one year. Now that they'd both agreed to go through with it, he wanted no doubt at all that it had been a true marriage in every sense of the word right from the first. And a marriage in every sense of the word included sex.

Still...

There was something...too public about the situation now. Though they'd all be minding their own business, there was no getting around the fact that he'd have his sister and the nanny and two armed men hanging around right outside the bedroom door.

He could wait.

Until tonight, when he would join his new wife in the large and comfortable—and very private—suite of rooms that he had chosen for her at Angel's Crest.

Waiting, though, presented one major problem: Emma herself.

She could be damn slippery when she chose to be. Witness the week of pure hell she'd put him through making up her mind to marry him in the first place. And the way she'd dug in her heels over the issue of bringing Mandy with them today. She'd won out, too. Against his better judgment, his sister was here, in Vegas, with them. He still hadn't completely gotten past his fury over the way she'd bested him on that score.

Emma had to be watched. He didn't dare let her out of his sight until he'd made certain she understood where she belonged—for the next twelve months, anyway. She was just hardheaded and morally upright enough to decide that sex should not be part of the contract they shared. He intended to disabuse her of that notion, and he meant to do it before the night was over.

But in the meantime, he had to keep her close and he needed to make sure she was occupied. He didn't want to give her a lot of time to think. She'd only make up her mind to do things that didn't fit in with his plans.

Ambrose was clearing his throat. "Ahem. Jonas. Emma. If you will step over here and sign the marriage license…"

Jonas offered Emma his arm.

She took it, looking up at him, her eyes soft, two charming spots of color staining her cheeks and her mouth just a little swollen from his kiss.

Just the way he wanted her.

Now, all he had to do was to keep her that way until tonight.

* * *

Starting with the kiss that sealed their wedding vows, things improved between Emma and Jonas. Enormously. Emma was so pleased.

Jonas seemed to have let go of his anger with her. He wrapped her fingers around his arm and led her to the table where they both signed the document that declared them man and wife.

Man and wife. She could hardly believe it. For a year, she would be Emma Lynn Bravo, wife of Jonas Bravo. It wouldn't, of course, be a marriage in the fullest sense. They did not love each other and they would not share a bed.

But they would live together at Angel's Crest. She would be a part of his and Mandy's lives for the next twelve months. And she hoped, by the time the marriage ended, that she might at least come close to accomplishing the tough task that Blythe had set for her.

The man in the gray suit said his goodbyes and Ambrose McAllister left, too.

Then Jonas said, "We have a few hours before we have to fly home. Would you like to take a look around the strip?"

Emma beamed at her new husband. "Oh, yes. Let's do that...."

Emma gave in when he argued that they should leave Mandy with Claudia, under the watchful eyes of his very able bodyguards. She had wanted the little one to be at the wedding. That had seemed important, somehow. But she didn't see any reason to drag her around the casinos. True, in recent years, Las Vegas *had* become a place where the whole family could have a great time. But Mandy was only two, a little young even for the theme park-style hotels like Treasure Island and the MGM Grand.

They changed clothes—Jonas into chinos and a polo shirt, Emma into a cap-sleeved tee with a keyhole neckline and a nice, snug pair of white stretch pants. Then he took her down to the lobby, under that incredible sculpture made of glass, and outside, where it was hot and bright and noisy and there were people everywhere.

They went to the New York-New York Hotel & Casino, saw the replica of the New York skyline and rode the Coney Island-style roller coaster. They visited the Mirage. Emma wanted to see the 20,000-gallon aquarium in the lobby, to have a look at the miniature ocean in there, complete with stingrays, sharks and even an octopus—not to mention the special habitat where Siegfried and Roy's white tigers lived.

At Circus Circus, while trapeze artists and high-wire unicyclists defied death over their heads, they even did some gambling. Emma played the dollar slots and Jonas bet on the spin of the roulette wheel. Emma lost fifty dollars. Jonas won a little over a thousand.

It was while Jonas was winning at roulette that Emma became aware of the two men watching them. One was short and round and balding, dressed in wrinkled khakis and a Hawaiian shirt. The other was tall and thin, in black jeans and a dark T-shirt, wispy hair pulled back into a ponytail. Danny DeVito and Peter Fonda, Emma thought—with cameras. They started snapping pictures soon after Emma spotted them.

Jonas grabbed her hand. "Time to go." He started walking fast. Emma had to run to keep up.

The dealer called, "Sir! Your winnings…"

Jonas didn't even pause. "Keep it. Call it a tip," he said over his shoulder.

The dealer shouted, "Thank you!"

Jonas didn't bother to reply. He was moving as fast as those long, strong legs would carry him. Emma hustled along at his side.

The two men followed them back to the hotel. They managed to get into the elevator and get the door closed before the men could hop in with them. When they got off the elevator several floors up, the pair were nowhere in sight.

"Keep moving." Jonas dragged her down the hall.

"Who were they?" Emma asked, as Jonas used his card key to get them in the door.

The green light blinked, Jonas turned the handle and the door swung inward. They stepped into the small entrance foyer of their suite and Jonas shut the door. "Photographers. Paparazzi. Expect to see your picture in the tabloids very soon."

Emma bit her lower lip and wondered what kind of stories would be written about them. The tabloids were so often full of wild exaggerations and sometimes even outright lies.

Jonas lightly touched the side of her face. "Sorry. You don't marry the Bravo Billionaire and expect to keep it out of the papers."

She gazed up at him. He gazed back with something that almost might have passed for fondness. Her heart did what hearts only did in love songs: it skipped a beat.

"Jonah. Emma. There you are." Mandy was standing in the arch that led to the living room of the suite, her plump hands on her two-year-old hips. "We have been waiting to fly away in the jet."

Jonas laughed. "Don't worry, sweetheart. We're leaving right away."

They managed to get down the back stairs and out

into the five-story parking structure without incident. A limousine was waiting there, engine idling, a second, smaller car right behind it. Mandy, Jonas, Emma and one of the two bodyguards piled in and headed for the airport. Claudia and the other man went in the second car.

They boarded the jet without any trouble. Apparently, they'd lost the two photographers at the hotel. In no time, they took off for L.A.

They got to LAX at a little after six in the evening. It took another forty-five minutes to reach the gate at Angel's Crest. Palmer, as always, greeted them at the front door. By then, Mandy was getting fussy. Claudia took her right upstairs.

Once the nanny and the child had left them, Jonas turned to Palmer. "Are Mrs. Bravo's rooms in order?"

Mrs. Bravo, Emma thought. That's me. How strange.

Also, she noted, he'd said, "Mrs. Bravo's rooms." She decided that meant he wouldn't be expecting her to sleep with him—which was good. They understood each other. There might be a certain attraction between them, but Jonas must have realized that getting involved in a love affair with her would only make everything all the more complicated. And Emma certainly did not need to be his lover to teach him the things he needed to learn.

It was all working out for the best. And she did *not* feel the least bit disappointed that she wouldn't be climbing all over him naked all night long.

"The suite is ready, sir," Palmer said. "Shall I show Mrs. Bravo the way?"

Jonas took her arm. His touch sent a hot little thrill coursing through her. "I'll take her up. She has a suitcase and a garment bag in the limo. See that they get to her room right away, will you?''

''Immediately.'' Palmer turned and left them.

Jonas wrapped her hand around his arm. She was getting kind of used to that, to her hand tucked nice and comfy around his forearm, which was warm and hard and dusted with shiny, springy brown hair. He led her up the stairs and down a couple of hallways, to a suite of rooms in the southwest corner of the house.

She loved the rooms on sight.

The large bed-sitting area had dove-gray walls, white woodwork and chairs upholstered in black and gold brocade. A black velvet skirt and white duvet covered the bed, which had mountains of pillows but no head or footboard. On the antique black and gold bed table stood a crystal vase filled with lush white peonies. A crystal chandelier glittered overhead and French doors led out to a terrace that overlooked the curving palm-lined drive. Farther out lay the sprawling grandeur of L.A. and beyond that, the endless Pacific.

There was also a walk-in closet, a dressing room the size of her bedroom at home and a bathroom tiled in vivid fuchsia, with touches of black, white and gold and a wall of mirrors over the twin sinks. The tub stood on a platform and was big enough for two—or three or four, if it came down to it.

Emma couldn't help wondering who'd been in that tub before. But then she reminded herself that there were several other bedroom suites at Angel's Crest. They probably all had tubs the size of this one, lots of room for rich folks to do things regular people only imagined in their wildest dreams.

''Is it acceptable?''

Emma turned. Jonas stood in the doorway to the dressing room.

"It's beautiful. Thank you."

"You're sure? There are other options—and you can have it all redone if you'd prefer."

That made her smile. "Blythe," she said, knowing that he would understand.

And he did. Something happened in his eyes. Something warm and a little bit sad. "My mother," he said. "She wanted to make the world a better place *and* she constantly wanted it redecorated."

Emma nodded. "I think she redid her own bedroom suite about—what?—at least six times in the past five years."

"Six would be about right. She never lasted more than a year before she wanted everything changed—in her rooms, anyway."

"It was part of her charm."

"Yes," he said softly. "I suppose that it was." He looked at her for a long moment. "You'll be all right here, then?"

"Yes, I will."

"Palmer will have your things sent up soon."

"I know."

"Dinner at eight?"

"I would like that." They would share a meal. That sounded very nice. They should do that often. It would give her a chance to get to know him better, to figure out ways to help him to open up.

"In the small dining room?"

"I think I can find my way there."

"There's an intercom box right ncxt to the hall door."

"I saw it."

"Just push the button if you have a problem. Palmer will see you get whatever you need."

"Okay."

"Until eight, then?"

"Yes. Until eight."

He turned and disappeared through the dressing room. She waited until he had time to get out into the hall and then she wandered back into to the main room, where she kicked off her high-heeled sandals and fell across the black-skirted white bed.

She was staring at the dangling crystals on the chandelier when she heard the discreet tap on the door. It was Palmer, with her things. He vanished into the walk-in closet carrying her suitcase and her garment bag. When he reappeared, he was empty-handed.

"Is there anything else right now, ma'am?"

"Nope. Thanks a bunch."

The butler made himself scarce.

Emma glanced at the bedside clock. Twenty after seven. She should probably give Deirdre a buzz, just to see how the workday had gone and to check on the Yorkies and Festus.

But she hesitated. If she called Deirdre, she'd get a lot of questions. Her friend would want details about the trip and the wedding itself, about how it had gone. Telling it all would take time, which Emma did not have right then. She wanted to shower and put on fresh makeup. And she had brought a very nice dinner dress. It was purple. Of silk shantung. A sleeveless curve-hugging sheath with a wide square neckline in her favorite length—short. She'd brought high-heeled dress sandals to match.

No. No time to call Deirdre. She'd do it later, after

dinner. Emma rose from the bed and headed for the bathroom, peeling off her clothes as she went.

When she came downstairs, Jonas was waiting for her. He'd dressed for dinner in another of those beautiful suits of his.

"Drink?" he asked.

"Well, why not?"

He ushered her into the living room off the grand foyer. She sat on one of the pretty sofas covered in blue-and-gray striped silk. Emma smiled to herself, thinking that the room had looked just the same five years ago, the first time she'd visited Blythe at the mansion. So many of the rooms had changed over the years, since Blythe was always redoing them. But this one, for some reason, she had left alone. Emma was glad. The room had gauzy white window coverings and walls that were a soothing shade between green and gray. There were beautiful rugs on the inlaid floors, all with intricate patterns woven in to them.

Family photos graced the tables, each in a beautiful, distinctive frame, pictures of Jonas and Blythe and Mandy. And older pictures, too. Of Jonas as a child, with his father Harry and a twenty-something Blythe. There was even one of Harry as a very young man, with his parents and with his younger brother, Blake. Emma shivered every time she looked at that one. Blake Bravo had the strangest, scariest pale eyes. Blythe had told her he had died years and years ago. And from some of the things Blythe had said he had done, well, maybe the world was a better place without Blake Bravo in it.

Jonas went to the liquor cart. "What can I get you?"

Emma turned from the picture of the man with the crazy eyes. "Hmm?"

"What will you have to drink?"

She confessed, "I like those kinds of drinks they always put umbrellas in. You know, the sweet, frozen kind."

He picked up a pitcher that was right there on the cart "Strawberry daiquiri?"

"Well that would be just fine." She wondered how he could have known to mix up her favorite kind of drink. And then she remembered. It was probably in her file.

He poured the drink into a tall glass and carried it to her.

"Thank you." She sipped. Oh, it was heaven. Thick as Italian ice and just a little bit tart.

He had the kind of drink she would have expected him to choose—three fingers of something from a crystal decanter. Maybe whiskey, maybe Scotch.

They sat for a while, sipping. Talking a little. It was pleasant and relaxing and when he offered her a second daiquiri, she took it.

Why not?

After a time, he led her through the foyer and into the small dining room, where the beautiful walnut table could seat up to twelve. The room had murals of tropical scenes adorning the walls and arches supported by marbleized columns. Jonas sat at the head of the table and Emma sat to his immediate right.

He offered wine.

She shook her head. Two daiquiris were more than enough. She felt warm and easy and very relaxed.

They ate. There was a creamy asparagus soup, then a wonderful salad with a dressing that tasted like oranges. The main course was lamb chops with dill and tiny red potatoes bathed in butter and herbs.

They had coffee after the meal—coffee sweetened with amaretto, which Emma couldn't bring herself to refuse. Palmer offered dessert, but Emma shook her head again and Jonas waved the butler away.

On the sideboard sat a clock made of some kind of green stone, with a gold face and black Roman numerals marking the hours. That clock said it was ten-thirty. Imagine that. The time had flown by. And tomorrow would be a workday, for both of them. Hadn't he mentioned an important meeting? He'd want to be rested for that.

Emma needed rest, too. She'd hardly slept a wink last night, she'd been such a bundle of nerves about today, about the whole unbelievable idea of getting married, about the passionate kisses she and Jonas had shared that were *not* going to go any farther than that.

Emma slid her linen napkin in at the side of her saucer. "It was a wonderful dinner, Jonas. Thank you."

He lowered his head in a slow nod of acknowledgement. "Tired?"

"A little. I think I'll just—" But he was already up, pulling out her chair for her. "Oh. Thanks."

He took her hand, wrapped her fingers around his sleeve. "Let's go upstairs."

He would walk her to her room. How thoughtful of him. He really could be a charmer when he put his mind to it.

They went together, as they had earlier that evening, up the stairs, down the two hallways, to the door of her bedroom suite. She turned to him. "Well, I...I hope that meeting of yours goes well tomorrow."

He deftly reached behind her and opened the door. "It's a simple acquisition we're discussing. Nothing too tricky."

"Oh. Well. Good." She backed into the beautiful pale gray room and Jonas came right along with her.

"Did I tell you I like that dress?" He turned a dial near the door. Wall sconces shaped like golden boughs on either side of the bed glowed to life. The chandelier came on too, but very low. She looked up and the teardrop crystals seemed to wink at her.

"Emma?"

"What? Oh. My dress? Thank you."

"Do you own a dress that isn't tight and short?"

"Not if I can help it." Somehow, he had backed her all the way across the big room, right through the sitting area, to the end of the bed. Her calves came up against the soft white duvet. "I like sexy clothes."

"I noticed."

"I think I look good in them."

"You do."

"Plenty of time to tone things down when I'm a little older."

"Do you see me arguing?"

"No." Since there was nowhere else to go, she dropped to the edge of the bed and then had to tip her head back to look up at him. "But I think, maybe, you disapprove of my clothes. Just a little."

One corner of his mouth tipped up. "I've found I'm becoming...accustomed to them." He turned and sat down beside her.

She looked over at him, and wondered if she should tell him that he had to leave now. She hadn't planned to let him in. But now he was here. And they were talking. And, well, certainly he'd be leaving in a minute or two.

She frowned at him. "You're not going to try to get

me to be more conservative in the way that I dress, are you?''

"Never."

"Well, good."

He lifted his hand and ran the back of his index finger down her bare arm, then slowly back up again. It felt...really good. Tender. And teasing and naughty in a distinctly delicious way.

"I do wonder, though," he said idly, as he kept on rubbing his finger up and down her arm. "Do you find you have trouble being taken seriously?"

"Nope. No trouble at all."

"What about men?"

"What about them?"

"Don't you wonder if they ever...get the wrong idea about you?"

"The wrong idea?"

"That's what I said."

"That's not real specific."

He shrugged, and he ran that finger up even higher, right over the curve of her shoulder. His hand reached her nape and lingered, fingers rubbing in a gentle massage.

Emma cleared her throat. "Uh. No. If men get any wrong ideas about me, I make sure they don't keep them for long. I never have troubles with men. Men are sweet—well, most men are, anyway."

He made a low sound. It might have been one of amusement. And he kept on massaging the back of her neck.

She sucked in a breath and ordered her spine to hold her up straighter. "It's all in how a woman carries herself. My aunt Cass taught me that."

"Your aunt Cass, I take it, was a very wise woman."

"Yes. She was. Very wise…"

He moved in closer, his hand sliding around to cup her other shoulder and bring her snug against his side. She should have pulled away. And she knew it. But it just felt so *good* to be sitting there, bucked up tight against him.

He touched her chin with his other hand, guiding it around so that she had to look at him.

Emma stared into those midnight eyes of his. "My aunt Cass…uh…she had a real good head on her shoulders."

"The way I heard it, she lost a ranch and a small business before you were even ten years old."

"Boy, those detectives of yours are pretty good."

"That's what I pay them for."

"The small business was a beauty shop. We had that after we lost the ranch. And it wasn't much of a ranch, anyway. You need a lot of land to run cattle in dry country. We barely had a thousand acres. And then we had a drought and beef prices dropped. So we lost the ranch and Aunt Cass scraped enough together to try the beauty shop. But that didn't work out either."

They were still sitting too close, still staring into each other's eyes. It probably should have become uncomfortable. But it hadn't.

He said, "Your aunt ended up a waitress, didn't she?"

Emma granted him a quick, firm nod. "Aunt Cass was a fine waitress. She always had the knack for taking care of folks. And she had a memory. You have to have a memory, to wait tables and be good at it. If she served you breakfast once, she'd always remember what you liked and how you liked it. You'd slide onto a stool at ner counter and she'd glance over at you and ask if you wanted the same as you had last time. If you said yes, you would get it. Because she really did remember. That's important to folks. That their preferences are remembered.''

He was watching her lips. It occurred to Emma that he was probably going to kiss her.

What would Aunt Cass think of that? Emma blinked. '''If passion drives, let reason hold the reins.' Aunt Cass used to say that.''

"I think Benjamin Franklin may have said it first," Jonas suggested softly. Yes, a kiss was definitely coming. His mouth was close, much closer than it ought to be.

"Benjamin Franklin?"

"That's right."

Emma felt a little hurt. "Aunt Cass never told me."

He shrugged again, an itty-bitty shrug, hardly lifting those fine shoulders at all. "Just an oversight, I'm sure."

She tried to put some starch in her tone. "Well, whoever said it, it is something to think about, don't you agree?"

"Absolutely." He laid his big, warm hand against her throat.

A hot shiver went through her. "Jonas…"

"Um?"

"I am…I am getting the feeling that reason is not holding the reins at this moment."

"Certainly it is."

"Uh. No. No, I don't think—"

"What we have to remember, is to let passion drive."

"No. I don't think so. I think you should go now. I think—"

And he did it. Right then. He bent that tiny bit closer, and his mouth met hers.

Oh, why did he have to go and do that?

She froze. She stayed utterly, completely still.

But he only went on kissing her, lightly, gently, tormentingly.

Until she could bear it no longer.

With a hungry cry, Emma wrapped her arms around those wonderful big shoulders and pulled him down with her across the bed.

Chapter 9

Getting her naked was a top priority. Jonas sensed that as long as she had that little purple dress on, she could continue to tell herself that kissing was all that was happening here.

He kept his mouth locked on hers as he repositioned them a little, pulling her along with him, until they both lay on their sides. He located the zipper at the back of the dress and he took it down in one quick stroke.

She jerked away and stared at him, eyes wide, cheeks charmingly flushed. "Oh, Jonas. No."

He gave her a puzzled frown, though he wasn't puzzled in the least. He knew exactly what that "No" had meant.

She let out a little groan. "I am sorry. I shouldn't have…" The words trailed off in midsentence.

He prompted, with great patience, he thought, "You shouldn't have what?"

"Kissed you back, when you kissed me. Pulled you

down here, across the bed. I was wrong. And, well, I think this is a bad idea."

Tenderly, he began slipping purple silk over the curve of her shoulder and down her arm.

"Jonas," she murmured reproachfully.

Her skin was wonderfully soft, smooth as a baby's. She was wearing a little purple nothing of a bra. He wanted that off her, too—though he had to admit, it looked pretty damn good on.

He thought about control—about how much he'd like to just let it go. Rip everything off her and bury himself in her. He wouldn't do that.

But the temptation was there. He was hard for her, achingly so, and he wanted her. Now.

Very gently, he pressed his mouth to the curve of her shoulder, breathing in the scent of her, "What's a bad idea?" he asked as if he didn't know.

"As if you didn't know," she said, in exactly the tone he had thought it. She slid the dress back in place on her shoulder. "You and me. Having sex. I think it's a bad idea."

Her back was bare, now he'd taken the zipper down. So he ran his hand down the center of it. She shivered. "Oh!" She moaned. "Don't..."

He guided her onto her back again and leaned over her. She had her eyes closed. "Emma."

"No. If I look at you, I'll only want to kiss you."

"Emma..."

Those long lashes fluttered open. "See? I was right." She hooked her arm around his neck and pulled him down again.

Yes. He did like the taste of her mouth. Moist and ripe and sweet as a peach. He ran his tongue along the inside of her upper lip. Wet silk.

She pushed him away again and narrowed her mostly-green eyes at him. "Jonas. I was not going to do this."

"But Emma. You *are* doing this."

"It's real weak and irresponsible of me. It sets a bad example."

"A bad example for whom?"

"Well, for you, of course. You're the one I'm supposed to be helping."

He took her meaning. After all, he knew his own mother. He did understand the nature of Blythe's scheme. In the year to come, the dog groomer from Texas was supposed to make of him a warmer, kinder, gentler man.

It wasn't going to happen. Jonas was who he was.

"Emma," he said gently. "I am thirty-six years old. Long past the age when I required an example."

"Still, it seems to me that—"

He put a finger against her soft mouth. "Listen." She pressed her lips together and nodded to show she was doing just that. He explained, "If you keep saying no, I'll start to think you mean it."

"But I *do* mean it."

He decided it was time to call her hand. "All right." He levered himself away from her and swung his feet to the floor.

She sat up, the purple dress sliding fetchingly down one shoulder, a platinum curl falling over her eye. "You're goin'?"

"Yes." He turned and started walking, sure of himself and of her for the first five or six steps, then not so sure, then absolutely certain he had blown it royally.

He got through the sitting area and was reaching for the brass handle on the door to the hall when she spoke from behind him.

"Jonas."

He turned and faced her.

At some point between his starting for the door and reaching it, she had kicked off her high-heeled sandals and jumped to her feet at the end of the bed. She stared at him, wide-eyed, her hand against her chest—which made her look doubly earnest and also appeared necessary in order to keep the purple dress from falling off.

Relief washed through him. It seemed that he had won this round, after all.

Jonas was right.

Emma *had* changed her mind.

She made herself confess, "I just admitted the truth to myself."

He lifted one eyebrow at her. "And that is?"

"I can't stand to see you go. We *are* married, after all, even if it is only a temporary thing. And, well, maybe we should. And maybe we shouldn't. I don't know anymore. I only know that I...well, I want my weddin' night."

He didn't move. He didn't speak. He just stood there by the door, looking at her with an expression that, to Emma's mind, could have meant just about anything.

Emma dropped her hand away from her chest. The top of the purple dress fell to her waist. She looked down at herself, at her lace and satin bra and the twin swells of her breasts. And then she looked back up at him, hopefully. She thought that maybe something happened in his eyes—something hot and hungry.

But he still had not moved.

Well, all right, then.

The dress was too snug to fall off by itself. So she shimmied it down the rest of the way. Once it lay in a pile around her ankles, she stepped out of it.

Then she stood tall and looked him square in the eye. "Jonas. Won't you please stay with me tonight?"

He answered by coming toward her again, loosening his tie, dropping his beautiful jacket to the floor, working at one cuff link and then the other, shoving them into a pocket of his slacks once he had gotten them off. When he reached her, he was already starting on the buttons of his shirt.

Emma bent and picked up her dress. She shook it out and turned to lay it over a chair.

Jonas grabbed her hand.

She stopped, turned, met his eyes—saw with a little surge of pleasure that he was worried she might have changed her mind again. "I'm not goin' anywhere."

He released her.

She laid out the dress and came back to him. He was naked to the waist by then, sitting on the end of the bed. He took off his finely made shoes, slid off his socks, rolled them up and stuck them inside the shoes.

She stood over him, in her bra and matching bikini panties and nothing else. He set the shoes on the pale, soft carpet. And then, still bent low, he wrapped his hand around her right ankle.

Emma had to lock her knees to keep from melting to the floor in a puddle of pure lust. She stared down at the curve of his powerful back, at the nape of his neck, at his dark, thick, close-cut hair.

He looked up then, craning his head back until their eyes could meet.

She wanted to bend down and put her mouth on his again, but then she caught herself. There was something important that hadn't been mentioned. "I don't have anything, for protection. I wasn't planning to—"

His hand tightened on her ankle. "No problem.

There's a drawer in the bed table. And condoms in the drawer.''

She couldn't help smiling. He was Jonas Bravo, after all. A man you didn't catch unprepared. "Well, okay then."

His hand started to move. It slid upward, over her calf, behind her knee, along the back of her thigh. "Oh, my, my…" she whispered.

And then she climbed into his lap.

"I think you should sit very still," he suggested in a pained whisper a few minutes later.

She sat in his lap, her legs folded along either side of his big thighs. He was pressed up against the satin crotch of her bikini panties. They were getting pretty wet, those panties.

And Emma was feeling very, very eager. "Oh, Jonas. I can't. I cannot sit still…." She rocked her hips against him, along the thick, tempting length of him. It felt real, real good.

He groaned aloud. She found she liked that—to hear him groan.

She put her mouth against his throat and moaned as she licked his skin. "You taste so good, Jonas."

He made a growling sound. And then he unhooked her bra.

"Oh!" she exclaimed as he peeled it away.

He threw it across the room. It landed somewhere by the sitting area, she thought—not that she had any interest in turning around to check.

He took her breasts in his hands and he said, "I'm sorry. Chances are, this will not be slow."

"It's all right." She hitched in a hungry breath. "Fast is good. Fast is just fine…."

His lifted her breasts. She took his signal and raised up to her knees. His mouth closed around her left nipple.

Emma found she was beginning to understand the kind of women who yelled and screamed during love-making. She could do a little yelling and screaming right now, oh she certainly could.

She moaned way too loudly and let her head fall back, spearing her fingers into his hair, pulling his big head in closer, harder, as he drew on her nipple and swirled his tongue around it and rolled it, grazing it oh so lightly, with his teeth.

He lowered himself back on the bed, pulling her down on top of him, letting go of her left nipple and then immediately latching right on to the other one. Emma crouched on her knees above him, holding his head to her breast, moaning so loudly by that time that anyone who heard would probably have called it a yell.

His hands moved along her rib cage, rubbing hard and hungrily. They grasped her panties and shoved them over her hips and down her thighs. She took it from there, holding his head to her breast with one hand, while she pushed the panties off with the other, managing by some miracle of eager and squirming dexterity, to get her left leg free of the hindering lace, until it slid down around her right ankle. She put her weight to the left and kicked the panties off at last with a triumphant little cry.

A cry that turned to a pleasured groan as he laid his hand against her belly, and then slid it lower, until he was cupping her sex. His fingers moved, parting, seeking—and sliding inside.

Ohmigoodness, Emma thought, moving like some wild thing, riding his hand. Already, she could feel herself, rising toward a high, hard climax as Jonas did incredible things with those fingers of his and his mouth slid upward, to capture her lips.

Oh, he was kissing her. Kissing her so hard and deep, she could swallow his tongue if he wasn't careful. His hand kept moving, tormenting and wonderful. And he caught her chin with his other hand as he sucked at her mouth.

Emma tried to speak, to tell him she was going over, but it was pretty hard to do, with his mouth devouring hers and his left hand holding her chin and his right hand....

Oh, his right hand...

She just kept riding that big hand, and kissing him back.

And she yelled. She did. She yelled the house down. Or she would have yelled, if he hadn't had his mouth so tight against hers.

Too late. Too wonderful. Too perfect. Too much...

The world started shimmering and her body started quivering and everything flew away but the hot, pulsing, electric sensation of coming.

It went on forever. It was way, way too short.

In the end, her legs could not hold her. She crumpled against his chest and then slid off, to lie on her back, her body limp as a rag doll, her eyes at first shut, then slowly drifting open. She sighed in blissful satisfaction and she stared at the chandelier overhead. Now, more than ever, the crystal drops on it seemed to be winking at her. Emma smiled to herself and laid her arm across her eyes.

Beside her, Jonas sat up. She glanced over. He was pushing off his slacks and his dark-colored briefs along with them.

She saw him. She saw *all* of him. "Oh, my, my..." she said.

He said nothing. He tossed the slacks and briefs away and he reached for the drawer in the stand by the bed. He took out a condom, removed the foil covering and rolled it down over himself.

She felt...so tenderly toward him right then. His every movement was so purposeful, so sure and so determined. His body was so strong and hard and big. Everything he did, he did better than anyone else.

He had a law degree from Stanford and some kind of business degree from one of those snooty eastern colleges—Blythe had told her, but now she couldn't recall which one. He had shot a charging rhino, wrestled alligators—or so the tabloids claimed. He'd made love to the most beautiful women in the world, taken his father's millions and turned them into billions.

And once, long, long ago, he had been six years old. A little boy. A boy who woke in the middle of the night and went into his baby brother's room.

No one ever knew why he went to the baby's room, or exactly what had happened there. The nanny had found him the next morning, out cold on the floor, a large bloody bruise on the left side of his head, near the crown.

And the baby? The baby had vanished—forever, as it turned out.

Jonas remained unconscious for three days. And when he finally woke up, he could recall nothing of what had happened that night. His father, Harry, had died of a heart attack six months after the kidnapping. Blythe had descended into a lengthy depression. And when she came out of it, she found she'd not only lost her baby and her husband. She'd lost her surviving son, as well.

The sweet and open boy Jonas had once been was no more....

The grown-up Jonas had finished with the business of insuring safe sex. He was looking at Emma. Emma gazed back at him, thinking of the little boy he'd been, the damage done, the losses suffered.

Jonas bent close to her. And then closer still. His mouth covered hers.

It was heaven, his kiss. He did it the way he did everything else, so thoroughly. So very, very well.

The tenderness inside her was a live thing, suddenly. It was warm and it was growing.

Emma thought, well, what is this? What is this that is happening here?

The kiss spun out for the longest, loveliest time. When it ended, Emma said what she had said before.

"Oh, my, my..."

Jonas didn't say anything. He loomed over her. She moved her legs apart, to make room for him, and she reached up her arms to pull him close against her heart.

Chapter 10

Several hours later, Emma fell asleep in her new husband's arms. She felt just wonderful. Just about the best she'd ever felt in her whole life, in fact.

Surely it had to be more than just good sex going on here. The whole world seemed brighter. Everything was magical and shining and...right.

Could it be love?

Was it possible that Blythe had had it figured out all along—that Emma and Jonas *were* meant for each other? Emma couldn't help but start to think that her dearest friend had been a very wise woman, after all.

Emma cuddled close to Jonas. He kissed her brow, whispered, "Go to sleep." So she did.

She woke the next morning as she always did—nice and early, at a quarter after six—to find herself alone in the bed.

She sat up and pushed back the white sheet that covered her. "Jonas?"

There was no answer.

She got up and stood by the edge of the bed. "Jonas?"

Silence. She looked around, at the unmade bed she'd just jumped out of, at her shoes and panties on the floor. Her bra was over there—a little swatch of lace and satin near the sitting area. And her dress was where she'd left it, by the bureau, laid over a chair. Jonas's clothes were nowhere to be seen. They had vanished—along with the man himself.

"Jonas?" She called his name one more time, though by then she had realized there would be no answer.

He had definitely gone.

Well, he had a busy day today, didn't he? That important meeting he'd mentioned, that must be it. It was probably an early meeting. He had needed to get ready.

And she had a lot to do herself today. It was moving day. She needed to bring her things here, to get Festus and the dogs settled in. And she had to spend at least a few hours at PetRitz. If she remembered right, there were two animals due in today who wouldn't sit still for anyone but Emma: a nervous toy poodle named Cleveland who belonged to a certain aging movie star, and a gorgeous white Persian cat with very sharp claws. The owners of both animals expected her to take care of them personally. And she would.

She looked down at herself: not a stitch on.

She smiled. Yes, it had been one beautiful wedding night. She turned and headed for the bathroom and a nice, hot shower.

"You are not leaving this office until I hear a few details."

Emma looked up from the stack of purchase orders

on her desk. Deirdre stood at the door, leaning back against it, apparently blocking the way should Emma try to flee.

"Deirdre..." Emma sighed. The phone beeped twice. Emma picked it up. "What?"

"There's another reporter out here." It was Pixie, at the front desk.

Emma sighed again. In the past few hours, she had sighed a whole lot. She had picked up the dogs and Festus from Deirdre's at eight that morning, thanking her friend profusely and promising to tell her all about the wedding later—when she had some time.

By ten, the animals had been moved into their new home. Emma then returned to her house, where she picked up enough of her wardrobe to tide her over for the next few days, along with a few photographs and knickknacks she especially treasured. She also talked to her neighbor, Mrs. Cowley, who owned the other half of her duplex. Mrs. Cowley promised to keep an eye on things while Emma was away.

Emma returned to the mansion, unpacked her clothes and then spent an hour with Mandy. Finally, at a little before one in the afternoon, she'd returned to PetRitz where she'd been ever since.

According to Pixie, the reporters had started dropping in around noon. Apparently, the two paparazzi from Vegas had been talking. Somehow, Emma's identity had been determined. And someone had leaked the information that Emma and the Bravo Billionaire were more than an item; they were husband and wife.

Emma said to Pixie, "Just tell him I don't have anything to say right now."

"But he says that he wants to give you a chance to tell him about the wedding in your own words."

"Pixie. Tell him no comment."

"Em," Pixie chided. "I gotta say. This one's kinda nice and you might want to—"

"According to you, they're *all* kinda nice. It's their job to be kinda nice, so that *you* will talk *me* into talking to *them*."

"No. No, this one really *is* nice and I think that you should—"

"Pixie. No comment."

"Oh, all right. Be that way." The line went dead.

Deirdre spoke up then from her position in front of the door. "You probably will have to talk to one reporter or another eventually, you know? They'll never leave you alone until you make some kind of statement."

Emma set the phone back in its cradle. "I know. But I want to discuss it with Jonas first, before I talk to anyone."

"Why?"

"He knows a lot more about handlin' the press than I do."

"Wait. Stop. Hold on. You just gave Jonas Bravo credit for something. You just, like, *deferred* to his judgment."

"So?"

"It's not like you. It's not like you at all. You've always said you didn't trust him. That you didn't even *like* him." Deirdre leaned forward and squinted suspiciously. Her spiky red hair seemed to stick out even farther. "Something's different about you." She looked up at the ceiling. She took two deep yoga-type breaths through her nose and let each one out slowly. Then she squinted at Emma again. "You're falling for him."

Emma coughed into her fist and signed another P.O.

"You are," said Deirdre. "You've got it and you've got it bad. For the Bravo Billionaire."

Emma looked up again. Her newly discovered love must have been shining in her eyes.

Deirdre groaned. "You spent the night in the same bed with him, didn't you?"

"Is that some kind of an accusation?"

"Didn't you?"

Emma was tempted to say that no, she had not. Technically, it might even have been true, since he had been gone when she woke and had very likely left before dawn.

Deirdre repeated, "Well? Didn't you?"

The truth went and found its way out her mouth. "And so what if I did? We are married, after all."

"Not *that* kind of married, you said so yourself."

"Deirdre. It...happened. And I'm *glad* that it happened."

"You're not up for a guy like that. Nobody's up for a guy like that. Think of all the women he's been with and not one of them has lasted."

"That was a long time ago, when he dated all those women. In the past few years, there's been hardly anyone."

"Em. We are talking the original heart of stone here. It is a known fact. And you. You are such a sucker sometimes."

"Well, and thank you very much."

"You are. What about Ridley, huh? What about Ridley Mays?"

"What do you mean?" Emma was offended—for Ridley's sake, mostly. "There was nothing wrong with Ridley. He was a sweetheart."

Emma didn't date a lot. And she rarely made the L.A.

club scene, where the young and ambitious hooked up with the opposite sex. But she had met Ridley on a night out with her friends at a certain very popular club. A talented actor who just never seemed to get a break, Ridley had been Emma's steady guy for two years. They'd drifted apart when he finally got a job—on an east coast soap, which had made it necessary for him to move to Manhattan.

Deirdre grunted. "Ridley was a loser. He still hasn't paid you back all the money he borrowed from you."

"So? I'm not worried about it."

"Em, I'm just saying, face facts. You are a good person with a big heart and men tend to take advantage of you."

"I beg your pardon. The only 'men' you are talkin' about is Ridley. And what I gave him, I gave him of my own free will."

Deirdre rolled her eyes and shook her spiky head. "Okay, okay. Let's forget about Ridley. Let's talk about Jonas Bravo, who is a control freak. We all know the type. He can run a multibillion-dollar corporation with one hand tied behind his back. He has to be the best. He has to *win*. And he has to be on top. If you fall for a guy like that, you're in trouble. You've given him all the power, and he'll just use it against you." Deirdre left the door and plunked herself down in one of the pink chairs on the far side of Emma's desk. "Look, I thought this whole idea of Blythe's was crazy when you told me about it the other night. Now, I'm starting to think it's plain impossible. How are you going to help Jonas Bravo become a better person if you're so gone on him, you can't see straight?"

"Well, you know, I haven't figured that out right yet."

"Like I said, I hope you know what you're doing."

"Oh, Deirdre. So do I."

At six, just as Emma was finishing up in her office, Pixie buzzed her again.

"Pix, if it's another reporter—"

"It's not. It's *him*. Jonas." Pixie cleared her throat and added, somewhat defensively, "He said that I should call him Jonas."

Emma picked up her pen, set it down, picked it up again. Her silly heart had started going a mile a minute. "He's here?"

"No. On line two."

"Thanks." Emma ordered her heart to slow down and punched the blinking light on her phone. "Hello?"

"Having trouble with reporters?"

She held the phone tight and smiled dreamily into space, images of the night before scrolling naughtily through her mind. "How did you know?"

"It was to be expected. And you're not alone. They're storming the gates here at the Bravo Building, too."

"Well, it's not too bad, honestly."

"Have you spoken to any of them?"

"Only to tell them no comment."

"That's good. I've sent a car, to take you to Angel's Crest tonight. It should be there any minute now, ready whenever you need it."

"But I have my own—"

"Leave it. You'll probably be followed. Might as well let a pro drive. I'll set up some kind of press conference in the next few days. We'll let them ask a few questions, take a few pictures. That should get them off our backs."

"All right," she said softly, wishing he were there, right then, in her office with her. She touched her lips, remembering. It seemed she could still feel the wonder of his kiss. "Jonas, I—"

The dial tone cut her off. He had already hung up.

Emma got back to Angel's Crest at a little after seven. Palmer told her that Jonas wouldn't be in until much later. He had meetings scheduled into the night.

Emma felt just a little wistful, a little let down. It occurred to her that if they didn't make an effort to see each other, they could easily live "together" in this huge house for the whole year set out for them in Blythe's will and hardly make contact at all.

He had his own rooms. And she had hers. That had seemed just dandy yesterday, before last night had happened and everything had changed.

Or, at least, she admitted ruefully, everything had changed as far as *she* was concerned.

"Shall I serve you dinner in the small dining room?"

Emma thanked Palmer and asked him to send a tray up to her rooms. "But let me buzz the kitchen when I'm ready, all right? I want to spend some time with Mandy first."

"Certainly."

Upstairs, she found that her bed had been made and her rooms set in perfect order. Fresh towels—the big, thick Egyptian cotton kind—hung in the bathroom. And there were white roses on the bedside table now instead of peonies. Festus was curled up asleep on one of the chairs in the sitting area and the Yorkies were eager for a walk.

Emma took the dogs down a servants' stairway not far from her rooms and out onto the big slope of lawn near the back patio. As she waited for the Yorkies to do their business, she spotted two of Jonas's bodyguards, one over by the loggia and one next to the pool. Both men wore wraparound sunglasses, so she couldn't see their eyes. But she knew they were watching her and she felt more than a little bit silly as she encouraged the dogs to hurry up and then used her scooper to clean up after them.

She took the dogs with her to Mandy's rooms. The little darling held out her arms, her adorable face lighting up with pleasure at the sight of a visitor.

"Emma! Come hug. Oh, look. The puppies! Mama's puppies are back!"

Emma had the Yorkies sit and then reintroduced them to Mandy. She showed the child how to greet a dog for the first time, hand low, palm up.

"So he can sniff you. That's one way a dog gets to know you. By sniffing."

Mandy giggled in delight when Ted licked her fingers. "See? Teddy knows me."

Too soon, it was eight o'clock and time for Mandy to get ready for bed.

"Stay for bath time, Emma," Mandy pleaded.

Emma and Claudia exchanged a smile and the nanny disappeared into her own room. Mandy had a number of small boats and little plastic people. She and Emma floated them all around in the bathtub, making putt-putting sounds. The dogs sat and watched for a while, twitching their ears, looking as if such play fascinated them. Eventually, though, they stretched out on the cool bathroom tiles for a snooze.

After the bath, Mandy brushed her teeth and demanded a story. Emma willingly complied.

It was well after nine when she turned off Mandy's light. The dogs were perfect. They came when she signaled them, slipping out into the hall with her right before she closed the door. She paused briefly to knock on Claudia's door and tell the nanny that Mandy was in bed.

Festus looked up and yawned when Emma entered her suite. "I missed you, too," she told him teasingly, and went to scratch the lazy guy around the ears the way he liked it.

She rang for her tray soon after that and ate while watching the news on CNN. Then, in an effort to relax, she took a long bath.

Relaxing didn't come easy. She couldn't stop listening for the sound of footsteps. Couldn't keep from wondering if Jonas would come to her when he arrived home, if she'd see him at all that night.

It was near eleven when she climbed into bed. Festus settled in at her feet and the Yorkies took their places, one on her left, one on her right. She turned off the light.

It took a while to get to sleep, a while to let go of her disappointment that he had not come. But eventually, she drifted off.

Emma woke suddenly some time later. The dogs had disturbed her. They were both sitting up and wagging their tails.

A man stood by the bed, looking down at her.

Jonas.

Excitement flooded through her, a lush sort of feeling, a feeling that had nothing to do with helping him become a better person and everything to do with what had happened between them last night—what, it appeared, would very likely happen again, right now.

Emma pulled herself up among the pillows. She glanced at the bedside clock. After midnight.

Jonas tapped the side of his leg with his hand. The

Yorkies jumped off the bed. He bent and greeted them, scratching each under the chin. They wagged their tails some more and made small, eager sounds in their throats.

Jonas stood. "Come." Tails wagging, they followed him to the sitting area. He snapped his fingers at the black and gold brocade sofa. The dogs jumped onto it. "Lie down." The Yorkies, knowing a master when they saw and heard one, obeyed.

Jonas turned and started toward Emma again, pulling at his tie and shrugging out of his jacket as he came. He tossed both toward a chair in the corner, not even glancing over to see if they hit their mark. They did. Festus got up, stretched and jumped down from the bed, as if he understood that very soon there would be no room for him there.

"Meetings went late," Jonas said. "I need a shower." The darkness hid the details of his face from her. She couldn't see his expression—and she had a feeling it didn't matter. If she *could* have seen him clearly, she would not have had a clue what he might be thinking.

He tipped his head, just slightly, in the direction of the bathroom. He was already working at his cuff links. "Do you mind?"

She shook her head.

He turned from her, pulling his shirttail free of his slacks as he went. She watched him go. Even after he'd vanished into the bathroom, she kept on staring like a long-gone fool at the place where he had been. Every atom of her body was attuned, humming. Yearning.

Twice, she reached for the light—and both times she pulled her hand back without switching it on. It seemed wrong, somchow, to push the darkness back.

Jonas emerged from the bathroom ten minutes after

he had entered it. His chest and legs were bare and he had one of those thick Egyptian cotton towels wrapped around his waist. He came straight for her, dropping the towel to the floor when he reached her. Emma held back the sheet and he joined her in the bed.

Chapter 11

Emma had on her turquoise satin shorty pajamas—or at least, she did for a minute or two. Jonas quickly set to work getting them off her. He dropped the top over the edge of the bed and tossed the bottoms somewhere near their feet.

His mouth was on hers, stealing her breath, banishing all possibility of rational thought—which, she probably should have been ashamed to admit, was just fine with her. She kissed him back, her hands roaming the hard terrain of his body. Oh, it was heaven....

Emma had had two serious boyfriends in her life so far—Ridley, the actor, and Elton DuBose, her high-school sweetheart, who had joined the air force right after graduation and ended up marrying a German girl he met while he was stationed in Berlin.

With both Ridley and Elton, Emma had found sex enjoyable. The way she saw it, sex was a natural activity. Like breathing and eating, it felt real good.

But she had not realized, not in all her twenty-six years of life, that sex could be like it was with Jonas, that desire could be something that ate a girl alive, that it could feel so incredible, just being consumed.

Jonas kissed his way down her body and she moaned and clutched his shoulders as he did things with his mouth and tongue that she had never known *could* be done. She went over the edge, with his head buried between her thighs. He kept his mouth there, sucking gently, as the aftershocks skittered through her.

A thin wedge of moonlight, glinting in through the French doors that led to the terrace, fell across the bed, turning everything silvery. Jonas looked up from between her spread thighs, mouth wet, eyes gleaming. He laid his hand over the moist dark-gold curls that covered her sex and whispered something tender about natural blondes.

She answered lazily, "Yes. I am an all-natural girl— at least from the neck down."

He chuckled. And began to caress her again.

She moaned and tried to brush his hand away. "Oh, don't. I am done for. I cannot move...."

He ignored her protests.

And very soon, she did move.

She wanted to touch him and kiss him and feel every part of him. So she did. She played with him as he had played with her. He lay back and she stretched her body over his, bending to his mouth, slipping her tongue between his lips, kissing him long and deep and slow.

She dragged her wet mouth down the center of him, and she captured him, sucking, until he gave in and bucked against her, pulsing. Spilling...

They rested, silent, all wrapped up in each other as the wedge of moonlight moved across the snowy sheets.

And then they began again—the two of them, all over each other in the wide white bed. He was in her and around her and nothing seemed to matter, nothing but the feel of his hands on her body, the way that he moved when he was inside her, the hot, open press of his mouth on her mouth, the burning dart of his tongue, reaching for the center of her, setting her on fire.

It was after two when she fell asleep again. She woke at three, briefly, and saw that she was alone.

She called for him once, "Jonas?" into the darkness. But she knew she'd get no answer. She knew that he had gone.

How smoothly the days that followed fell into a pattern. He came to her at night, most often waking her from sleep. They would make love. And when she woke in the morning, he would be gone. Emma went to the doctor, got a prescription for birth control pills, but she never told Jonas.

Because they never talked, not really, during the night. If he had something to say to her, he would call her at PetRitz, usually in the afternoon.

Two days after they were married, he called to set up the press conference that was supposed to get all those reporters to stop following them everywhere they went. The press conference worked. It succeeded in getting the reporters and shutter-happy paparazzi to back off.

Unfortunately, the resulting articles made Emma want to gag. They had headlines like "The Blond Bombshell and the Bravo Billionaire...True Love at Last?" and "Bravo Billionaire Brought to Heel By Sexy Dog Trainer." It was so insulting. They couldn't even get her job title right. Everybody at PetRitz teased her about it. It got old real fast

She decided to talk to Jonas about the articles and how much they bothered her. They were lying in her bed, naked as usual, and satisfied, for the moment, though Emma knew that very soon it would start all over again.

She told him that she had read some of the articles about the two of them and that she had hated them.

He shrugged. "Don't read them."

She glared at him. "That's it? That's all you have to tell me, don't read them?"

"That's right."

"But it's so…rude. The things they're allowed to print for the whole world to see. I have half a mind to sue them, I sincerely do."

He canted up on an elbow and bent over her. "Emma…"

She saw the look in his eyes and she knew just what it meant. "Don't. Don't you touch me, not right now. I am tryin' to talk to you about something that is a problem for me and I—"

"Listen," he whispered, his voice like warm honey, pouring over her, making everything thick and sweet and slow. Making her stupid—there was no other word for it. All he had to do was look at her, speak to her, put a hand on her, and she got real stupid, real fast.

He instructed, "Do not read them. Don't read them and don't think about them. Act as if they don't exist. And they won't."

"I can't help thinking about them. I get razzed about them all day long."

"You get razzed because the people who razz you know that it bothers you. Don't let them know, and they'll leave you alone."

"But I—"

And then he kissed her.

That was the end of that conversation.

She did take his advice. She stopped reading the tabloids.

Surprisingly, she found that he was right. She pretended that the articles didn't exist and after a very short time, she found she could almost believe it. When folks teased her, she just smiled and nodded and let it go. They stopped teasing.

In bed a couple of nights later, she told Jonas that his advice was working. She thanked him.

He bent close. "Let's see just how grateful you really are...."

Well, and what could she do, but show him?

The next afternoon, he called PetRitz to tell her that he would be gone for a few days. He was flying to New York for a series of meetings that had something to do with buying a high-rise in Dallas. He gave her the news, said goodbye and hung up.

Emma sat at her desk with the dial tone buzzing in her ear and wondered why he couldn't have told her that last night.

The answer was disgustingly obvious, even to a woman made terminally stupid by love or desire or whatever you wanted to call what was going on between her and her new husband.

Jonas couldn't hang up when he was in bed with her. If he talked to her about anything important while he was actually in her presence, there was always the chance that she might talk back. He'd have to get up and put on his clothes and leave to get away from her. That could get awkward, so he just called her, said what he had to say—and then said goodbye.

Emma set the phone down, her mind turning to those warnings of Deirdre's.

*Let's talk about Jonas Bravo, who is a control freak...
If you fall for a guy like that, you're in trouble. You've
given him all the power, and he'll just use it against
you....*

They had been married for less than a week. True,
that was only a tiny fraction of the year Blythe had given
her to make Jonas Bravo into a different kind of man.
It would be easy to tell herself that she still had plenty
of time—and it would be true. She *did* have plenty of
time.

But she hadn't gotten off to much of a start, now, had
she?

She'd let him do exactly what Deirdre had predicted
he would—take control and use her own craving for him
against her. She'd allowed him to set up their marriage
just the way he wanted it.

Jonas got back from New York on Tuesday. Emma
knew he'd returned because he called to tell her he
wanted to have dinner with her that evening at eight
o'clock in the small dining room.

Emma said, "Oh, Jonas, I'd love that," feeling all
warm and hopeful inside, thinking that *this* was more
like it.

Jonas said, "Good. See you at eight," and hung up.

Emma dressed with great care that evening, in her one
little black dress, which was much simpler and less provocative than the clothes she usually wore. Yes, it clung
to her curves just as all her dresses did, but it fell to her
knees rather than mid-thigh. It had a simple scoop neck
and cap sleeves and seemed to her to be the kind of
dress that would give off serious signals—signals that

said she'd enjoy a little conversation with her new husband for once, thank you very much.

She stood before the mirror in her dressing room and shook her head. "Real pathetic. Married for one whole week and you only see him in bed."

Even on the weekends, Jonas had proved elusive. This last weekend, he'd been in New York. And the one before, well, Emma had no idea where he'd been, exactly. Maybe working. She knew he worked very long hours during the week. He probably worked weekends, too. And he'd spent some of the time with Mandy—Claudia had told her that. But somehow, he managed never to go to Mandy's rooms when Emma was there.

Well. Tonight would be different than the other nights. Tonight, Emma and her husband would *talk.*

What she hadn't counted on was how the sight of him hollowed her out, how all he had to do was put his hand on her arm and the blood seemed to rush up to the surface of her skin where he touched her, as if it only wanted to be closer to him.

Pathetic, she thought. Downright pitiful.

He led her to the living room where they'd shared drinks on their wedding night. He had the daiquiris ready—banana flavored this time. The golden, icy confection tempted her.

But Emma couldn't afford to get any more stupid than his mere presence was already making her. Banana daiquiris were out. "No, thanks," she said.

He slanted her a look—watchful, knowing. And he shrugged. He poured himself whatever he'd poured himself the last time, three fingers of something richly amber in color.

He raised his glass to her and he drank. And then he came toward her.

Oh, she wished he wouldn't do that. The closer he came, the more tangled up in yearning she got. And the more downright dazed. She was standing in front of one of the striped silk sofas, since she hadn't quite gotten around to sitting down yet. And then she couldn't sit down. Her legs felt spindly and weak as those of a newborn calf, yet at the same time, she could not get them to bend.

He stopped about a foot from her. It was way too close—and it wasn't nearly close enough. She could smell him. He smelled so good, of some really nice aftershave and of healthiness and of something else, something that was just *him,* something that stunned her and drew her and made her want to grab him and run—straight up the stairs to her bed.

"Dinner can wait," he said. He turned to set his half-finished drink on the little table next to the sofa. She just stood there, longing moving through her like a pulse, thinking how pathetic she was—and at the same time, too aroused to even care.

He faced her again. "Ready?" He offered his arm.

She hooked her hand through it. They turned for the door to the grand foyer and the stairs.

"An attractive dress," he said, when he was taking it off of her. "It suits you, in a whole new way."

She actually opened her mouth then, to say what had been on her mind. "Well, I wore it because I thought it looked serious."

"Serious?" He had the zipper down. He put his hands on her shoulders.

"Yes. I was planning to talk to you about—"

"What?" He pushed the dress off her shoulders, his hands stroking down her arms.

"I thought—"

And he kissed her.

So much for thought.

He took away the dress, and her black bra and her pretty high-heeled shoes and even the pantyhose she had worn because they had seemed a kind of protection, a way to be more covered than usual around him.

Oh, well. So much for her plans for the evening.

He took off his own clothes and the two of them fell to the bed and after that there was nothing but sighing and moaning and some yelling, as well.

Emma knew that she needed a good talking-to. She needed someone to tell her what-for.

For the first twenty or so years of her life, she had had her aunt Cass for times like these. And after Aunt Cass had succumbed to that melanoma she got because she'd always been so big on getting nice and tan, she'd had Blythe. Thinking about the wise things either of those two women might say now was like ripping open a healing wound. It made Emma's throat close up and her chest feel too tight.

Well, Aunt Cass and Blythe were gone. If Emma wanted wise words, she'd have to look elsewhere.

She and Deirdre had coffee and bagels together in Emma's office at PetRitz the morning after Jonas returned from New York. They talked a little about the workday ahead and then some about a new guy Deirdre was seeing, an accountant of all things. He sounded like a pretty decent fella, and Emma told her friend so.

Then Deirdre asked, "So, how's life at the mansion?"

Emma told all—well, not the *details,* but the main points.

It was awful, putting it right out there, how in just over one week of marriage, she'd had nothing that even came close to a real conversation with her new husband, that his touch caused her IQ to drop fifty points. How he came to her late in the night, and left before dawn.

"I swear, Deirdre," Emma cried, "if he sleeps at all, it's never with me."

Deirdre shook her red head and munched her raisin bagel with raspberry-flavored cream cheese and said, "It's not like I didn't warn you."

Emma set down her coffee and made a low noise in her throat. "Oh, gee. Thanks. Say 'I told you so.' That is a big help—and what are you laughing about?"

"It's too delicious." For a minute, Emma thought Deirdre meant the cream cheese, which she was licking from her fingers. But then she added, "My boss, the sex toy."

Emma sat back in her swivel chair and tried to look dignified. "You are just too mean to live."

"What if the tabloids got ahold of what you just told me? Wouldn't that be rich? I can see it now, 'Dog Trainer Willing Sex Slave of Bravo Billionaire.'"

"Oh, I am *so* glad I talked to you about this," Emma muttered under her breath.

"All right." Deirdre had finished laughing. She leaned toward Emma. "So what are you going to do?"

Emma swiveled her chair back and forth. "I was hopin' that you'd have a suggestion."

Deirdre shrugged. "Get a backbone?"

"I've tried."

"Try harder."

Oh, where were Aunt Cass and Blythe when a woman needed them?

Deirdre was squinting across the desk now. "You're serious? You want advice? From me."

"Yes, I do."

"Well, then." Deirdre sipped coffee, took another bite of her bagel. Finally, she came out with it. "I'd say, try to talk to him one more time. But use a different approach."

"Different?"

"Yeah. Come at it a new way. Maybe don't try to talk to him right at first, when he shows up at the side of your bed. Get the edge off first, so to speak."

"The edge off?"

"Emma. You know what I mean. Make love, once or twice. And when you're both relaxed and satisfied..."

"Try to talk to him then."

"Exactly."

"And if that doesn't work?"

Deirdre swore. "What is the *point* with this guy? I gotta ask you, why don't you just enjoy the mindless sex thing while it lasts and then—"

"That is not what this is about."

"Oh. Right. Sorry, I forgot."

"Just stop being sarcastic and tell me the rest."

"The rest?"

"The rest of your advice, what to do if I still can't get him to talk to me."

Deirdre paused long enough for a few of her yoga breaths. Then she slumped in her chair. "All right. If you can't get him to talk to you, then I'd go for action."

"Action?"

"Yeah, and don't ask me *what* action. You'll have to figure that out for yourself."

* * *

That night, Emma waited. She bided her time. When her husband came to her, she didn't even try to get him to talk to her right at first. She let him lead the Yorkies and Festus away. Then she opened her arms to him and pulled him down onto the bed with her. She made love to him—passionately, tenderly. She gave it her all.

Twice.

And then a third time.

Finally, well past one in the morning, he did what he always did, brushing her hair away from her temple, whispering so softly, "Go to sleep."

Surprisingly, she found she felt clearheaded, for once. As if her resolve to reach out to him had finally become strong enough to override her overwhelming lust for the man.

Emma took the hand that smoothed her hair and kissed it. Then she sat up. She reached over and turned on the bedside lamp.

The light helped, it really did. She felt more sure of herself than she did in the dark.

Jonas had sat up, too. He was frowning at her.

She gave him a big smile. "Jonas, have you noticed that we never seem to talk?"

He looked at her for a long time. And then he smiled. It was a very slow smile and a totally sexual one. "I don't think we need to talk."

Oh, now, how did he do that? How could just his voice and his smile turn her into a quivering mass of burning desire?

Hold on, she was thinking. Don't go under. Don't give in.

She sat up straighter and pulled the sheet tight around

her bare breasts. "There," she said. "Look what you're doin'. Aren't you ashamed of yourself?"

"No." With a finger, he traced the tops of her breasts, right above the sheet, causing hot little goose bumps to erupt where he touched.

"Well, you certainly should be." She took his hand and gently pushed it away. "This is crazy, this thing between us."

He sat back a little—which was good. The farther back he sat, the clearer her mind got. He said, "As far as I'm concerned, this thing between us is working out just fine."

She straightened the sheet a little, huffed in a breath. "Jonas. It is not working out just fine. We're *married*. We don't act like married folks. Not one bit."

"Why should we? This is hardly your average marriage."

"Well, you are dead right there, mister. If you ask me, it is a very strange kind of marriage. You come to my bed in the night. We make love. You leave. If you have something to say to me, you call me at work. We both know why you do that. So that you can hang up as soon as you're done talkin'. So I won't have a chance to say anything you don't want to hear.

"Maybe you're happy with the way things are goin'. I'm not. Even if it is for only a year, I would like it to be the best year it can be. I would like more than beautiful lovemakin'. The way I see it, if there's gonna be lovemakin', there should be sleepin' afterward—you and me, I mean, sleepin'. Together. And there should be talking. I want you to really *talk* to me."

He studied her face for a long, painful moment. Then he said, "Good night, Emma." He pushed back the covers and swung his legs off the bed.

She folded her arms over the sheet. "Just tell me, Jonas. Does this mean I'm not gettin' through to you?"

He sent her the kind of look he was famous for—cold and dangerous as the blade of a knife.

She kept her chin high. "Aunt Cass used to say, 'Treat a man as he is, and he will remain as he is. Treat a man as he can and should be, and he will become what he can and should be.'"

He grunted. "Goethe," he said.

She frowned. "Huh? Gurta?"

"Johann Wolfgang von Goethe, German poet and dramatist. That quote came from him."

"Well, fine. Whoever said it, I am doin' it. I am treatin' you as you can and should be, Jonas Bravo. By the time our year is over, you won't be what you were."

He said something under his breath, something nasty, she just knew it. Then he started getting dressed. He did it swiftly and efficiently. No wasted movement whatsoever.

In two minutes from the time he'd left the bed, he was striding to the door, fully clothed. He went out, closing it quietly behind him.

Emma stared at the door he had shut on her.

Okay Jonas, she thought. I have tried to get through to you with talk. Talk has not worked. Now action is called for.

Chapter 12

Jonas called Emma at PetRitz twice the next day. Once in the morning and once in the early afternoon. She didn't answer her phone either time. He ended up talking to Pixie, who told him, both times, that Emma was busy and couldn't come to the phone right then.

"Busy doing what?" he demanded on the second call.

"Well, she didn't tell me that. She just said to tell you that she was busy."

"Just busy."

"That's right. I'd be glad to give her a message for you, Jonas."

"No, thank you, Pixie," he replied, thinking that *he* was the one getting the message here. And the message was, if he wanted to talk to his wife, he'd better think of some other way to do it than by phone. He added, "I'll try again later," knowing he would do no such thing.

''Well, you just go ahead and do that,'' Pixie chirped out, sounding insolent enough to set his teeth on edge.

There wasn't a thing more to say right then, so he hung up.

He decided to give her cell phone a try. It rang for a long time, then a recorded voice picked up, told him that the customer was not available at the moment and invited him to leave a message.

He didn't.

It was barely seven when Jonas returned to Angel's Crest that evening. He'd gone ahead and rescheduled his dinner engagement with Ledger DelVecchio, an independent film producer, a fellow who always amused him and whose offbeat movies Jonas often backed.

Though he never made any real money doing it, Jonas frequently contributed to the arts, both as an investor and through outright donations. He supposed he had some of his mother in him, after all. Now and then it felt good to do a thing just because somebody with money *had* to do it or it wouldn't *get* done.

But Ledger would have to wait until tomorrow night. Tonight, Jonas wanted to get things straight with Emma. He had his driver drop him off at the side entrance nearest her rooms. He planned to make a few things crystal clear to his temporary wife. And after he had explained how things were going to be, he planned to ask her to have dinner with him.

Night before last they'd never managed to get around to dinner. He regretted that now. But he'd taken one look at her in that damn demure little back dress, and all he could think about was getting it off of her.

And yes. All right. Maybe he shouldn't have walked

out on her last night. He was willing, he'd realized to-day, to expend a little effort to keep Emma happy.

Because, on the whole, Emma kept *him* happy. In ways he'd never known a man *could* be happy. The woman was a find. In the end, he supposed, there was something to be said for sincerity—for frankness and honesty, for giving a hundred percent.

Emma made love like that: sincerely, frankly, one hundred percent. After the past nine stimulating nights, Jonas had discovered he could actually imagine lasting out the whole year without becoming the least bit bored.

He only had to make it clear to her that heart-to-heart talks and staying the whole night in her bed were not part of the deal. He was willing to bend. A little. He'd spend more time with her clothed, if she wanted it that way. They'd share meals a few times a week.

He'd even take her out, if that would please her, though in his opinion, going out would be far more trou-ble than it could possibly be worth. Right now, the two of them were something of an item with the press. Which meant they'd probably be hounded unmercifully by reporters should they dare anything so outrageous as trying to share a meal in a restaurant.

Jonas climbed the servants' stairway to the second floor, telling himself that if Emma wanted a few nights on the town, she would have them. Because he was a fair man and he took care of the people who took care of him. And as exasperating as the woman could be now and then, Emma Lynn definitely knew how to take care of him.

He emerged from the stairwell into a side hall, strode down it and turned a corner to find himself at the door to Emma's suite. He reached for the door handle—and then hesitated.

Strange. Every night, he went into her room without so much as a thought for knocking first.

But right now, he felt that that would be wrong. Rude. An invasion of her privacy.

Maybe it was the slowly sinking sun whose orange rays still glowed in the fan-lighted window at the far end of the hall. He never came to her when the sun was up. Daylight, somehow, seemed a time when he had no claim on her.

He shrugged. Whatever. And then he knocked.

And after that, he waited.

She didn't answer.

He called her name, "Emma," and knocked again.

Nothing.

It hadn't occurred to him that she might not be in her rooms. She had always been there, waiting, whenever he wanted her.

The absurdity of his assumption dawned on him then. He'd never before come to her at seven in the evening. This, as they say, was a whole new ball game. She might be anywhere—including on the other side of the door, ignoring his knock.

He took hold of the door handle. It turned, so he pushed the door inward. "Emma," he said, "there's no need to be childish about—"

He cut himself off. She did not appear to be in the room.

He went in and quietly shut the door behind him. "Emma?"

No answer. He went into the dressing room and the bath, as well. No sign of her. Or of the dogs, for that matter. Or even of that sleepy-eyed black-and-white cat.

It came to him. Mandy's room. She'd taken the animals and gone to visit his sister.

Well all right, then. He'd seek her out there. That might work well, now he thought about it. If she remained irritated with him about last night, she would try not to let her feelings show around the sprite. She'd make an effort to be civil to him, and that would be a start. They could spend some time with Mandy, and then he could lead her away to say the things he meant to say.

He started for the door again—and then paused near the foot of the black-skirted bed. Something wasn't right.

His gaze fell on the gilded black Empire table that served as a nightstand. Last night, there had been two framed pictures on that table, one of his mother and the Yorkies and Mandy. And one of a handsome, deeply tanned woman in a tight-fitting blue chambray shirt and Western-cut vest: the legendary Aunt Cass.

Neither picture was there now.

Jonas turned slowly, taking in every aspect of the large room. He found not one single item of Emma's in sight. No pictures, none of those little bits of bric-a-brac she had brought with her when she moved in, things like a saucer full of shells she'd probably gathered on some beach somewhere and a three-inch figurine of a raccoon standing on its haunches, prehensile paws tucked under its chin, staring out at the world coyly through surprisingly lifelike black glass eyes.

Jonas spun on his heel and strode to the dressing room. He threw back the door to the walk-in closet.

Not a single, skimpy dayglow-colored dress. No leopard-skin pants, no peekaboo blouses, no rows of sexy high-heeled shoes. Nothing. Empty. Just a faint, faraway echo of roses, the smell of her lingering, and that was all.

Jonas very carefully shut the closet door.

He was absolutely furious. He'd been willing to compromise, damn it—within reason, anyway. She should have given him a chance.

What the hell kind of game did she think she was playing? She knew that they had to live together for the entire year. She had *agreed* that they would live together.

She had no right at all to move out on him. None. Zero. Zip. They were abiding by the terms of his mother's will and she was not going to be allowed to screw things up.

Now, he would have to go out and find her and drag her back where she belonged.

He strode to the door. Halfway down the hallway, he stopped.

He really was furious. Maybe too furious.

He needed to give himself a chance to cool off a little, before he went after his wayward wife.

So all right. First, he'd pay a visit to the sprite. Being around Mandy always soothed him. He'd see his little sister, listen to her childish laughter, let her boss him around for a while, and when he went after Emma, he'd be calmer.

Not so likely to wring her smooth white neck.

The door to the nursery stood open when he got there.

And he knew. Before he went into the playroom, the bedroom, the nanny's room, the bathroom with its big white tub where Mandy liked to float her plastic boats....

He knew that she was gone.

He strode from one room to the next, charting the emptiness, telling himself to be calm, to think clearly, not to jump to conclusions.

But the past was alive in him, all of a sudden, gnawing

at him from the inside, a rat with big, sharp bloody teeth, chewing its way out of his chest.

He dropped to the rocker in his sister's bedroom, let his head fall back, sucked in long, slow breaths through his nose.

This was not real. He refused to believe it. It simply could not be happening again. No one had broken in. It was impossible. This wasn't thirty years ago. Now, his men prowled the grounds. No intruder could get through twice—to make his way in *and* to make good an escape.

His sister had not been stolen. He had not lost her. He had not failed in his duty to keep her safe. She would not vanish from his life as if she had never been. It could not be. He would not allow it. He would not—

His mind spun to a stop.

He lifted his head, sat up straight, muttered one word. Her name.

"Emma."

Of course. Emma was behind this. She had not only run off when she had no right to do such a thing—but she'd also dared to take his little sister with her.

Terror no longer gnawed away inside his chest. Now rage burned there.

He was furious all over again. More furious than ever. At Emma.

Palmer chose that moment to appear in the doorway to the hall. "There you are, sir."

Jonas stood. "What is it, Palmer?"

"Sir, your driver told me you'd gone in by the side entrance." Palmer stepped into the room. He carried a legal-sized envelope in his right hand. He held it out. "Ms. Emma asked me to see that you got this the minute you arrived home."

Jonas took the envelope, tore it open and unfolded the note it contained.

Jonas,

In your mother's will, it says that I get to choose where we live. I have decided that I choose my own house. I'm taking Mandy there, and her nanny, too. Poor Claudia. She's real upset. She thinks you're not going to be too happy about this. But I told her not to worry. I told her I knew exactly what I was doing. I told Palmer the same thing. And what could either of them say? After all, I am your wife and I ought to know what's okay with you and what's not. Right?

So we're waiting for you. At my house.

See you soon and don't forget your toothbrush,

Emma

"Is...everything all right, sir?" Palmer asked.

Jonas glanced up. The butler looked distinctly apprehensive.

"Everything's just fine," Jonas said. "This letter tells me all I need to know."

And it did. It told him where he had to go to get his hands on her.

"Have my driver bring my car back around to the front, will you please, Palmer?"

"Immediately, sir."

Chapter 13

Jonas descended on Emma's duplex at seven forty-seven. He beat on the door with his fist. When she didn't get there to open it fast enough for him, he started shouting.

"Damn you, Emma! Open this door!"

The Yorkies ran to the door and began barking at it frantically. Claudia came running down the hall. "It is him, Ms. Emma. It's Mr. Jonas. Ah, *Dios mío...*" She paused to make the sign of the cross and then to press her fingertips to her lips. "We are in big trouble now. He will kill us, I swear to you—"

"Now you just relax," Emma said, proud that none of the apprehension she felt came through in her voice. Jonas went on pounding and the Yorkies went on barking.

Emma took the nanny by the shoulders and turned her around so that she was facing the hall. "Go on. Go back to Mandy. She's probably scared out of her skin with all this racket going on.''

"But Ms. Emma, we can't—"

"Emma! Now!" He pounded some more. The Yorkies yipped and ran in circles.

"Don't you worry, just go on along now." Emma gave Claudia a gentle push. The nanny scurried back the way she had come.

"Emma!" More pounding. It was a solid-core door, but it wouldn't hold up forever under such a brutal assault.

"Stop that!" she shouted back at him. "I am coming! I want to put the dogs out! Just you hold on!"

There was silence. The Yorkies had turned to stare at her, their big brown eyes saucer-wide behind the wispy fringes of brown fur that drooped from their foreheads.

She slapped her thigh with authority. "Bob. Ted. Come." They scampered behind her to the sliding glass door that opened onto the patio. "Out." They went through and she shut and latched the door. Then she marched back to her small entrance area, slid back the dead bolt and pulled the door wide.

He was standing on the other side and he did not look happy.

Well, she wasn't very happy with him, either. "I hope you know you've probably scared your baby sister clean into next Tuesday. And poor Claudia. She was callin' on her maker, speakin' in Spanish, drawin' the sign of the cross. Dear old Mrs. Cowley, who owns the other half of this duplex, has probably already called 911. And besides all that, you have stirred up my dogs."

He just looked at her, that burning look he could get now and then. Usually, he got that look when they were making love. She found it very arousing then. However, since there wasn't any lovemaking going on at the moment, the look made her more than a little bit nervous.

She moved back. "All right. Come in."

He stepped over her threshold. She shut the door behind him.

"I expect you to act like a civilized human being," she warned. "And the minute you throw something, you are out of here. Understand?"

He didn't bother to answer. His glance flicked over her living room and came back to settle on her. "Get your things. Get Mandy's things. And Claudia's. We are all going home. Now. You and I will have a nice, long talk after we get there."

Emma folded her arms under her breasts. "I gave Palmer a note to give to you."

"So?"

"Did you get that note?"

"Yes, I got that note."

"Did you *read* that note?"

"Yes, Emma, I did."

"Well. Then you know very well that I'm not leavin' this house. I am the one who gets to make the choice about where we live. And I have decided that we will live here."

He kept that burning gaze right on her—and he started walking toward her.

"Wait," she said. "Stop. Just you stop right there."

He kept on coming. She told herself to stand firm, but her legs seemed to move of their own accord.

She gave ground—backing toward the kitchen, under the arch, across her red-tiled floor. He kept pace with her. It worked out fine until she ran out of floor and into her refrigerator, which was thick with magnets in various animal shapes. She bumped a couple of them. They clattered to the floor.

She glanced down at the magnets—a chicken and a Scottie dog—then back up at him. "Jonas..."

Very carefully, sliding magnets out of his way to do it, he laid one big hand on either side of her head.

She knew what to do, and she did it fast, too, bending her knees, bolting under his restraining arm.

But he was faster. He blocked her escape by lowering that arm and extending his opposite knee until it met the refrigerator. More magnets fell.

With great dignity, Emma straightened her legs again. "This is what happens when you're big and strong and rich, huh? You think it's your God-given right to push people around."

"I am just trying to get your attention."

"Well, guess what? You got it."

"Good."

"What happens now?"

"Now, you listen."

"Okay, fine. I am listenin'."

"Are you sure?"

She decided that question didn't deserve an answer. She waited, thinking that he was way too close, too big, too warm, too...everything. She wished he would back off.

And at the same time, she wished he would press himself against her, just grind himself right into her, let the magnets fall where they may.

Oh, Deirdre was right. For a self-starting independent take-charge woman, she sure did a good impression of a sex toy.

Finally, he spoke. "We cannot live here. It is impossible.'' He said each word slowly and softly, right into her face.

She dredged up a scoffing sound. ''Exaggerate a little, why don't you, Jonas? Of course, we *can* live here. There is a kitchen, three bedrooms, two bathrooms. A roof over our heads. Even a livin' room with a workin' fireplace and a twenty-seven-inch TV. It may not be Bel Air, but we *can* live here, I promise you that.''

''Why?''

''Why what?''

''Why the hell are you doing this?''

''Because your house is too darn big and it's too easy for you to hide when you're there.''

That seemed to get to him. He dropped his imprisoning arms and stepped away from her.

She waited for him to say something. He didn't. She looked down at the magnets around her feet. Kneeling, she gathered them up, the chicken, the Scottie, two cats and a frog. The frog had been injured in the fall—a crack right down the middle of its white belly.

''Emma.''

She didn't answer. Instead, she straightened, turned and stuck the magnets back where they belonged.

She felt rather than heard him move toward her again. All at once, he was right behind her. She tried to steel herself. It didn't do much good. Her midsection was melting. The blood in her veins pounded out his name.

''Hide from what?'' he whispered much too tenderly, his breath warm against her ear.

''It's not a 'what,' it's a 'who,''' she replied, low and a little bit angrily. ''And you know it, too.''

He put those big hands of his at her waist, very lightly. She was wearing toreador pants and a crop top, which meant he was touching bare skin—skin that warmed and softened and seemed to melt like the rest of her at his slightest touch.

His lips were against her hair. "You mean it's a 'whom.'"

She pressed her forehead to the cool freezer compartment door. The coolness didn't help. The rest of her was burning up—with wanting him. "Who, whom, what's the difference? It's me, Jonas. You are hiding from me."

He pulled her, slowly, and so gently, back against him, tucking her into him, letting her feel that he wanted her as she wanted him. Then he loosened his hold a fraction and pressed his lips to her nape. She made it easy for him, bending her head, giving in to him—as she always did. All he had to do was touch her, speak to her in that low, private voice that seemed to be meant only for her. And she was a goner.

Pathetic. Pitiful.

It had to stop.

She lifted her head. It was a start. He stopped kissing the back of her neck.

"I have never even seen your bedroom, Jonas. I have not seen where you sleep, your private place. We are *married* and I haven't seen it."

He let go of her waist—and put his hands on her shoulders instead. "You want to see my bedroom?" he whispered in her ear.

She kept her back straight, her chin high. "Yes, I do."

His hands were on the move again. They slipped beneath her arms. His fingers grazed the side swells of her breasts. She had to press her lips together to keep from letting out a hungry moan.

"All right," he said. "Come home. I'll show you my bedroom."

"You'll *show* it to me?"

"That's right."

"That's not enough."

"You want more?"

"I sure do."

"Name it." He cupped her breasts. She moaned at that, but very softly—and then it occurred to her that this was not her room at Angel's Crest. This was her kitchen in North Hollywood and Claudia could come flying down the hall, Mandy in tow, any minute now.

She turned in his embrace and captured those wonderful hands of his. "Not now…" She sent a glance toward the arch that led to the hall.

He took her meaning and nodded. "You're right."

She let go of his hands. He had the grace to move away a few steps.

She told him what else she wanted. "I want us to share a bedroom, Jonas. I don't care whose bedroom, yours or mine. It doesn't matter. Just as long as we start spendin' whole nights together."

Something changed in his face. It seemed to close against her. All at once, his eyes were looking right through her. Emma shivered as if a cold wind had blown through the room.

"I sleep alone, Emma." He said it flatly, as something that was beyond discussion or dispute.

"Oh," she said. "Well, that sounds pretty final."

"It is."

Emma felt like a blind person who'd run up on a wall, just squashed herself flat against it with no prior warning.

She tried not to sound as disconcerted as she felt. "Okay," she said cheerfully. "As I said a few minutes ago, there are three bedrooms here. Claudia and Mandy have two of them. I've got the master. And you are very welcome to share my room with me any time you get tired of sleepin' on the sofa.''

He looked at her as if he doubted she had any brains at all. ''I told you. We cannot stay here.''

''That's right, you told me. But you didn't bother to say why.''

''You know damn well why. It's not safe. There's no security.''

''Sure, there is. I have an alarm system.''

''A box by the door and a couple of sensors in the windows? Come on, Emma. Any idiot could get through a system like yours. To even call it a system is pretty damn ludicrous.''

''Jonas. This is your paranoia speaking, that's what this is.''

''If I'm paranoid, I have my reasons. And you know damn well what they are.''

Emma blinked. It was the first time in their entire acquaintance that he had referred of his own accord, even indirectly, to the tragedy of thirty years ago. Could this be called progress?

''Yes,'' she said carefully. ''I do know. And what happened thirty years ago is not going to happen now.''

He turned his head away from her, so he seemed to be studying the cabinets above the stove. ''If you'd asked my parents back then, they probably would have said the same thing—that it couldn't happen. It wouldn't happen. To them. But it did. It happened to them. To me. To my brother.'' He looked at her again—or at least, he looked in her direction. His eyes were worlds away. ''We never found him.''

She wanted to say something wise and comforting and helpful, but all that came out was, ''I know. Oh, and I am so very sorry…''

"It killed my father. He had a heart attack, but we all knew what caused it. To lose a son like that, to have him stolen from my father's house, right out from under his nose. My father was a man who believed, with some reason, that he had a certain degree of power in the world. But then he was forced to learn the true meaning of powerlessness. It killed him, that's all. And my mother, well, you know all about what happened to her."

Emma nodded. She felt she didn't dare speak. Though she had heard it all before, from Blythe, it still hurt, to hear these hard things. How much more it must hurt him, to say them.

Jonas said, "I have a detective agency, the best in the city, on retainer. I've had one agency or another on retainer ever since I was old enough to *hire* a damn agency. They not only check out individuals for me, they keep an open file on my brother's kidnapping. They've come up with leads, now and then. Leads that go nowhere. The fact is, we still don't have a clue where my brother went, who took him, if he's long dead and buried in some shallow grave somewhere—or if he's alive, a grown man now. Walking the earth somewhere, not knowing who he really is, where he came from, who his people are…"

His eyes were focused on her again, determined and so sure. "That's why we cannot stay here. You are not just Emma Lynn Hewitt anymore. You have married the Bravo Billionaire. And you will put all of us at risk if you continue to insist that we live with you here, where I can't guarantee that you and Mandy will be safe."

He straightened from the counter, came close again, put both big hands gently on her shoulders. "Now. I want you to go and pack up whatever needs packing. As soon as you're ready, we can go.''

Emma stared up at him. She felt warm all over, a new kind of warmth. A warmth from more than the promise of great sex. It had happened. For the first time.

Jonas had *talked* to her. Maybe, at last, they were getting somewhere—and it was a good thing, too. They had such a long way to go.

"Oh, Jonas," she said. "No. We are not going back to that mansion of yours. Do what you have to do to make this house safe. Put in a state-of-the-art alarm system. That's fine with me. Get all those bodyguards of yours to hang around outside in the pyracantha bushes, ready, willin' and able to jump anybody who tries to threaten us. Whatever. But we are stayin' here for a while."

He dropped his hands from her shoulders. "Didn't you understand a word of what I just told you?"

"I did. I understood, but—"

"And yet you'd put us all in jeopardy anyway?"

"But we *won't* be in jeopardy. I am not going to believe that. Nobody is after us. It's been thirty years since your brother was kidnapped, and nobody's tried to hurt you or your family since then. It is not going to happen again."

"Easy for you to say."

"Jonas, you can protect us here—as much as we really need protectin', anyway. Please. Just give staying at my house a chance."

He stepped back, started to turn. "I'm taking Mandy with me. We are leaving now."

"Oh, wait…" She grabbed his arm.

He froze, looked down at her hand where it gripped his forearm, then slowly into her eyes.

She let go of him. "You know what Blythe's will says. You have to live with me, where I say we will live, for one year. If you don't—"

"Are you threatening me, Emma?"

"No. I am...remindin' you of our situation. And I am, well, I am willin' to compromise."

Coward, a voice in her head taunted. Lily-livered ninny. Yellow-bellied fool...

Should she stand firm? Well, okay. Maybe.

But if he took Mandy and returned to the mansion, where would they be but right back where they'd started? Yes, she could sue him, and maybe somehow save Mandy—from what, it was becoming less and less clear to her.

From her brother's overbearing protectiveness, maybe. From a life locked away at Angel's Crest.

But even if by some miracle she managed to wrestle custody from him and save Mandy, well, who would save Jonas?

His eyes had gotten warier—but he hadn't turned away again. "Compromise, how?"

"We'll go back to Angel's Crest with you now, all of us."

"And?"

"And from now on...we share a bedroom, you and me."

He made a low, disbelieving sound. "I told you—"

"I know you did. You sleep alone. But that's my offer. What do you say?"

He said nothing.

"You know, Jonas. I can't say as I'm flattered at how bad you *don't* want to sleep with me."

"Emma..."

"No. I'm not done yet. I'm gonna go further. *Don't*

sleep with me. But don't come to my room nights, either."

He made that noise in his throat again, the one of total and complete disbelief. "You're not serious. You don't want that any more than I do."

"Well, thank you for admittin' it."

"I haven't made any secret of the fact that I want to be in your bed."

"Right. You just don't want to *stay* there for very long."

"Emma—"

"Wait. I am not finished. This is my last offer. Mandy and I will go back with you to Angel's Crest. And you will not come to my bed again unless you're plannin' on stayin' in it till dawn."

He swore.

She told him, "There's more."

"Great. I cannot wait to hear it."

"We will have…time. Together. You and me. And Mandy, too. I know you are a busy man. I'm not gonna ask for the impossible. Say, ten hours, total, a week. And three of those ten hours will include Mandy. We can have dinner together, meet for lunch, take in a movie, go for nice, long walks. Whatever. But there won't be any lovemakin' going on, not until you decide to—"

He put up a hand. "I get the picture."

"Well, then. Do you agree?"

"Yes. I'll stay out of your bed unless I plan on sleeping there—or unless you change your mind."

She didn't like the look on his face. It was much too self-satisfied. "Wait a minute. I never said anything about changin' my mind."

"No, Emma, you didn't. I was the one who said that."

Chapter 14

When they got back to Angel's Crest, Jonas asked Emma to have dinner with him. She accepted. After the meal, he walked her up to her room.

"That's two hours you have spent with me," she said when they got to her door. "Eight more to go by next Thursday." She looked very determined—and utterly adorable.

He allowed himself a smile. "Keeping score, are you?"

"Just keeping our agreement."

"Change your mind anytime."

"Stay the night."

Jonas shook his head with a great deal more regret than he wanted to feel. "Sleep well, Emma."

"Don't you worry. I will."

The next day, Friday, she dropped in on him at Bravo, Incorporated. He found it vaguely irritating, the thrill that shivered through him when his receptionist buzzed him to say that Mrs. Bravo would like to see him.

He was alone in his office, with no appointments or meetings for the next hour. Good timing on her part, he supposed—not that it wouldn't have been a simple matter to let her cool her heels a little, to tell the receptionist he didn't want to be disturbed.

He said nothing of the kind. He didn't even stall. He was too damn anxious for the sight of her. "Send her in."

She strolled into his office in her spiky-heeled shoes and dropped into one of the two leather wing chairs opposite his desk. She crossed those long legs and folded her hands loosely in her lap.

"I have come to ask if we can take Mandy to the zoo on Saturday," she announced. "I know I should have asked you last night. But I didn't think of it until this morning. And then, well, I thought maybe I'd be more likely to convince you if I came in person. So here I am." He watched that beauty mark by her mouth. "Or Sunday," she added, eyes round with apprehension. "We can go Sunday if that would be better for you...."

What would be better for him? Easy: for her to give up this foolishness and let him back into her bed.

"Jonas, please can't we do this? I think Mandy will love it, seein' the animals, gettin' out for a while..."

She must have noticed he was staring at her legs. She coughed and recrossed them. "Jonas?"

He looked into her sweet, flushed face.

And he couldn't help thinking that a one-time excursion wouldn't be all that risky. Criminals, after all, studied—and made use of—the routines of their victims. Being at the same public place at the same time of day on a regular basis, or living in a house that could not be secured—those were two of the most effective ways to court trouble. Anyone out to do harm could learn with relative ease where to find his victim and when. But a one-shot deal? He and Emma and Mandy would have their day at the zoo and be back at Angel's Crest before anyone was the wiser. They might end up dogged by a reporter or two, but he could handle that.

"All right," he said. "Tomorrow."

That tiny mole disappeared into the shadow of her cheek as she beamed him a thousand-watt smile. "That is just great. I thought we could maybe leave around ten, if that's all right, grab a chili dog or something while we're at the zoo."

"Sounds good to me."

"Oh, I am so glad." She stood.

He realized he shouldn't have agreed so swiftly. Now she would leave. "Wait…"

She blinked those eyes, which he swore right then were the color of emeralds. And after she blinked, she just stood there, between the leather wing chair and the extensive mahogany expanse of his desk, giving him a chance to tell her why he had asked her to wait.

The invitation seemed to come out of his mouth all by itself. "Tonight, I'm having a friend in for dinner." It was the independent film producer he'd had to put off the night before. "I'd like you to join us."

The dark lashes swept down again, then up. He saw pure pleasure in her eyes. "Well, that would be real nice. Thank you, Jonas."

"We'll have drinks in the front room. Around eight."

"I will be there." She started to turn.

He decided he ought to give her more information. "His name's Ledger DelVecchio and—"

She spun back to him. "The movie director?"

She had succeeded in surprising him again. "Director and producer. You've heard of him?"

"Sure. Blythe said once that she thought he was very talented."

Jonas had met Ledger through Blythe. Years ago, the moviemaker had been one of her strays, a very skinny kid from San Pedro with big dreams and a battered Super 8 movie camera constantly running in front of his face.

Emma said, "After all the great things Blythe said about him, I went out and rented one of his movies— the one about the dog that saved New York."

"*Sparky.*"

"That's right. Oh, and the one about the aliens—both the space kind and the *illegal* kind, and the border patrol and the mutated bananas. I saw that, too. *Fruit of Venus,* wasn't that it?"

"I believe so."

"I like a movie where everything doesn't get wrapped up all nice and neat at the end."

"Ledger's movies certainly qualify on that score."

She chuckled. So did he. But then the laughter faded and they were left looking at each other across the too-wide desk.

"Well," she said finally. "I guess I ought to let you get back to work."

He was sick of the damn desk between them. He stood and went around it. "There's no rush. Want some coffee?"

"I would love some—I mean, if you are sure that I am not interrupting anything." She sat back down again.

He buzzed his secretary and asked her to send in a coffee tray. Then he dropped into the other wing chair, the one right next to hers. They talked—about Ledger and his strange movies. About how much Mandy was going to enjoy her first trip to the zoo. About how if they didn't watch it, they'd use up their ten hours long before the week was out.

"There's no reason we can't spend *more* than ten hours together, is there?" he heard himself asking.

And she said, "Well, of course there isn't. No reason at all...."

Ledger DelVecchio was part Mexican, part African-American, part Italian and part Irish—or so he claimed. "I am the *real* America," he was fond of informing anyone who would listen. "Does that make you nervous?"

In Jonas's opinion, Ledger was too scrawny to make anyone nervous. He stood six-foot-three and weighed perhaps one hundred and fifty pounds, possibly less. He had skin the warm brown of a walnut shell and black eyes. Once his hair had been black, too. But for over a decade now, he had dyed it an improbable shade of blond and shaved it off even with the tops of his ears, so that it looked like a lemon-yellow bird's nest turned upside down on the crown of his head.

He and Emma hit it off from the first, which Jonas had somehow suspected they might. Emma told Ledger how much she admired *Sparky* and *Fruit of Venus*. Then the two of them spent perhaps a half an hour discussing the lovable personality and amazing scenting ability of the bassett hound—Sparky, the star of the film by that name, had been a bassett hound.

By the time they sat down to the table, Ledger was off and running on the subject of his latest project, which Jonas had already figured out he would end up paying for, and which Emma appeared to find absolutely fascinating.

"Oh, no, you are kiddin' me. I do not believe it. And then what happens next?"

Ledger told her, in detail, in that basso profundo voice of his that sounded impossible coming out of a man so damn skinny.

After the meal, they retired to the media room. Ledger showed them a few clips he had brought. Ledger always stayed late into the night when he visited. He drank Chivas when he partied and he could put the stuff away, never seeming to get the least bit drunk, simply becoming more relaxed and expansive as the hours went by.

Emma left them at a little after one.

Ledger hardly let her get out of the room before he was singing her praises. "She's an original, Jonas. You are one lucky man. Someone *real,* with a heart to match her bra size. What you needed. Open you up a little, get you to chill some. And that accent, jus' sweet as a li'l ole piece of country pie. Blythe found her, didn't she? Leave it to Blythe..." His black eyes misted over. "Damn it, why is it the good ones are always gone too soon?"

Jonas said he wished he knew and offered more Chivas. Ledger didn't say no. Jonas poured them each another drink. And then another after that...

Ledger stayed until well after three, at which time Jonas invited him to make himself comfortable in one of the guest suites.

Ledger refused, as he always did. "It's one thing to drink your booze, to help myself to your caviar and hearts of palm. But I got to keep my edge. Can't weaken too much, can't start lying myself down in the decadent mansions of the white power establishment."

Jonas had one of his drivers take Ledger home. Then, alone in the living room off the grand foyer, feeling slightly drowsy and more than a little bit buzzed, he poured himself one more drink. As always, he'd enjoyed seeing Ledger and he didn't even mind parting with the few hundred thousand it was going to cost him to help make Ledger's latest dream a celluloid reality.

What he did mind was going up to his room without stopping in to visit his wife first.

Jonas swore, though there was no one else in the room to hear it. He sipped that last drink, which he knew damn well he should not have poured. As he sipped, he reminded himself that it had not even been thirty-six hours since they'd come to the agreement that kept him out of her bed, that *she* was the one who would change her mind eventually. All he had to do was wait awhile.

He dropped to a sofa, swirled the ice cubes around in his glass, listened to the cheerful clinking sounds they made. He would finish this drink and go up to bed.

His bed.

He drank the last of it, then set the glass on the side table near his elbow. But he didn't get up. He found himself studying an old family photo on the low table in front of him: his grandmother and his grandfather, his father and his uncle Blake, who had been disinherited at the age of twenty—and died in an apartment fire not many years later. Blake's weird pale eyes seemed to glitter at him, full of malice and evil intent.

Jonas grunted. He looked away from the old photograph, stared into the middle distance, pondering.

Maybe it was the booze, breaking down his defenses, clouding his judgment, but right now, he found he couldn't help wondering...

Was it really all that important to sleep alone?

He blinked, shifted on the sofa. Damn right it was important. He had always slept alone. He had trouble getting to sleep in the first place. And once he managed that, he tossed and turned a lot.

He might whack Emma in the face with a flung-out arm. He might kick her. He would unquestionably hog the bed and take all the covers. The truth was, when he did finally drop off to sleep, he was usually out of control. He knew this because of the state of his bed when he woke.

And sometimes, when he had a certain dream—a dream he could never actually remember—things could get very ugly indeed.

Jonas waved his hand in front of his face and instructed aloud, ''Forget the damn dream.''

He hadn't had it in a long time now—except for that once, the night Blythe died, which was pretty understandable. Before that, it had been over a year. And since the night of his mother's death…nothing. The odds were he wouldn't have the dream again for a long time to come. Maybe never.

Yeah. No reason he couldn't forget the damn dream.

Jonas smiled to himself.

They got along pretty well, he and Emma. Tomorrow, by God, they were going to the L.A. zoo with Mandy. Just like a family. And wasn't *that* something new and completely different?

Not that it was anything lasting. No, nothing permanent. And that was part of the charm of it.

What was it Ledger had said tonight? That Emma was *real,* that she was just what he needed, to ''open him up a little,'' to help him to ''chill.'' That was pretty much, he imagined, what his mother had thought when she'd

cooked up this whole crazy plan to marry him off to her
for a year.

And maybe it was working. A little.

Right now—so late at night it couldn't be called anything but tomorrow, after an evening of good company
and a couple more whiskeys than he should have allowed himself—it didn't seem like anything but good
news that his eccentric mother's bizarre marriage
scheme was working out all right, after all.

Jonas looked down at his shoes. The handwoven rug
underneath them had a medallion pattern. The medal-
lions seemed to be…shifting. Hell. The whole room was
shifting.

But only a little. Like a boat gently rocking on a
placid sea.

He spoke again to the empty room. "Bed. Now."

Carefully, he raised himself up off the sofa.

Once on his feet, he sucked in a couple of slow, deep
breaths. Yes. It was all right. He was drunk, but not so
drunk he couldn't make it where he needed to go.

He started for the tall doors that led to the grand foyer.

When he reached the top of the staircase, he had a
choice: go left, to his own bedroom suite. Or right. He
went right.

When he got to her door, he put his hand on the knob.
It turned. She hadn't locked it.

But then he let go without opening it.

No. It wouldn't be right, to wander into her bedroom
now at—he braced one hand on the doorframe and lifted
the wrist of his other hand to squint at his watch—
4:03 a.m.

Not right. Not a good thing, so late at night it was

morning already, reeking of whiskey, weaving when he walked.

Better to just go on along to his own room, deal with all this—Emma, their agreement, whether or not he wanted to back down on this issue—tomorrow, with a clear head.

But then, his feet didn't want to start walking again. It seemed a huge, impossible distance, all the way to his own suite of rooms. His feet weighed a thousand pounds each and everything was slowly, lazily spinning around....

He grunted, turned, braced himself against the wall right next to the door and slowly slid down it, until he was sitting cross-legged on the geometrically patterned runner that ran the length of the hall.

Well, and now he was down there, he didn't see any reason to remain in a sitting position. Why not relax a little? Whom was it gonna hurt?

Whom...

He let out a low laugh, thinking of Emma, yesterday, telling him it wasn't a "what" but a "who."

He had corrected her. *You mean it's a "whom."*

Who, whom, what's the difference? It's me, Jonas. You are hiding from me....

Jonas shook his head. Hiding, was he?

The hell he was. He was right out here, at her door, sitting on the floor.

He listed to the left, and went on listing, until he was lying on his side. He tucked his arm under his head. Better. And then he closed his eyes.

The next thing he knew there was movement at his back—the door swinging open. He didn't even have to look. He knew she was there. Who the hell else would it be?

And besides, he could feel her there, right behind him, looking down at him. He could smell her, as well. Dewy roses...

"Jonas? Are you all right?"

He rolled to his back and blinked up at her. "Hi."

The light was dim, provided by low-wattage bulbs in wall sconces placed at intervals along the hallway. But he could see her just fine. That gold and silver hair formed an enchanting sleep-mussed halo around her face and she was wearing one of those little skimpy bits of nothing she always wore to bed—a hot pink bit of nothing, to be precise.

He wrapped his arm around her smooth bare ankle and laid his hand on her foot. It always felt so good, just to have his hand on her somewhere. He had a very nice view, up over her shins and her knees, her strong thighs to the hot pink hem of the little bit of nothing. It was kind of shadowed, beyond that, but he'd seen what was up there. It was burned into his brain.

She said, "Looks like you and Ledger had a real good time."

He nodded and idly fiddled with her toes. "We did. Drank too much."

"No kidding."

"I've been thinking..."

"Oh?"

"Yeah. There are some negatives you should know about."

"Well, okay. Shoot."

"I'm a bad sleeper."

She looked puzzled.

So he elaborated. "Restless, you know. I might hit you, steal the covers, that kind of thing."

A soft smile bloomed on her mouth. "It doesn't matter."

"It doesn't?"

She shook her head.

He said, "Well then, the truth is, I came here to sleep with you."

"You did?" Her face got softer. Damn. What a woman. A disgusting drunk said he wanted to sleep with her and she got all soft and sweet over it.

"Yeah. But then I thought...too drunk, y'know? So I was going to leave. But then I decided to sit down for a minute..."

She knelt, which meant she was closer. Hey. Fine with him. "Come on..." She slid her hand under his neck as if she wanted him to sit up.

He wasn't so sure about that. He looked at those gorgeous breasts of hers, which were very close to eye level right then. "Come on where?"

She had her arm under his shoulders now. She gave a gentle nudge. "To bed."

"Ugh." All at once, he was sitting up. He didn't like it much. But she had said something interesting. "That would be...*your* bed?"

"That's right."

"Oh. Well, then. Let's go."

It was not easy, but he was properly motivated now. With her help, he found himself on his feet. "Ugh," he said again.

"Come on, don't stop." She wrapped his arm around her shoulders and tucked herself up tight against his side.

They were through the door—she shoved it shut as they went by—past the sitting area and weaving at the foot of the bed in no time. As usual, the Yorkies were sitting among the tangle of sheets, waiting for instructions, apparently. Emma clicked her tongue at them and gestured with a toss of her head. They jumped down from the bed. He didn't see where they went next. He really didn't care. The black-and-white cat was curled on a chair by a bureau. It looked up, yawned, and rested its head back on its paws.

Emma got them turned around. "Okay, sit." They dropped to the bed together. When he got there, he just went on falling. He would have taken her with him, but she let go of his arm, so he went down alone.

Flat on his back, he stared up at the chandelier overhead. It twinkled and swayed, though he knew very well that it was not really moving.

She slid off the bed and started fooling with his feet— taking off his shoes and socks, he realized after a minute. Once she had that handled, she came up on the bed with him again and started taking off everything else.

He let her do it, not helping her much, lifting various parts of himself whenever she told him to, letting those same parts flop back to the bed as soon as she pulled free whatever piece of clothing she was trying to get off him. She had him down to his briefs in very little time. Then she made him move to the side so she could get the blankets out from under him.

"Emma?"

"Hmm?"

"Can we stop moving soon?"

She settled the sheet over him. "Yes, Jonas. We are stopping. We are stopping right now." He turned on his side with a groan.

She switched off the bedside lamp and slid in beside him. He reached for her. She came in against him, curving her back and bottom into the cradle he made by bending his thighs.

"You left my damn underwear on." He breathed the accusation against her hair.

She laughed, a low laugh. "If I take them off you, there will be more movement."

"Oh," he said. "Don't want that."

"I didn't think so."

"Emma?"

"Hmm?"

"Want to make love...don't think I can."

She felt for his hand, kissed it, tucked it between her breasts, so he had a handful of her all wrapped in silk. Hot pink silk...

"Good night, Jonas."

"Yeah, Emma. It is now."

Jonas woke at a little after ten in the morning with a doozy of a hangover. Emma rang for Palmer and ordered a pitcher of ice water and some extra-strength Tylenol.

They agreed that the trip to the zoo could wait until Sunday and spent most of the day in Emma's rooms. She pampered him. He enjoyed that. She brought him cool wet cloths to put over his eyes and urged him to drink lots of water. She ordered them brunch in the early afternoon. He didn't eat a lot of it, but what he did eat helped. The hangover seemed to be passing.

By four, he felt almost normal. There remained that shaky, edgy sensation to remind him of why he usually had sense enough to drink sparingly, if at all.

Emma had dinner ordered up to the nursery. They ate with Mandy, a picnic on the playroom floor. Then they hung around for bath time and to take turns reading her a bedtime story. They left the nursery at about eight-thirty.

From the nursery, he took Emma to his rooms. "Because you wanted to see them."

She stroked the curved arms of the Biedermeier chairs and admired the view from the terrace. "Very nice," she said, rather shyly. "Thank you for showing me."

And they returned to her rooms.

She told him that night that she'd gone on the Pill and that it would be safe, at least as far as pregnancy was concerned, to stop using condoms. They kicked their shoes off and sat on the bed together, each of them cross-legged, facing each other. She said that there had been two men so far in her life: an actor named Ridley and a high school sweetheart.

"I never messed up with Ridley," she told him. "We always used protection. I did mess up once or twice with Elton, and it worried me, you know, that I hadn't been careful, even though we were so young and Elton always swore there was never anyone before me, and we lived in a small town where folks generally considered themselves immune to things like sexually transmitted diseases. But Aunt Cass pretty much drilled it into to me. She always used to say, 'I'm not gonna try to tell you that you should never do what comes naturally. But when the time comes, you put a raincoat on it. Women are always getting pregnant when they thought it was a safe time and AIDS doesn't care if you're a nice girl or not.'" She wrinkled her nose at him. "I suppose you're going to tell me someone else said that first."

"Not on your life."

"Well, good. Anyway, Aunt Cass was real big on bein' safe in order not to end up bein' sorry. And since there were those few times with Elton that were not safe, I had a test, a couple of years ago, just to check. It was negative."

She looked at him hopefully and he realized it was his turn to lay it on the line as regarded his sexual history.

He cleared his throat. "There have been more than two," he confessed.

She groaned and rolled those almost-green eyes. "Yes, I know. And you don't need to go rattlin' off a list of their names. It will only depress me. And it could take half the night."

He wanted to defend himself a little. But what could he say? She already knew what she needed to know on this point, that he had bedded a lot of women in the past and that none of them had mattered much. They might as well leave it at that.

"All right," he said. "I won't go get the list."

She looked at him narrowly for a moment—and then it hit her that he was kidding. "Oh, you..." She fisted her hand and lightly punched him in the shoulder.

He said, "There *is* some good news."

"Hit me with it."

"I have always practiced safe sex."

She made a low noise of disbelief in her throat. "Oh, come on. *Always?*"

"All right. I seem to remember one indiscretion."

"Oh, holy cow. Just one?"

"I don't like the way you said that."

"Well, pardon me. But I am impressed. I mean, with all the opportunities you've had, to have only messed up once. Jonas. That is just excellent."

"Well. Thank you."

"You are welcome."

He explained, "I was nineteen. It happened under the stands at a football game—Stanford/UCLA, I believe it was."

"People get way too excited at sports events."

"Don't they? After that, though, I have made it my business to always be prepared. And I have not, as you put it, 'messed up,' again."

"Well, then." She looked very pleased—with herself. With him. "Don't you think that, as long as we agree that there won't be anyone else for the time that we're married…" She hesitated, her cheeks turning the most enchanting shade of pink. "I mean, that is, if it was just going to be you and me, while we are married, then we probably could…"

He reached out, hooked his hand around the back of her neck and pulled her mouth right up to his. "We could what?"

She was blushing furiously now. "But then, maybe we should just…play it safe, anyway. Maybe that's the responsible thing to do."

He took pity and gave her a little distance, letting go of her smooth, warm neck, sitting back on his side of the bed. "Maybe it comes down to…do we believe each other and can we trust each other?"

"Yes." Her face seemed to light up from within. "That's right. That's what…married people have to do. Believe. And trust. And, though we are only married for a year, it is still a *real* marriage, isn't it? For as long as it lasts?"

He nodded.

She said, "Well. *I* believe *you.* I can't say as I trust you, Jonas, not about *everything.* You are a difficult man and you like to be in control and sometimes, I think, if it's to your advantage, you might stretch the truth a tad. But about this, well, I have no doubts. I just know you are bein' straight."

He felt absurdly pleased at her confidence in him—

even qualified as it was. He returned the favor, said, "I trust you on this." And he did, which stunned him a little, now he thought about it. He'd never trusted any woman to take care of contraception. He never planned to have children, and the last thing he needed was to have some ex-lover slap him with a paternity suit.

"Well," she said. "Okay then..."

He echoed, "Okay."

They were still sitting cross-legged, facing each other. He leaned forward and so did she. She sighed when their lips met, opening for him instantly, her tongue meeting his, wrapping around it. After the sigh, she moaned.

So did he.

They undressed, kissing as they did it, buttons slipping from holes, zippers sliding down. They were naked in no time, their clothes strewn around the sides of the bed.

He guided her down among the pile of pillows. And then, for a while, they just lay there, on their sides, facing each other, kissing some more. It was slow and lazy and very, very good. Maybe they could just go on like this forever, lying together on the white bed, mouths permanently fused.

He touched her as he kissed her. Touching her gave him limitless pleasure. He liked to run his index finger down her spine, tracing each bone. He liked to cup her bottom, to curve his palm over the silky swell of her hip.

She stroked him in return, her soft hand moving down, finding him, closing around him. He groaned into her mouth.

And then she was pulling at his shoulders, urging him to cover her. He put his hand on her, delved in. She was slick and wet and ready. He wanted to taste her.

But she wasn't having that. Not right then. When he

tried to lower his head, she dragged him back up and claimed his mouth once again.

She wrapped those incredible legs around him and at that point, he couldn't have held back if he'd wanted to. In one sharp stroke, he was inside.

She froze. So did he. He pulled his mouth from hers, and he looked at her. She stared straight back at him.

They started to move, at first slowly, then picking up rhythm, faster and faster—then slowly again. She was so tight and so wet around him. He thought, with whatever part of his brain still able to function, that this was the best place to be in the whole of the world.

The rhythm picked up again. He looked down into her face, watched her climax break over her, her mouth going so soft, eyes far away and dazed.

The sight finished him. He stiffened. She pushed herself tight against him, her body bowing right off the mattress.

The pulsing of his own release began.

A few minutes later, she pulled the white sheet over them. He wrapped his arms around her. They slept.

He woke at six-ten the next morning and realized he had slept over eight hours straight through, which just might have amounted to some sort of record for him. Emma told him he had slept peacefully, as far as she knew.

"You didn't hit me or kick me," she declared. "You didn't even steal my covers. You did just fine."

He could hardly believe it. "I did?"

"Yep."

"Well, what do you know?"

She leaned over and kissed him. He kissed her back

and that led where it usually led—to soft moans and tender sighs.

They had breakfast together out on the loggia, the long roofed gallery not far from the pool. And at ten, they took Mandy and left for the zoo. The weather was perfect—the kind of weather L.A. has always been famous for, bright and beautiful, the temperature in the low seventies.

Mandy had a ball. She rode on Jonas's shoulders a lot of the day, pointing and crowing in delight as she recognized the various animals. ''Oh, look! Giraffe! See that? Monkeys!''

The best part of the zoo trip was what didn't happen.

No one seemed to recognize them. Or if anyone did, they behaved like civilized human beings and respected their privacy. Not a single shutter-happy reporter stuck a camera in their faces the entire day.

They got back to Angel's Crest at a little after three. Mandy had fallen asleep in the car, so they took her right up to the nursery and turned her over to Claudia.

Jonas had a few things to deal with at Bravo, Incorporated, things that just couldn't wait another day. ''If I'm lucky, I can get back by nine or so tonight.''

Emma kissed him and told him she'd be waiting for him, whatever time he returned.

He entered her rooms at nine on the nose. She had ordered a light supper for them. They ate and then they showered together, ending up making very wet love under the shower spray.

Jonas fell asleep in Emma's arms some time after midnight.

Some time after that, the dream came for him.

He woke as he always did when the dream got him—sitting bolt upright, the sweat streaming off of him, shouting the word, "No!"

Chapter 15

"Jonas?" Emma was sitting up beside him.

His heart was beating like a trip-hammer. He could not breathe.

"Jonas, what is it?"

He shoved her gentle hand away, threw back the sheet and jumped from the bed.

"Jonas..."

With superhuman effort, he tried to suck in air. It was like breathing through a flattened straw. Relax, he thought. Easy. It's all in your mind....

He bent at the waist, put his hands on his thighs, waited for his windpipe to open—or to pass out.

All in your mind. Bad dream. Not real...

Still, his windpipe felt smashed flat. He sank to his knees. If he was going to lose consciousness, the closer to the floor the better.

Slowly, over a period of seconds that felt like years,

his windpipe began to relax. The air started getting in. He sucked in one slow, careful breath. And then another.

All right. It appeared that he would not pass out this time, after all.

Carefully, he straightened to his height.

Emma was standing, very still, about two feet from him. He hadn't even heard her leave the bed.

"Better?" she asked softly.

He managed a nod—and concentrated on the job of drawing one breath after another. It got easier with each one.

She waited, standing so still, naked as he was, her body like a white flame in the darkness, until he could breathe close to normally again.

Then she asked, "What can I get for you?"

He could smell himself—the sour, cornered-animal smell of pure terror. His skin was still clammy with it, with nightmare sweat. "Shower," he croaked in a voice not his own.

"I'll get the water goin'." She turned and left him.

As soon as he was certain his legs wouldn't give out on him, he followed her. She had the water running. When he entered the bathroom, she pulled open the shower door. Welcoming steam billowed out. He got in there, in the heat and the steam, let the water cascade over him, even drank a few gulps of it, to ease his shredded throat.

When he got out, she was waiting with a towel. She dried him, massaging as she wiped the water away. By the time she was done, he felt almost human again.

"Come on." She took his hand, led him back to the bed. The Yorkies were there, sitting among the tangled sheets, looking up at them, tails thumping out a hopeful rhythm. They never gave up trying to reclaim the privilege of sleeping with Emma. Inevitably, they headed straight for the bed any time it was vacant.

Emma clicked her tongue. Droopy-eared and downcast, they rose on all fours to jump down.

"Hell," he said. "All right. They can stay—but I don't want them on top of me."

Two sets of ears perked up. Emma sent him a tender smile and then snapped her fingers. The dogs moved to either corner at the end of the bed, each of them walking in a circle and then settling down, noses resting on front paws, eyes bright and grateful under all the eyebrow fringe.

Emma got into the bed and so did he. She settled the sheet over them and pulled him close, guiding his head to rest on her breasts. She stroked his hair.

"You want to talk about it?" She kissed his brow.

He started to answer no automatically, but the word stopped itself somewhere short of sound.

For the first time in thirty years, he found he *did* want to talk about it.

He moved back a little, so he wasn't resting right on top of her anymore. But he kept his hand on her, fingers wrapped around her ribcage, arm resting across the lower part of her chest, right under her breasts. It felt good, as always, to be touching her.

"It's a nightmare I've been having on and off, since the kidnapping. I know it has something to do with the kidnapping—I believe it actually *is* the kidnapping. That I relive it, in the dream."

She asked gently, "You *believe?*"

"I can't say for sure. When I wake up, I don't remember what the nightmare was. I hear myself shouting the word, *No.* And then, once the word is out, I can't breathe. I run sweat. You saw it...."

She turned on her side. He moved his arm to accommodate her, sliding his hand down a little until it lay in the cove of her waist. She reached up, stroked the hair at his temple. "That's the real reason you sleep alone, isn't it? You don't want anyone to see you, to see what it's like for you, how awful it is for you. You think it makes you look weak."

"I don't just *think* it, Emma. It's a fact. I *am* weak, when the dream gets me." He was a little stunned he had said it, that he'd admitted it out loud.

But he had. And the world hadn't ended.

Emma was watching him tenderly, her palm resting against the side of his face. "If you could remember the dream, then you would be remembering what happened that night, right?"

"Could be. But I've learned not to get my hopes up." He took her hand, kissed it, twined his fingers with hers. "Tell me something."

"Anything."

"How much do you know about the kidnapping, anyway?"

She lifted her shoulder in a shrug. "Blythe used to talk about it sometimes. About how awful it was, about the terrible effects it had on your family."

"But I mean the specifics of what happened. Do you know that I went into my brother's room that night, that somehow I was knocked unconscious?"

"Yes. I know that."

"Apparently, I fought. There were bruises, on my arms and legs, over my ribs. And on my neck."

"As if someone had tried to strangle you...and don't you think maybe that explains why, when you have that dream, you wake up and you can't breathe?"

"It's more than possible. But I don't remember. I

don't remember a damn thing about that night. And I've been questioned by the best, believe me, by what seemed like a never-ending chain of police detectives and police psychologists. And after the police were through with me, there were all the specialists my parents hired to try to pry open my mind and get to the secrets locked away in there—everything from psychiatrists to hypnotists to a few fringe types who claimed to have psychic powers. Nothing worked.''

"But Jonas, you do *want* to remember. Some part of you must. Some part of you has been tryin' to remember for thirty years.''

"Maybe so. But the fact remains that I don't remember. And whoever took my brother didn't make many mistakes. The police never found any real evidence that they could use to track down whoever did it. Whoever it was broke the lock on the door to the east entry, apparently got up the servants' stairway there and got in to the nursery without being spotted. It wasn't that far, just a few feet down the hall once the kidnapper made it up the stairs. And then it would have been so easy, to go back by the same route. I was the only glitch in the plan. And not that much of glitch, the way it turned out. A good whack on the side of the head, and my memory of what happened was wiped out.''

"Not completely wiped out. Just…trapped inside your head.''

"We assume. We don't even know that for certain, since I never remember the dream. It *could* be about something else altogether.''

"You don't believe that.''

"No. No, I don't.''

She gently pulled her fingers from his. "It sounds like

the kidnapper had been in the house before, knew where to go in, the straightest way to the nursery..."

"Yes, it does. Or maybe he—or she or they—bribed a servant. Though I have to say that the police found no evidence to that effect. And to open up a whole new chain of possibilities, there had been a piece in *Gracious Homes* magazine just a few months before, a ten-page spread on Angel's Crest—including the basic floor plan and lots of pictures. It's possible that the kidnapper could have gotten enough information from that to get in and get to the nursery without being caught."

"Oh, Jonas. Any one of those explanations makes sense."

"That's what I'm telling you. We have never even gotten close to learning who took my brother, who claimed two million in diamonds as a ransom—and then never brought him back to us."

"Two million in diamonds," Emma whispered in a musing tone.

"That's right. No one ever saw them again, either."

"What about the nanny—I'm assuming you and your brother had one?"

"We did. Like Claudia does now, she slept in a room right next to the baby's room. The police interrogated her. Extensively. They got nothing from her but tears and remorse that she didn't wake up when the whole thing went down."

Emma traced his eyebrows, one and then the other, and idly asked, "You've moved the nursery, since then?"

"Hell yes. We use those rooms for storage, have ever since we accepted the fact that Russell wasn't coming back."

"Russell," she repeated his brother's name softly.

"Blythe said he was a good baby, big and healthy. That he had a cute little cleft in his chin...."

"Yeah," he said, not wanting to go any farther along that line. He didn't remember much about his baby brother. And what he did remember hurt. It was all loss and emptiness. Darkness. Fear. And in the end, a deep and abiding certainty that he should have done better, he should have done *something* to keep his brother safe.

He knew it was classic stuff, that a six-year-old kid couldn't be expected to hold his own against an adult criminal with a two-million-dollar ransom on his—or her—mind. But unfortunately, what logic told him didn't go all that far toward allowing him to forgive himself.

Emma put her finger on the tip of his chin. "You have it, too. That cute cleft right here."

"FYI, a man is not thrilled when a woman calls him cute."

"Oh, well, Jonas, whatever you say, especially since you are the most manly man..."

"That's better—and it runs in the family."

"Manliness?" She touched the groove in his chin a second time. "Or do you mean this cleft?"

He grunted. "My father had it. And I have a certain second cousin, met him in Wyoming years and years ago. Name's Zach. He's got it—or he did when I was five and he was, oh about eight or nine, I guess..."

"I didn't know you had a cousin in Wyoming."

"What? Something my mother *didn't* share with you?"

"That's right. Tell me about your Wyoming cousin."

"Cousins. Plural. My great-great-grandfather homesteaded there, in northeastern Wyoming. Near a little town called Medicine Creek. The original homesteader's cabin is still on the ranch—or at least it was, when I was five. We only visited once, before Russell was born. I think we planned to go back, but then, well, life got pretty tough for the L.A. branch of the family. Somehow, years have gone by. Haven't been back yet.''

"So your great-great-grandfather..."

"Had a son."

"Who had a son, who—"

"Uh-uh. My *great*-grandfather had *four* sons. Ross, Gregory, Jonas and James. Ross, who had a few sons of his own, stayed in Wyoming. The other three didn't. Can't tell you offhand what happened to James. I think that Gregory ended up in northern California. *He* had a son, who had a son, who had two daughters. Maybe you remember that Blythe heard from one of those daughters not too long ago?''

Green eyes gleamed. "I do remember. Jenna's her name. Blythe told me all about her.''

"What a surprise.''

She went on, undaunted by his teasing. "Blythe said that Jenna even went to school here, at UCLA. And Jenna's sister lived in Los Angeles for a few years, too. But they didn't even realize they were kin to the L.A. Bravos. The connection had been broken over the years, Blythe said.''

"My mother was an only child of older parents. She didn't have much family. I think she wanted to reestablish connections with the other branches of the Bravo family, especially the past few years.''

"She and Jenna were plannin' to meet, weren't they? But then Blythe got so sick...''

"Death can do that. Really gets in the way.''

She wrapped her hand around the back of his neck and threaded her fingers into his hair. "You have been doin' so well. Don't go gettin' cynical on me. Please...''

How the hell could a man resist a request like that? For an answer, he moved his head close enough that he could kiss the tip of her nose.

She grinned at him. "Much better. Now, tell me about your grandfather—whose name was Jonas, right, just like you?"

"Right. My grandfather Jonas came here, to southern California. He invested in real estate. And he made a bundle. He built Angel's Crest. And he had two sons. The oldest, Harry..."

"Your father."

He nodded. "And four years later..."

Emma shivered. "The evil Blake."

"With whom we do not have to concern ourselves. He was dead in an apartment fire at the age of twenty-six."

"Blythe said he was really a terrible man. That he was a cheat and a thief from the time he was little. That he would have gone to prison for manslaughter because he killed some poor fella in a barroom brawl."

"That's right. He was out on bail when he died."

"And that was—what—just a few years before Russell was kidnapped?"

"I'm not sure, exactly. Two or three years, yes."

"Your poor father. No wonder he had a stroke. Too many awful things happened to him, in too short a time."

"Same for my mother. My father's death was the final straw for her. She withdrew—to the inside of her own head."

"And that left you, didn't it Jonas? In all the ways that matter, for four years, you were all alone."

"There were people to take care of me."

"But in your heart, you felt alone."

He moved closer to her. She was so warm, so *alive*, and she smelled so good. "Kiss me, Emma...."

"Jonas, didn't you feel alone?"

"You won't give up until I admit it, will you?"

"Nope."

"And then will you kiss me?"

"You bet."

"All right. I admit it. I felt alone."

"You got used to things that way."

"Putting words in my mouth? I'd rather have your tongue there."

"Oh, you are so bad...."

"Do I get my kiss now?"

She lifted her mouth for him. He took it, reaching out, wrapping his arms around her and pulling her as close as he could possibly get her.

Eventually, he slept again—straight through, that time, until dawn. If he had dreams, they were good ones. Because he woke to a feeling of lightness, a sense that, at that moment, in bed next to Emma early on a Monday morning, all was right with the world.

Jonas went on another business trip, to Dallas that time, on Tuesday. He was back by Thursday. He shared dinner with Emma that night in the small dining room and afterward, they went upstairs together, to Emma's bed.

They were asleep by eleven and the dream did not come for him. He woke at dawn, refreshed. That Saturday, they took Mandy to Griffith Park. And the next Saturday, they all flew to San Francisco, just for fun.

Those were lovely days, days that Emma stored in her heart, to treasure forever, the days after Jonas gave in and came to her bed to stay for the whole night.

Sometimes, in the mornings at the breakfast table, or in the evenings at dinner—or on weekends, when they strolled the paths at Griffith Park or fed the seals at Fisherman's Wharf, it began to seem to Emma that they truly were a family, a married couple with a toddler, in love and blissfully happy with the life they had made.

Maybe she shouldn't have, but somehow she couldn't stop herself from hoping that someday soon Jonas would speak of love to her, that he would confess he had no intention of ending their marriage when the year was up.

But the wonderful days went by. He was open and loving with her, yet he did not say the words she longed to hear.

Then again, neither did she.

And maybe that was the best way, for now. To take this time as it came to them, take each day as a gift. There would be ample opportunity in the months to come to talk of what might happen when a year had passed.

On Monday, the day after their return from San Francisco, at eleven-thirty in the morning, Jonas sent a car to pick Emma up at PetRitz. He had two hours for lunch—from twelve to two—and she had arranged to take the same time off herself. They'd agreed to spend that time together, sharing a catered meal in his office. Emma rode to their rendezvous with a naughty feeling of anticipation making her stomach all fluttery, causing her heart to beat just a little too fast.

She'd seen the way he looked at her the last time she visited him at Bravo, Incorporated. That had been before he agreed to sleep with her, when he was keeping hands off. Today, it would be different. They would lock the door and he would tell his secretary not to disturb them.

Anything could happen.

My, my, my. In an office penthouse suite, forty stories up. And it was such a *big* desk he had....

She had the driver let her out at the main entrance to the Bravo Building. She went in through the giant glass turnstile door, marched across the pale marble floor and right up to the high desk where two security guards were waiting.

"Mrs. Bravo," said one of the guards. His name was Bert McCandless. It said so on his nametag, which was pinned to the breast pocket of his very official-looking blue uniform. Bert was smiling, a big, welcoming smile. "I believe you are expected."

"I sure am, Officer McCandless."

"Call me Bert."

"Will do, Bert." She beamed at the other guard, sneaking a peak at his nametag, as well. "And how are you today, Todd?"

"Mrs. Bravo, I am just fine."

"Let me escort you up." Bert started to come out from behind the desk.

Emma waved him back. "Don't you bother yourself. I know the way." She started to turn for the elevators.

A hand brushed her left arm. "Excuse me. Mrs. Bravo? Mrs. *Jonas* Bravo?"

Emma turned toward the voice, saw that it belonged to a tall, lean man with wavy brown hair and the face of a poet or maybe a rock star—a face that was somehow vaguely familiar.

The two guards had stiffened. Hands went to weapons. "Step away from Mrs. Bravo," Bert commanded.

Emma whirled on him. "Oh, stop that."

"Mrs. Bravo, please," Bert instructed in a warning tone. "Let us handle this guy."

Emma glared at him. "Bert, I am serious as liver failure here. Back off. This man is not plannin' to do me any harm.'' She sent a narrow-eyed glance at the man in question again. ''Are you?''

The man was carrying a briefcase. He slid it between his legs on the floor and put up both hands, palms out. ''No way,'' he said, somehow managing to sound both ironical and sincere.

And Emma knew. Right then, somehow, she knew. Though his eyes were brown, not deepest blue, though his chin didn't have the slightest hint of a cleft. A Bravo. Yes. There was something about him, something she couldn't put her finger on. Maybe it was the way he carried himself, or something in the shape of his face, or in the determined set of his strong jaw. Maybe it was a combination of those things. Whatever. Emma was certain that this man and Jonas shared a blood connection.

The man said, ''I only want to talk—to your husband. Last week, I called several times. No one would put me through to him and he never returned my calls. So I flew to Los Angeles. I came in here first thing this morning, hoping I might accomplish in person what I couldn't seem to do by phone. I was told to wait. I *have* waited. For about three hours now. Everyone keeps telling me I'll have to *keep* waiting. That Mr. Bravo is a very busy man. That—''

''Oh, put your hands down,'' Emma said. The man shrugged and lowered them to his sides, then bent to pick up the briefcase again.

Emma asked, ''What's your name?''

''Marsh Bravo.''

Delighted, Emma clapped her hands together. ''Oh, I knew it. You have that look.''

Marsh Bravo frowned.

Emma explained, "You just…you look like a Bravo, that's all."

"I see," he said warily.

"Are you from Wyoming?"

"No. Oklahoma."

"Hmm." Emma couldn't remember either Blythe or Jonas mentioning that any of the Bravos had settled in Oklahoma, and this man had nothing of Oklahoma in his voice. "I'm a west Texas girl myself—and you sound a lot like a Yankee to me."

"I lived for several years in Chicago. I just moved back to my hometown a few months ago."

"Well, now. That would explain it, I guess." Emma rested an elbow on the desk. People went in and out of the turnstile door, got on the elevators, and got off. They all minded their own business, though—well, except for Bert and Todd. The two guards were leaning on their side of the desk, looking from Emma to Marsh Bravo and back again, like spectators at a tennis match.

Emma said, "And you are a second cousin, of Jonas's?"

"No. A first cousin. My father and your husband's father were brothers."

Emma couldn't quite believe what she'd just heard. "But…Jonas's father only had one brother."

"Right."

"You are tryin' to tell me that Blake Bravo was your father?"

"Yes. I'm afraid that's exactly what I'm telling you." He did not look particularly pleased to admit it.

And Emma didn't see how it could be true. "But Blake…well, he died a long time ago. And I do not believe that he had any children."

That fine poet's face looked bleaker by the moment. "The truth is, Blake did have at least one child. Me."

Emma just didn't get it. "At least? You don't know for certain if you're an only child?"

"I've learned that I can never be sure of anything— not if it involved my father. When I was growing up, he'd disappear for long periods of time. We never knew where he went. And when he came back, he certainly never told my mother or me what he'd been up to. He was...mysterious, to put it mildly. So that's why I say that he might have had *more* children. I could have brothers and sisters I don't even know about."

It didn't add up. "Wait a minute. You said 'when you were growing up.' You make it sound like your father was there when you were a child."

"He was."

"But...how old are you?"

"Twenty-eight."

"Well then, Mr. Marsh Bravo, you are a miracle baby for sure, because Blake Bravo has been dead for over thirty years."

"No, he hasn't," Marsh Bravo replied. "My father died five months ago, on the second of May."

Chapter 16

Emma said, "Marsh Bravo, I think you're right. You need to have a nice, long talk with Jonas. And I'm takin' you to him right now."

Bert and Todd stopped leaning on the desk and snapped to attention. Bert announced, "Mrs. Bravo, we'll have to search this man first—and have a look through that briefcase."

Todd chimed in, "It's policy. Uninvited, unknown visitors don't get past the first floor without submitting to a thorough search."

Emma frowned. "A thorough search for what?"

"Weapons, among other things."

Emma decided she didn't really need to know what "other things" they thought they might find. She gave Marsh a sheepish smile. "My husband is, well, he's a real bear about security. It probably doesn't help much to say this, but he does have his reasons."

"It's all right," said Marsh.

Something in his tone led Emma to believe that this new cousin of Jonas's knew about what had happened thirty years ago, that he understood the devastating effects the tragedy had had on Jonas's branch of the Bravo family. She asked, "Do you think you could just...?"

Marsh hefted the briefcase onto the counter. He worked the combination locks, popped the latches and took everything out of it himself. There were stacks of papers and something that looked like an old photo album. Once white, it had yellowed with age.

Bert and Todd pawed through all of it, studying the papers, thumbing through the album, which had the word "Surprise" on plain white paper, taped to the front of it.

It appeared to be some sort of scrapbook. There were a lot of newspaper clippings inside. Emma caught sight of a few headlines as Bert turned the pages. She saw Blythe's name. And Jonas's.

A scrapbook about the Bravo family, then?

The top of the briefcase contained a built-in accordion-style file pocket. "What's in that pocket there?" Bert demanded after he and Todd had inspected everything else.

Marsh unhooked the snap closure and pulled the pocket wide. There was nothing inside.

"Let's have a closer look at that." Bert started to reach for the case.

Emma stepped forward. "Bert, it's all right."

"Mrs. Bravo, I am under orders to—"

"You are not going to tear the poor man's briefcase apart, and that is that."

"It's my responsibility to—"

"*I'll* take responsibility, so you can just let it go now."

Bert and Todd exchanged a look. Then Todd announced, "We'll still have to do the body search before he goes upstairs."

Emma groaned.

Marsh said, "No problem." He had already piled everything back into the briefcase. He snapped it closed and spun the locks. "Mrs. Bravo, will you hold this for a minute?"

"I want you to call me Emma—and I'll be happy too."

He handed it over.

Todd said, "Step back from the desk, please."

Marsh did as he'd been told. Todd emerged from behind the desk and performed the search.

Evidently, a body search wasn't all that common around the Bravo Building. It actually succeeded in drawing some attention from passersby on their way to and from the elevators. More than one of them paused to frown and to stare.

But it was over in less than a minute. Todd nodded at Bert. "He's okay."

Emma sighed. The endless security precautions did get old. But she had to remember that the two men were only doing their jobs. She smiled at each of the guards. "Thank you, Todd, Bert."

The guards smiled back. Bert said, "You have a real nice afternoon, Mrs. Bravo."

Emma handed Marsh his briefcase. "Let's go."

The secretary who sat at the desk not far from Jonas's door frowned as Emma and Marsh approached. Evidently, she'd gotten a call from the guards downstairs. "Mrs. Bravo—"

"It's all right," Emma told her. "He's with me. And Jonas is expecting me. We'll just go on in."

"But—"

Emma didn't stick around to listen to objections. She'd heard enough of those downstairs. "This way, Marsh." She led him through the doors into the huge corner office with its stunning views of Los Angeles.

Jonas was sitting at his giant-sized desk, his back to one of the two walls of windows. Behind him and to his right, the city seemed to go on for miles, an endless sprawl silvered with smog and dotted with gleaming towers of steel and glass.

Jonas rose from the desk, his midnight glance flicking from Emma to the man at her side, then back to Emma again. "Emma." His tone teased her. His eyes did not. "You should have mentioned you were bringing a guest." He came around from behind the desk and extended his hand. "I'm Jonas."

The other man took it. "Marsh Bravo."

Jonas shot Emma another glance. This one had *What the hell is going on here?* written all over it.

"I...met Marsh down in the lobby. He's been trying to get hold of you. He called and called and couldn't get through. So he came in person, early this morning. He's been waiting downstairs for hours."

"I see," Jonas replied, using the same words—and the same guarded inflection—that Marsh had used earlier, when Emma had told him he looked like a Bravo. Jonas turned to Marsh. "You'll forgive my people." His tone was courteous, but not especially apologetic. "I pay them to be cautious. Sometimes they get a little carried away."

Marsh nodded. "I understand."

A silence ensued, an awkward one.

Jonas broke the silence with another by-rote courtesy. "Will you join us for lunch?" The food was all laid out on the table in the small dining nook where the two inner walls met—the meal that was supposed to have been for just Emma and Jonas. "I can get us another place setting."

Marsh seemed no more eager to share their lunch than Jonas had been to offer it. "Thank you. But no."

"Have a seat, then." Jonas led them to the sitting area, near an inner wall not far from where the food waited.

Emma perched on the couch. Jonas sat beside her.

Marsh took one of the wing chairs across the glass-topped coffee table from them. He set his briefcase on the coffee table, then rested back in his chair.

"Damn. I can't believe it. I'm here. And now I don't know where to begin."

Emma had to order her body not to squirm—and her mouth to stay shut. She'd gotten him up here. Surely he could manage everything else on his own. No doubt he would prefer it that way.

But Jonas was not looking terribly receptive. He was sitting too still, his face way too composed.

Well, and what, exactly, had she expected? For him to offer up a nice, big hug the minute Marsh had said that his last name was Bravo? Sometimes, lately, since she and Jonas had grown closer, Emma actually forgot what a cold and careful man he could be.

Marsh said, "The first thing I need to tell you, I think, is what I told your wife down in the lobby. That my father was Blake Bravo. And that he didn't die thirty-two years ago in that apartment fire as I'm sure you were told."

Jonas glanced Emma's way again. The look he gave

her was far from a pleased one. He didn't believe what he'd just heard. He also didn't appreciate that she'd dragged Marsh up here.

Well, too bad. Marsh was here. And Jonas was going to listen to what he had to say.

Emma granted her husband her sweetest, most reassuring smile.

Jonas did not smile back. He looked at Marsh again. "Excuse me? I'm sure I didn't hear you right."

"Unfortunately, you did."

"You expect me to believe—"

"Listen. From what I can piece together, my father faked his own death—to get past a manslaughter rap, I think. I'd guess that the man who died in his place must have been some poor vagrant, someone my father thought wouldn't be missed."

Jonas sat forward. "But the body was identified. Positively. As Blake's."

Marsh shook his head. "According to newspaper accounts of the fire, the body was burned beyond recognition."

Jonas still wasn't going for it. "Dental records proved—"

"He must have found a way to fake them. That's the only answer that makes any sense. We'll probably never know exactly how he pulled it off. But he *did* pull it off."

"You seem certain of this."

"I am."

Maybe Marsh was certain. Jonas clearly wasn't. "Where is your father now?" He put just enough emphasis on the word "father" to make it clear he doubted even that part of Marsh's story.

"Dead." Marsh said the word without expression.

"He wasn't dead *then*—but he is now?"

"That's right."

"You're positive?"

"I am."

Jonas made a low sound in his throat, one that spoke all too clearly of his total disbelief. "As I just pointed out to you, we were all pretty positive that Blake died thirty-two years ago. What makes this second 'death' any different?"

"This time the body was…intact. Identifiable."

"You identified it?"

"Yes. My father died—*really* died—five months ago in Norman, Oklahoma, at the hospital there. He died of a second massive heart attack after open-heart surgery. I saw the body afterward. It was my father's body—and if you'll only bear with me for a few minutes here, I think I can prove what I'm telling you."

"You're saying that you have evidence to support this claim?"

"Yes."

"Show me."

"I will. In a moment. But first, let me—"

Jonas cut him off. "I'd like to see the evidence. Now."

"Jonas, don't!" The words just kind of popped out of Emma's mouth. She sincerely had not meant to interfere. But how could she help it? Someone had to get this conversation moving on the right track.

Jonas said nothing, only looked at her, the kind of look meant to shut her up but good.

Too bad. He ought to know by now that there was no shutting her up when something needed saying. "You have got to quit givin' the man the third degree and let him tell it his own way."

"Oh, do I?"

"Yes. You do. It is called *listening*, Jonas Bravo. And I think you should try it. Now."

He stared at her hard and long. She stared right back. Finally, he turned to Marsh again. "My wife seems to think there's something to what you have to say."

Marsh raised both hands, palms up. "Just *let* me say it, let me get it all out. Then decide for yourself."

Jonas took what seemed like forever to answer. But in the end, he nodded. "All right. Have it your way."

"Thank you." With a hard exhalation of breath, Marsh forged on. "I think you do need to know that my father and I were not close. In fact, I wanted nothing to do with anything that was his. Which is why it's taken me so long to get here. I swear to you, I would have come sooner, if I had only known..." Marsh speared his hand back through his thick dark hair. "There's too damn much to explain. And I'm doing it badly."

Emma just ached for him. She started to speak—to grant him a few words of reassurance. But Jonas caught her eye. He shook his head. She held her tongue.

Marsh spoke again. "I guess I'm...making excuses for myself. Apologizing for not getting here months ago, right after my father died, when I should have gone to his house and..." He glanced away, then faced Jonas once more. "Look. I knew this wouldn't be easy. But it's worse than I expected. Just...bear with me. Please."

"I assure you. I am trying." Jonas's voice was so cold. Emma wanted to reach over and give him a good shake. But she held herself in check.

In her heart, she felt certain that Marsh was every bit as much a Bravo as the man sitting at her side. But Jonas was more careful. How could he help it, after all he'd been through? He needed further convincing. Emma really couldn't blame him for being more cautious than she.

Marsh said, "About a week ago, I finally decided to go and clean out the shack that my father called home. There was a certain room in that house, the room my father called his 'office.' He always kept it padlocked. No one was ever allowed in there. What we found in that room—"

"We?"

"Yes. My wife went with me. Her name is Tory." Marsh's bleak expression lightened a little. A soft gleam came into his eyes. Emma recognized the look. Marsh Bravo loved his wife deeply.

Marsh said, "Together, Tory and I went through that office of my father's. Once we realized what we'd found there, I considered taking everything to the police. I suppose I probably should have done exactly that. But I honestly do not believe there's a hell of a lot the police are going to be able to do at this point. No one is...at risk anymore. My father—the guilty party—is dead. So much time has passed. And the truth is, I couldn't help thinking that if our positions were reversed, yours and mine, I'd rather you brought everything straight to me."

Jonas said nothing. He only sat there, utterly still. Waiting.

Marsh reached for his briefcase. He worked the locks, popped the latches and propped open the top. "In that room I just told you about, my wife and I found this." He handed Jonas the age-yellowed photo album.

Jonas read the word taped to the front of it. He sent a baffled glance at Marsh. "Surprise?"

Marsh shrugged. "My father's sick sense of humor. Before he died, he kept telling me he had a big *surprise* for me. That book was it—or at least, a crucial part of it.''

Jonas opened the book and slowly began turning pages. It started with family photos—of the L.A. Bravos years before Jonas had even been born. Emma recognized the young Harry and Harry's father and mother from the pictures she had seen of them at Angel's Crest. She also recognized Blake. Who could ever forget that man's wolfish pale eyes?

Marsh reached across the coffee table and pointed at Blake in one of those early family pictures. ''That is my father.''

Jonas looked up.

Marsh went on, ''He got older. Craggier. Meaner, if that's possible. But those eyes never changed.''

The men stared at each other—and something shifted. Emma was sure of it. Right at that moment, Jonas began to believe.

Jonas resumed turning pages. The family photos ended and the newspaper clippings began. ''Blake Bravo Indicted on Manslaughter Charges,'' one headline read. And then there were several articles about the fire that had supposedly claimed Blake's life. ''Disinherited Bravo Dies in Apartment Blaze'' and ''Fire Claims Life of Younger Bravo Son.''

There were pages and pages of clippings concerning Russell's kidnapping, a long series of ugly headlines including, ''Bravo Baby Vanishes'' and ''Two Million in Diamonds Paid in Ransom for Bravo Baby,'' and ''No Leads in Bravo Baby Case.'' After that, there were clippings about Harry's death, about Blythe's mental collapse.

And it didn't end there. The stories continued, down the years, stories cut not only from the tabloids, but also

from the *L.A. Times* and the *Daily News*, the *San Francisco Chronicle* and the *Examiner*. Stories about Jonas,
growing up, attending Stanford and Yale, hunting in the
Sudan, dating an endless succession of beautiful women,
settling down to make billions with Bravo, Incorporated.

There were stories about Blythe and her charitable
activities: "Blythe Bravo Campaigns for Animal
Rights," "Bravo Matriarch Contributes One Million to
Save Street Kids," "Blythe Bravo, Angel of Angel's
Crest."

And finally, near the end, there were clippings about
Mandy: "Billionaire Baby" and "Blythe Bravo: Proud
New Mom at 58" and "The Littlest Bravo: Amanda
Eloise."

An icy shiver crawled down Emma's spine. Just to
think of that man with those terrible eyes, cutting out
articles about Mandy, carefully pasting them into the
yellowed book...

It was enough to make her decide that maybe Jonas
wasn't so paranoid, after all.

"My God," Jonas said quietly. "This is a trophy
book."

"Exactly," said Marsh, his voice bleak. "My father's
little souvenir. A way for him to relive his greatest ac-
complishments. Faking his own death..."

Jonas looked up and met Marsh's eyes. "...And kidnapping his brother's child without ever getting caught."

"That's right," said Marsh. "Look at the last page."

Jonas turned to it. "Something was taped here."

"A key. To a safe-deposit box. My wife and I went
to the bank where my father kept that box." Marsh unhooked the snap in the top of the briefcase, the snap that
held the accordion file shut. He pulled the file open. It
was empty, as before.

But then he reached in and raised the back wall of the file from the base, revealing a pocket concealed behind it.

Nestled in that pocket was a black jeweler's bag. Emma felt for Jonas's hand then. He let her have it without hesitation. She gave a squeeze and he squeezed back.

Marsh said, "Right before he died, my father got a lot of pleasure out of making cryptic references to my 'inheritance,' to some 'big, *glittering* surprise' I was going to get as soon as he was gone. I didn't have a clue what he was talking about. As I said earlier, I didn't want to know. I wanted to forget..." Marsh's voice trailed off.

He made himself continue. "I wanted to forget everything that had to do with my father, from the hell that was my childhood, to all the things he had stolen from me. And there were a lot of those, of things that he stole. Things other people take for granted. Things like hope, things like happiness. Things like love..."

Marsh took the bag from its hiding place, pressed the back wall of the file into place and hooked the snap that anchored it shut. Then he closed the briefcase and pressed the latches shut, as well.

When all that was done, he spoke again. "After my father died, I did find happiness. I found the love I had thought lost to me forever. And I found the daughter I didn't even know that I had. For a while, I ignored the past. I told myself it was behind me, that I'd let it go. In a strange way, my father had returned what he'd stolen from me, by calling me back to my hometown when he was dying."

Marsh hefted the bag in his hand. "So for a while, I was able to tell myself that the past was over and done with. But it nagged at me. And finally, after several months, I discovered I was ready to deal with it. That's when my wife and I went to my father's house. That's when we found that scrapbook and the key to a deposit box. That's when we went to the bank, with the key and my birth certificate and my father's will, which left everything to me. The bank officer verified that I had a right to the contents of the box. He took me into the vault, helped me open the box. And then he left me alone to do as I wanted with whatever was inside.

"Which was this bag." Marsh loosened the drawstring that held the bag shut. Very carefully, he shook the contents of the bag onto the coffee table.

Emma already knew what would fall out. Still, she couldn't hold back a gasp as the sparkling trail of diamonds spilled across the glass.

Chapter 17

"The ransom." Jonas's voice was hushed and low.

Marsh nodded.

Jonas said, "He never spent it."

"I'm sure *having* it was what it was all about to him. He could go to that safe deposit box any time—and there it was, a fortune in diamonds—"

"—And another trophy, like the scrapbook."

"That's right." Carefully, Marsh gathered up the stones and returned them to the velvet bag. "Have an expert take a look at these, compare them to whatever records you have of the diamonds your father bought to ransom your brother. I'm certain that they're one and the same. But I think you'll agree it's best to make absolutely sure." He tightened the drawstring, securing the treasure inside. "Here."

Jonas extended his hand.

Marsh dropped the diamonds into it. "Talk about irony. I think my old man imagined it was going to be some huge temptation for me—whether to keep my 'big, glittering surprise,' or not.'' He smiled. Emma thought it was the saddest smile she'd ever seen. "The minute I looked in that bag,'' he said, "the minute I saw what it contained, all I wanted was to return it, to start making right what the old man had made so very wrong.'' Jonas rose. Marsh picked up the scrapbook. "Better put this away, too.''

Jonas took the book and the diamonds and left through an inner door. He emerged empty-handed a few minutes later. "I hope you'll change your mind, Marsh. Have lunch with us, after all?'' It was a sincere invitation this time.

Marsh said, "I'd like that.''

Jonas buzzed his secretary and ordered another place setting. They all three sat down to eat.

Emma was the one who dared to broach the subject that she knew was on all of their minds. "I wonder...''

Both men looked at her.

So she laid it right out there. "Do you all think that maybe, in Blake's office, or in his things somewhere, there could be something more, something you and Tory missed, Marsh. Something that might help us to find out what happened to Russell?''

Marsh set down his fork and said just what Emma had known he would say. "I've been wondering the same thing.''

Jonas sipped from his water glass. "Well, there's only one way to find out.''

Emma grinned. "A trip to Oklahoma.''

Jonas turned to Marsh. "That's where this house of your father's is?''

"Yes. In Norman, Oklahoma. It's a university town, about twenty miles south of Oklahoma City.''

"And you live...?"

"In Norman, too."

Emma prompted, "With your wife, Tory, and your daughter...?"

"Kimberly. Tory wanted to make this trip with me. But Kimmy's in school. And Tory owns a florist shop. It's hard for her to leave on short notice. I'm a little more flexible right now. I own a limousine service that I started in Chicago. I'm opening a new branch in Oklahoma City, and I have managers in place at both locations—OKC and Chicago—so they can cover for me."

Jonas said, "But I imagine you'll be glad to get home."

"Yes, I will."

"All right. I'll need the rest of the day to deal with a few things that can't wait here. But tomorrow, I'll be ready to go—what about you, Emma?"

"As if I would miss it."

"Good. First thing tomorrow then, we're on our way. Marsh, you'll be our guest tonight."

"If you're sure. I don't want to—"

Jonas didn't allow him to finish. "I wouldn't have it any other way."

After Marsh left them, Emma and Jonas moved back to the couch in the sitting area. Emma shucked off her shoes and tucked her legs up to the side. "You had me worried there for a while, Jonas Bravo. I thought you were never going to listen to what Marsh had to say."

He wrapped his hand around her neck, pulled her close and kissed her right between the eyes. "You're too damn trusting."

"Well, but I *was* right. About Marsh. Wasn't I?"

He rested his brow against hers—head to head. "Yes, Emma. You were right."

She grinned. "Say that again…"

"Don't get pushy. Once is enough." He wrapped his arm around her and settled her in close.

She rubbed her cheek against the fine fabric of his jacket. "I think we'll have to take Mandy. She'll get lonely, if we're gone for too long."

"Emma." His chest rose and fell beneath her ear as he sighed. "We can't be gone for more than two or three days at the most. We both have businesses to run. We'll have to learn what we can as quickly as we can. And then, very soon, we'll have to turn everything over to the professionals."

The professionals. She sat up straight. "You mean the police?"

"And my detectives."

"Maybe…" She hesitated, reluctant to say what she couldn't stop herself from thinking.

"Maybe what?"

"Well, maybe we ought to just turn it over to the professionals right now."

He looked at her levelly. "Maybe you're right."

For about a half a second, she thought that he might have changed his mind about the trip—but then she saw that gleam in his eyes. "You're not foolin' me. You couldn't stand it, not to have a look around that 'office' of Blake's yourself. You just have to see what you might find there."

He shook his head slowly, as if he couldn't believe his own foolishness. "That's right. But what we're doing—mucking around in the evidence of a capital crime—I can't say I approve of it."

"Well, yeah, but what are the police going to *do* now,

anyway, since all this time has passed? And *which* police? The kidnapping happened in California. Blake's house is in Oklahoma..."

"I know," he said. "I've been thinking all the same things."

She reached over and took his hand. "It is kind of all in the family, now, isn't it? It looks like there's no one for the police to arrest, anyway, since Blake is dead. And if Russell's still alive somewhere—and I am prayin' with all my heart and soul that it might be true—well, he can't be in any danger, can he? I mean, not because of anything to do with what happened all those years and years ago."

He looked at their joined hands and then he looked in her eyes again. "You're saying the same thing I keep telling myself. That we have the right to do this."

"Well, and we do—or at least, *you* do. And since you invited me, I get to be involved, too."

He chuckled. "Are you always so sure that right is on your side?"

"Well, now, I just said I'm not really *sure.* But if a person is goin' to do a thing, she might as well do it with all of her heart."

"Don't tell me. Your aunt Cass said that, right?"

"Right—and okay. I can see your point. Maybe we won't have much time to take care of Mandy while we're playin' at bein' detectives in Norman, Oklahoma."

"I'm so glad you see it my way."

"Only this once."

"I'll try not to get cocky."

"Smart thinkin'—and we also have to consider the Yorkies and Festus."

"Palmer will take care of them."

"Palmer's just about the most efficient human bein' I have met in all my days. But he's not an animal person. I think I'll just get Deirdre to baby-sit them. She can stay in my rooms at the mansion, or she can take them to her place, whatever works better for her."

"However you want it."

She leaned closer. "Say that again."

He obliged, softly, "However you want it...."

"Come here. I'll show you how I want it." She offered her mouth. "Kiss me."

He did. She sighed. He guided her back onto the sofa.

And then the phone on his desk started buzzing.

Jonas lifted his head and swore under his breath. "My two o'clock appointment has apparently arrived."

Her arms were wrapped around his shoulders. She craned up enough to look at her watch. He was right. Two on the nose. They didn't even have time for a quickie. "And I had so many exciting plans for today."

"We'll have to do it again sometime."

"Is that a promise?"

He planted one more hard kiss on her mouth—a swift one that time. "It is a solemn vow."

Later in the afternoon, Jonas consulted a diamond broker. The broker assured him that the diamonds in the bag and those described in the documents were the same, though several appeared to be missing from the original count.

That evening, when the three of them—Marsh, Jonas and Emma—sat down to dinner, Jonas mentioned the missing diamonds.

Marsh frowned. "I swear to you, I gave you all the diamonds I found in that safe-deposit box."

"I'm sure you did. Your father probably spent a few now and then, don't you think?"

"Maybe. As I said earlier, I think he prized the diamonds for themselves, as physical proof of what he'd managed to get away with. And he was no fool. I'd guess that he figured out from the first that putting two million in diamonds on the market was a pretty good way to get caught."

"But still," Jonas argued, "he could have sold a diamond or two, when he needed cash and couldn't get it any other way. That wouldn't have been too dangerous for him. And he'd still have had the bulk of them left to gloat over."

Marsh shrugged. "I suppose."

They talked more of Blake, and of the kidnapping, Marsh and Jonas sharing what they knew in hopes that somehow, by combining what information each of them possessed, something more about what had happened to Russell might come to light.

Marsh said, "My father didn't work, at least not that I ever saw. My mother was the one who worked. I always assumed that what little we had came from her. But then she died, when I was sixteen. And somehow, my father never had any real problem getting by."

"Getting by? I take it you mean there wasn't a lot."

"You take it right. My father drove the same rattletrap pickup for over twenty years. And after he died, when I went in that shack we lived in, I found the same dingy brown carpet that had been there all my life, the same ancient television with a pair of rabbit ears on top. But in that office of his..."

"What?"

"A state-of-the-art computer hooked up to the Internet, a computer he used—along with the stacks and stacks of newspapers and magazines piled up in that room—to gather something that *was* important to him.''

''Information,'' Jonas said.

Marsh nodded. ''He was a secretive man, about himself. Maybe keeping track of people he knew gave him a feeling of power—and control.''

''So careful, when it came to the diamonds,'' said Jonas. ''And the way you describe him, he kept a pretty low profile for most of his life. Yet he had to be damned arrogant. To live under his own name—even if everyone he'd known in California thought he was dead.''

Marsh said, ''I'd be willing to bet he lived under a variety of aliases for a while, anyway—after he engineered his own 'death' and after the kidnapping.'' He sipped from his water glass. ''I managed to get myself something of a college education. Took a psychology course or two. I've come to the conclusion that my father was a psychopath, one with a truly diabolical mind and a surprising degree of impulse control—when it suited him to exercise it.''

''My mother always claimed he was just plain evil,'' Jonas said.

Marsh didn't argue. ''Maybe it's as simple as that.''

Jonas chuckled. ''And this is adding up to a lot of maybes.''

''I know. The fact is, I doubt we'll ever get at the root of what drove my father.''

Jonas agreed. ''I'm afraid you're probably right, though I think his motivation for kidnapping my brother is pretty clear.''

Marsh grunted. ''To you, maybe.''

''Oldest motive in the book—revenge.''

''Against...?''

''My father.''

"But wait a minute," Emma said. "I thought it was your Grandfather Jonas who disinherited Blake. And didn't he pass away before Russell was kidnapped?"

"That's right."

"But then, why would Blake take his revenge on his *brother?*"

"Because Blake blamed Harry just as much as he blamed my grandfather." Jonas picked up his wineglass, took a thoughtful sip. "The way I heard the story, at first, after my grandfather cut Blake off, my father kept in contact with him. My father gave Blake money whenever he showed up with his hand out. But then Blake ran into my grandfather one day here at Angel's Crest, when Blake came to try to talk my father into giving him another 'loan.'

"My grandfather ordered Blake out. Blake lost his temper. He beat my grandfather, and pretty badly, too. My father came in on it. He tore Blake off of my grandfather and the brothers fought. My father won. He had Blake tossed out and gave orders that he was never to be let beyond the gates of Angel's Crest again."

"Oh, yeah," said Marsh. "For something like that, Blake Bravo would have to claim some major revenge."

"And how perfect," added Jonas. "Blake was the second son. And so was Russell."

"Perfect?" Emma wrinkled her nose at her husband. "It's all just plain creepy, if you ask me."

"But it makes a sick kind of sense," said Marsh, "given the way that my father's mind worked. *His* father had disinherited his second son, so in effect, the first Jonas Bravo ended up minus one son. And so Blake saw to it that Harry lost a son, too."

Emma couldn't help but say it. "For the first time in

my life, I am *glad* that someone is dead. A man like Blake Bravo deserves to be dead."

Jonas woke that night shouting, "No!"

Blinking into the darkness, Emma sat up beside him as he threw back the covers. He surged from the bed and then stopped, bent at the waist, his back to her. The sweat was streaming off him, the powerful muscles of his back flexing and jerking, as he tried with all his considerable strength to get air, sucking in through his closed-up windpipe with all his might, making a horrible tight gasping sound.

Emma jumped from the bed and then just stood there, debating with herself as she had debated the last time this happened. Should she intervene? It looked like he was getting *some* air. She knew her first aid. If he was getting air at all, she was supposed to leave him alone—wasn't she?

He went on, bent at the waist, hands on his thighs, making that horrible desperate wheezing sound.

It was too much. She would dial 911. Emma turned toward the phone—and then whirled back around again as Jonas sank to his knees.

He fell over on his side and his big body went lax.

He was still. And the gasping had stopped.

"Jonas?" Emma dropped to her own knees beside him and put her fingers at the pulse point on his neck.

A good, strong heartbeat. Thank God.

She got down there with him, all the way down. She lay on her side, her nose a few inches from his and she felt his warm breath against her face.

Breathing normally. Better all the time.

She waited. And in a few minutes, she was rewarded. His eyes opened. They looked glazed.

He spoke, his voice a rough rasp. "My red truck..."
He blinked. She watched as his vision cleared.
"Emma?" He frowned at her. "What...?"

"Shh." She smoothed the hair at his temple. It was
soaked with sweat—like the rest of him. "You had the
dream."

He winced, swallowed, winced again. "Damn. The
dream..."

They lay there, on the pale, soft carpet. Emma stroked
his face, his neck, his shoulder, down his arm. Eventually, she asked, "Shower?"

"Yeah."

She got up and went to turn on the water for him.

She waited until they were back in bed and cuddled
close under the sheet before she asked him if, just
maybe, he remembered something this time.

He answered flatly, "No."

"You said somethin', when you first came out of it.
You said, 'My red truck.' Does that mean anything to
you?"

He closed his eyes, sighed, and then opened them
again. "Not a damn thing."

"Jonas..."

"Um?"

She hesitated. She had a feeling he'd resist the suggestion she was about to make.

"Just say it," he whispered gruffly, and rubbed his
forehead against her shoulder.

"Well, have you ever considered maybe talkin' to a
doctor about this? I mean, someone who is trained to
deal with things like this?"

"A psychiatrist, you mean?"

She couldn't tell if he sounded amused—or irritated.

"Well, yes. Some kind of therapist. Someone who would know how to help you."

"Help me, how, exactly?"

"Well, to get to the root of the dream. And then to get past it, so you can stop havin' it."

He pulled free of her embrace and canted up on an elbow. They looked at each other through the darkness. His eyes, she thought, looked very deep. There were shadows of fatigue, like dark bruises, beneath them.

"Jonas, are you...okay?"

"Fine," he said. "And as to seeing a therapist, I thought I explained that. I *have* seen a therapist. An endless series of them, as a matter of fact. None of them got anywhere with this little problem of mine."

"But that was years ago."

"So?"

"Things might be different now. I'm sure therapy is like anything else. They learn new things all the time, they improve their...techniques."

"Emma."

"What?"

"Been there, done that. Not again."

"Oh, Jonas..."

"Not again. Clear?"

"But—"

"Clear?"

She made a face at him. "Oh, all right." She reached for him. "Come back here."

He settled in close once more, his head on her shoulder. They lay there, wrapped around each other, the silence punctuated by the faint snoring of one of the Yorkies at the foot of the bed. Emma smiled and closed her eyes.

And then he was rubbing his forehead against her shoulder again.

"Jonas, what is it?"

"Nothing. Headache."

"Since when?"

"Had it all night. Thought it would pass, but it seems to be getting worse..."

"I'll get you somethin' for it." She started to rise.

He lifted his head and kissed her chin. "No. You stay here. I'll get it myself."

"I don't mind."

He put a finger to her lips. "Shh. Stay here. I'll take care of it."

He was back in no time. She held the sheet out to welcome him. He came down to her, wrapped his arms around her.

"Jonas?"

"What?"

"I have this feeling. It's really strong."

"And what is your feeling?"

"We're going to find your brother. I just know we are."

"And will we find him alive?" Again, she couldn't read his tone. Was he irritated? Disbelieving? Before she could say anything, he sighed. "Never mind. Don't tell me. Let it be a surprise."

"You mean you believe me? You think we'll find him, too?"

He didn't reply, only pulled her closer.

Tenderly, she combed her fingers through his thick hair and considered the question he hadn't let her answer.

And will we find him alive?

About that, she had no hunch at all. "Jonas?"

Again, he gave no reply. And she didn't press him. After a time, his breathing evened out.

Emma lay in the darkness, staring up at the shadowed crystal teardrops that dangled from the chandelier, holding her sleeping husband close and trying to imagine what kind of man Russell Bravo would have become. Trying to picture someone who might be a brother to Jonas—someone big and strong, someone a little overbearing who liked to give the orders, someone with midnight eyes and a cleft in his chin.

Trying *not* to think of a small bare skull, a bit of baby blanket, a few sad little white bones...

Chapter 18

They arrived at Will Rogers World Airport in Oklahoma City at just a little after noon the next day. Tory, Marsh's wife, was waiting for them. She was a tall, slender woman with a mane of curly red hair and a sprinkling of freckles across her nose.

The drive to the nearby university town of Norman took less than half an hour. They caravanned, Marsh and Tory in the lead, Emma and Jonas following them in a rented Chrysler 300M—and a pair of Jonas's bodyguards taking up the rear.

"I've been wondering what Marsh's wife would be like," Emma told Jonas as they sped down the interstate. "Tory's got...dignity, don't you think? Dignity and a warm heart. I liked her the minute I set eyes on her."

"Emma. You like everyone the minute you set eyes on them."

"No, Jonas. I do not. I never did like you—until recently."

He sent her a look. "You're saying you do like me now?"

"Yes, indeed I do."

Marsh and Tory Bravo lived in a handsome brick house on the corner of a wide tree-lined street. They had a comfortable guest bedroom and they insisted that Jonas and Emma make use of it.

"You'll have to share the hall bathroom with Kimberly," Tory said. "I hope that's all right."

Emma waited for Jonas to insist that they couldn't stay there. Security was clearly nonexistent. And where would the bodyguards sleep?

But either his paranoia was slipping a little, or, since Mandy wasn't with them, he felt willing to take a chance on spending a whole night—or maybe even two—in an unguarded house.

He smiled at Tory. "Sounds fine to me."

Tory smiled back. "And this is a quiet neighborhood. Nothing bad is going to happen here. Maybe you could just send those bodyguards to a hotel?"

The bodyguards in question were waiting in their rental car in front of the house.

"Maybe I could," Jonas agreed.

And he did it. He went out and told the men to make themselves scarce. They were to find lodging for themselves and remain available at all times by cell phone, in case he needed them. But they didn't have to shadow their employer's every move.

"Way to go, Jonas," Emma said over her shoulder when he came back into the house and found her in the guest room unpacking their things.

He came up behind her, took her by the waist and nibbled on her ear. "Proud of me, are you?"

"You'd better believe it."

He nuzzled her hair. "Prove it."

"I will—later."

"You'll have to do it quietly," he whispered. "There'll be a nine-year-old sleeping just down the hall." They'd be meeting Marsh's daughter later in the afternoon, when she came home from school.

Emma turned in his embrace and twined her arms around his neck. "You think I can't do it quietly?"

"I'm willing to watch you try." He was grinning—but he still had those dark circles under his eyes.

She brushed her fingers between his brows, where the skin looked drawn with tension. "Still got that headache?"

"It comes and goes. It's not too bad right now."

"Maybe you ought to take a—"

"Emma. I'm fine. Let it be—and I think Tory is holding lunch for us. Come on." He snared her hand and pulled her out into the hall.

Tory did have a light meal waiting for them. They sat down to sandwiches, fruit salad and iced tea.

After lunch, Tory left them to return to her florist shop and Marsh said he'd drive them out to his father's house.

Ten minutes after getting into Marsh's roomy sedan, they had left the town of Norman behind. Woods of oak and hickory, turning gold now with the colors of fall, surrounded them, interspersed with fields where rough brown grasses grew and cattle and horses grazed. The October sun shone down and the day was mild, the air fresh and clear.

The houses were far apart, some old and run-down, some big and brand-new. The new ones, Marsh told them, were mostly the dream homes of folks who worked in the city and didn't mind an hour's drive to and from work if they could live out in the country.

"When I was kid," he said, "this was all ranch and forest land. But in the past ten years or so, as you can see, that has changed. They've broken a lot of it up into five-acre parcels. And people with money are building out here."

Marsh turned onto a slightly narrower road where the trees grew closer in, branches meeting overhead, forming a lacy canopy of green and gold. Driveways wound off into the trees, most of them marked by mailboxes.

"Here it is." Marsh turned the wheel again, into a driveway with no mailbox beside it, one so overgrown, someone who didn't know it was there would probably never have spotted it.

The driveway was rutted and unpaved. They bumped along it slowly. Branches scraped the car's roof and a couple of bushy-tailed squirrels darted across the road in front of them, easily making cover on the other side before the car got close enough to be a threat to them. Soon enough, they came to the end of the driveway. Marsh parked behind an old pickup, which sat under a carport built off the side of a tumbledown shed.

Beyond the carport lay a cleared space. And beyond the cleared space stood the house. It was a plain wood-sided structure with an asphalt-shingle roof. At one time it might have been white. But most of the paint had long ago peeled off, leaving the wood to weather down to an ugly gray. There was a lot of junk stacked against the side of the shed and near the house—old tires and broken tools, empty plastic containers and bins full of aluminum cans.

Growing up in Alta Lobo, Emma had seen similar places, ramshackle run-down houses with a lot of junk around. But most people did something to try to make even the poorest house a home. They'd put a violet in the window, or some silly statue in the yard.

There was nothing like that here, nothing that would make this bleak place a home. Just junk and red dirt— a shed, a house and an old pickup truck. The pickup wasn't even any kind of real color. It had a coat of rusting gray primer on it, and nothing more.

Marsh turned off the engine and muttered dryly, "As I think I might have mentioned, my father never cared a whole lot about living well."

They got out of the car, crossed the cleared space and entered the house under the sagging overhang that served as a front porch.

It was no more inviting inside than out. The front door opened into a living room with brown carpet, brown chairs and a brown couch. The smell of mildew hung in the air and not a single picture graced the dingy walls.

"This way." Marsh led them down a dark, narrow hallway, past two bedrooms on the right. The hallway jogged left at the end. A few steps and they confronted a padlocked door.

Marsh had the key.

They entered Blake's "office." It consisted of a battered desk with a computer on top, a wall lined with metal bookcases, some scarred file cabinets, an old portable typewriter on a cheap stand, a window air conditioner and a closet. Emma opened the closet door. Like the metal bookcases, the closet was stacked high with old newspapers and magazines.

Marsh booted up the computer, then offered the squeaky swivel chair to Jonas. "Be my guest." Jonas took the chair. The computer required a password, which Marsh provided. "It's 'surprise.'"

Jonas typed in the word at the prompt and he was in. "Your father gave you the password before he died?"

"No. He gave hints. The hints were in certain things he said to me—and of course, the word was pasted on the front of his scrapbook. But he never told me directly. What fun would that have been for him?"

Jonas swore. "Your father had one sick idea of fun."

"You'll get no argument from me on that point."

Jonas began to explore the computer, checking through the different programs stored inside, scrolling through files, seeking some hint of something that would lead him to something else, some clue that might end up helping him to discover what had happened to a baby who had vanished three decades ago.

Emma went through the file cabinets, which Marsh said Tory had already looked through once. She found file folders full of clippings—articles about everything from how to build your own storm cellar to a thousand and one uses for old newsprint. She found folders with Blake's bills in them—utility bills, grocery receipts, bills for meals at places like Pizza Hut and Taco Bell. It looked as if the man had kept every piece of paper he ever got his hands on.

She also found folders with people's names on them. Most of the names she didn't know. But there was a folder for Marsh and one for Jonas. One for Tory and one for Kimberly. One for Blythe and one for Amanda. There were folders for other Bravos, too: Jenna and her sister, the three Wyoming cousins and their families and several more that Emma didn't recognize offhand.

As a rule, the folders with people's names on them were empty. But Blythe's folder held a couple of clippings, both of them less than a year old. And Jonas's contained one clipping, about some business deal he'd made back in March.

She showed the clippings to Marsh and Jonas.

"He probably planned to paste them into that book of his," Marsh said. "But he died before he got around to it."

The computer, like the file cabinet, contained hundreds of files labeled with people's names. In those files were phone numbers and addresses, notes about places of business, likes and dislikes, hobbies and pastimes. As in the cabinet, there was a file on Marsh and each member of his family—and on Jonas and Blythe and Mandy.

"What was he plannin' to *do* with all this information?" Emma asked no one in particular after they'd been in that room for about an hour and a half, getting nowhere, looking through dusty papers and scanning computer files that seemed to have no other purpose than the secret invasion of other people's privacy.

"Whatever it was, he won't be doing it anymore," Marsh said. He was leaning over Jonas's shoulder as Jonas opened folders and scrolled through files. "I don't know about the two of you, but I find that very reassuring."

"It's just too bad he didn't keep a file on Russell," Emma said. "Except in the scrapbook, we haven't seen that name anywhere."

Marsh made a noise of agreement in his throat and glanced her way. She thought that he was thinking just what she was right then. That there was no file on Russell because he had died three decades ago. What would be the point in keeping track of the dead?

Jonas pressed his fingers to his forehead.

Emma put her hand on his shoulder. "That headache is still bothering you, isn't it?"

"It's all right, Emma." He gently shrugged her off. "We need a nerd," he said. "Someone who can get in here deeper than I know how to."

Marsh was nodding. "You're right. The old man must have deleted things, and maybe some of what he got rid of would be of use to us now. An expert might be able to retrieve it."

"I know one or two bona fide computer geniuses," Jonas said. "I'll make a few calls tonight, see if one of them would be willing to fly out here tomorrow morning and have a look."

"Sounds like a plan."

"In the meantime, I see he's got a port here for a Zip disk. Maybe we ought to make a backup copy of everything on his hard drive—just in case something happens to this computer."

"Good idea," said Marsh. "I think I saw some of those bigger disks around here somewhere...." He knelt and pulled several of them from one of the lower left-hand desk drawers. "Here we go." He set the fat gray disks on the desk. Jonas picked up the top one, removed it from its case and inserted it into the port.

Emma turned to the file cabinet again and started in on the *N*'s. Marsh had already gone back to thumbing through the dusty stacks of newspapers and magazines. Jonas completed his task of copying the contents of the computer onto the Zip disks. Then he remained at the computer, scrolling through file after file.

It was after five when he sat back in the swivel chair. "That's it." He rolled his shoulders, as if to loosen the tension gathered there. "I've opened every file in this damn machine—at least every one I can manage to access. And I have found zero. Nada. Nothing at all that might get us any closer to figuring out what happened to my brother."

Emma had found nothing, either. She shut the bottom file drawer and brushed off her hands as Marsh tossed the magazine he'd been thumbing through back onto one of the dusty stacks.

Jonas rubbed at his eyes. "I can call around, as I said, for someone to get out here and have a closer look at this computer. But after that..."

Marsh sank to the edge of the battered desk. "We've kind of run out of places to search, haven't we?"

"Don't forget the rest of the house," Emma reminded them. "Nobody's gone through the kitchen drawers, or your father's bedroom, have they?"

"No," Marsh said. "And you're right. We should go through the whole place. I would have guessed, if there were anything more for us to find, it would have been in this room. But you never know..."

Jonas stood. "We'll check the rest of the house tomorrow. And go through the shed." He shrugged. Emma thought he looked very tired—and way too resigned.

He didn't think they were going to find anything. She could see that in the weary lines of his face, hear it in the flat tone of his voice.

At Marsh's house, they met Kimberly, as well as the little girl's cat, a good-natured gray tabby named Mr. Pickles. Kimberly was very pleased to learn she had a cousin from Los Angeles.

"I think we'll have to come and visit you, Cousin Jonas," Kimberly announced. "It'll work out great. We can go to Disneyland and Universal Studios while we're there."

Jonas said he'd look forward to that visit and really seemed to mean it. He told Kimberly about Mandy.

Emma watched him with the little girl, noted the warmth in his eyes and the openness of his smile. He really had come a very long way since their marriage. Blythe would be proud.

Now, if they could just find Russell…

But a day of fruitless searching had created serious doubts on that score. After Kimberly had gone to bed, the grown-ups made themselves comfortable in the family room and discussed the situation.

Jonas said, "I think we've already got all the clues Blake left for us."

Marsh concurred. "I'm afraid you're right. The scrapbook and the diamonds. Just enough to rub our noses in what he did—and nothing else. No way to track down your brother, no hint at all as to how to find out what the hell happened to him."

"A whole new aspect to his revenge. He as good as confesses, but there's no way we can get to him, no way he pays for what he did, no way we ever learn where my brother is now."

"Right. The locked room, the computer, the files, the stacks of old magazines and yellowed newspapers. I'm sure it gave him a hell of a good laugh, before he died, picturing me going through everything, imagining how it might go, if I decided to give up the diamonds and take what I knew to you or to the police. How we'd tear that office of his apart trying to find some indication of where Russell might be now…"

"And how we'd come up with nothing."

"Exactly." Marsh fisted his hand and tapped it on the arm of his char. "Damn. The old man brings new mean-

ing to the word *diabolical*—and I noticed you didn't try
to contact your computer expert.''

Jonas shrugged. ''The more I considered it, the more
it seems to me that there's no more in that computer
than what we've already found.''

Emma couldn't help speaking up then. ''Come on,
you guys. Don't give up yet. You never know. We still
might find something.''

Jonas sent her a tender, indulgent look. ''Emma, it's
not very damn likely.''

''Maybe it's not. But do you mind if I stick with a
positive attitude?''

''Be my guest. Tomorrow, we'll look through the rest
of the house and that shed. And then on Thursday, I
think it's time we turned over what we've got to the
authorities. Let them do whatever they're willing to do
at this point.''

They went to bed at a little after eleven. Jonas didn't
complain of his headache, but Emma could see it was
bothering him. The skin beneath his eyes looked more
bruised than ever. She asked him if he'd taken anything
for it. He told her not to worry, that he was fine.

She knew very well that he was not fine.

And she also knew it wouldn't help to keep nagging
him about it. She pressed her lips together to keep from
fussing over him any more than she already had, turned
off the light and tucked herself up against him, spoon-
fashion. He nuzzled her ear affectionately and she
rubbed her foot down the front of his hairy leg, sighed
at the feel of his warm breath in her hair.

She thought of how they had teased each other earlier,
the little challenge he'd thrown out, that he'd like to see
her try making love without doing any shouting. But that

had been before they'd spent the afternoon in Blake's dingy office, seeking some little hint that might lead them to Russell—and finding nothing at all.

She could not even imagine what it must be like for him. To get his hopes up after all these years. And to have to live through the death of those hopes all over again.

It wasn't easy, when a person learned to open up. Being opened up meant you were more likely to get hurt.

Emma did understand that. There was a price, for openness. It was called pain.

But then, as Aunt Cass used to say, *You also get joy and love and tenderness. Only people who open their hearts get those things.*

Jonas's arm lay across her waist. She took his hand, twined her fingers in his and pressed their joined hands close to her heart. He slid a leg between her legs, pulled her in closer against his body.

Emma closed her eyes. The day had been a long one. And she was very tired....

Jonas lay awake, listening as the sound of Emma's breathing became shallow and slow, feeling her fingers go lax in his. Good. At least one of them would get a little damn sleep.

His head felt as if someone had turned a demon loose in there—a sadistic little devil with a ball peen hammer and a yen to batter his way right out of Jonas's skull.

It hurt.

But not as much as the thought that they probably weren't going to find Russell, after all. Not by themselves, anyway—and most likely not even with the help of the authorities.

They were out of their depth with this. They should

have turned it all over to the police yesterday, right after Marsh gave him the scrapbook and the diamonds. Hell. They might even have destroyed evidence, poking around in Blake's things, though he doubted it. Everything they'd touched today was thirty years and half a continent removed from what had happened to his brother. But still. It was a possibility.

And it was also water over the dam, at this point. They had done what they had done—and tomorrow, they would do more. Because somewhere deep inside him, hope still burned, a pinpoint of golden light that wouldn't give up, though he knew it was bound, in the end, to be swallowed by the looming shadow of disappointment.

Jonas closed his eyes. He breathed in the sweet scent of the woman in his arms, took what comfort he could from the warmth of her body, the tender feel of her fingers in his, the twin swells of her breasts pressing soft and full against his forearm.

His headache faded a little. He closed his eyes with a long sigh. Sleep came creeping over him, light as a mist or a shadow not quite seen, so that he hardly knew he had slipped the moorings of consciousness and drifted out into the dark sea that was the dream.

Chapter 19

One moment Jonas lay in the guest room of his cousin's house, with Emma in his arms.

And the next moment, he was home. At Angel's Crest. Home in his bedroom, with the moon shining through the tall palm trees outside making funny, scary shadows against the walls. Like big fish fins, or strange arms, the shadows of the palm branches...

He was awake, though he knew he had been asleep just a moment ago. He looked at the glowing dial of the Mickey Mouse clock by his bed. Mickey's long arm was on the one and his short arm pointed at the two. That meant two o'clock. Five minutes after two o'clock.

Yeah. That was right. Very late. Too late to be awake.

"Go back to sleep, young man," his daddy would say, if he knew that Jonas had opened his eyes.

And his mom would shake her head. "Jonas, darling. It's the middle of the night..."

He closed his eyes. He was going to go back to sleep. He really was.

But then he remembered.

His eyes popped open again.

He knew what had woken him up. His new red truck, the fire engine truck that made a siren sound when the wheels turned and had a working ladder that could stand up and pull out, get longer so the firemen could save people from burning buildings and rescue scared cats trapped in tall trees...

His new red truck was in Russy's room. Under Russy's crib. He'd left it there yesterday, when he was playing in Russy's room and he'd revved it up and let it go and it rolled right under the crib. And then Paloma, his nanny, who was also Russy's nanny now, had said he could hold Russy.

Jonas really liked that, sitting in the rocking chair and holding Russy, who was just a tiny baby, only three months old. It made Jonas feel very big and grown-up.

So he'd sat in the rocker and Paloma gave him Russy. He was very careful. Very gentle. He rocked only a little and he looked down at Russy's pink face and his little baby mouth and he whispered, "You are my brother and when you get a little older I will teach you how to write your name and how to tell what time it is...."

Jonas liked having a brother. He liked it a lot. He wanted more brothers. And even maybe a sister, too. Their house was a very big house and it would take a lot of kids to fill it up. Jonas would always be the oldest, though. The first one. He would be a big brother. And he would take care of the littler ones.

This always pleased him, to think of himself as the oldest of a whole bunch of Bravo kids. It made him feel proud and big and real good about himself.

That was probably it, why he went and forgot the red fire truck. He was too busy thinking about being a big brother. And then his mom came and told him to go and wash his hands for dinner.

"Let's have that little sweetheart." She'd bent over him, smelling so good, like she always did. She kissed him—just touched her soft lips to his cheek—and at the same time scooped Russy right up into her arms. Russy made one of those googly, smiley sounds. Jonas's mom had laughed. "Oh, you are a happy boy." She looked at Jonas, her face all soft. "Go on now, wash your hands." Her words told him what to do, but her voice said that she loved him so much.

"Mom. You love me, don't you?"

"I certainly do."

"That's good. 'Cause I love you, too."

He had slid off the rocker and gone to wash for dinner. And he had forgotten all about the red truck.

Until now. Until five minutes after two in the middle of the night.

He should go back to sleep. He knew that. He could get it later. After the sun came out, at a time when a boy was supposed to be awake.

But it just bothered him. He wanted that truck.

Jonas sat up in bed. The wind was blowing outside a little, moving the tree branches so that the shadows waved at him from the wall of his room. He decided not to look at them. Not to think about how late it was and how dark and if there was such a thing as a creature in the closet or a monster under the bed, well, this would be the right time for something like that to be awake and looking for a kid to grab and carry away somewhere, wherever monsters came from, the dark places, the scary places, where a kid would never see his mom or dad again.

Stop thinking about monsters, he told himself silently. There are no monsters. No creatures in the closet. No such thing. Not in real life. Uh-uh. Nosiree.

Jonas pushed back the covers and swung his bare feet to the floor.

Slippers. He thought about slippers and then decided to skip them. He could tiptoe a lot better without them, and he did want to be quiet when he went into Russy's room. He didn't want to wake up the baby—or Paloma, who slept in the room on the other side of Russy's. If he woke Russy, Russy might cry. And if he woke up Paloma, or if Russy's crying woke her up, he might get in trouble.

He wasn't sure about that, about the trouble part. He hadn't exactly done this kind of thing before, so he'd never been told that it was a wrong thing to do, sneaking into Russy's room in the middle of the night.

He'd never been *told* it was wrong. But he thought maybe it might be. So he decided it would be better if he just kept real quiet, snuck in, got his red truck and snuck back to his bed. No one would ever have to know, and the getting in trouble part wouldn't even have a chance to happen.

Careful not to look at the swaying shadows on the wall, Jonas tiptoed to the door that opened onto the hall-way. He wrapped his hand around the doorknob and turned it, very carefully. The door gave inward as he pulled on it. It didn't make a single sound. He stepped out into the hall, onto the hall rug, which had pictures of leaves and flowers all over it, though right then, in the dark, the leaves and flowers were hard to see. They looked a little like snakes in the dark, snakes in the rug, wiggling and wrapping all around each other, snakes that might come alive in the rug, come alive and curl around his ankles, slither up his legs and—

No. Stop. No scary thoughts.

The rug was just the rug. It had flowers and leaves on it and he wasn't even going to look at it anymore right now.

There were small lamps on the walls, with lightbulbs shaped like candle flames at the top of them. But they didn't help any, because they were all turned off. The only light came from either end of the hall, silvery moonlight glowing in the high windows there. It wasn't much, but it was enough that Jonas could see where he was going.

Very quietly, keeping to the middle of the rug where he imagined he'd be less likely to cause any creaking sounds, he moved down the dark hall toward his baby brother's bedroom. It wasn't far. There was his room and then the big playroom where he kept most of his toys, and where there was also a table for studying. He was old enough now that he had to study sometimes. He was "very bright." His mother said so and his teachers did, too. Most people, when they were six, were in first grade. But he was studying some things that a lot of kids learned in third.

And someday, he and Russy would share the playroom. And when his other brothers came, and his sister, they would share it, too.

Sharing, he thought. That would be another thing that he would have to teach them. Little kids needed to learn how to share. He would say things like, "This is my red truck. If you promise not to break it, you can play with it, too." Jonas smiled to himself, pleased to think what a good big brother he would be, how he would—

He blinked. And his plans for his future as a big brother flew right out of his head. Something wasn't right. His brother's door was open. There was a shadow of emptiness, the darkness of Russy's room, where the closed door should have been.

Well, and that was okay. Wasn't it?

He wasn't sure. For some reason, it didn't feel very okay.

He thought he could hear noises in there, in Russy's dark room—rustling noises, noises that spoke of secrets and of hurrying. The kind of noises the monster under the bed might make—or the creature from the closet.

He tiptoed closer. Then, without even really deciding to do it, he stepped toward the wall and flattened himself against it, right next to the dark hole that was the doorway to Russy's room.

More rustling. Something fell to the floor—one of Russy's rattles. Jonas recognized the sound it made.

As the rattle dropped, a man whispered in a voice that sounded like a snake hissing, "Damn you, Lorraine. Quiet."

Jonas shrank against the wall, biting his lip to hold back a whimper. There were no monsters in his brother's room. There were *strangers* in there.

Jonas wanted to turn and race away down the hall. He wanted to hide, somewhere safe, where the man with the snake-hiss voice could never find him. And he wanted to get his daddy. To get his daddy to protect him. Protect him and Russy from the strangers in Russy's room.

But his daddy and mommy were sleeping two long hallways away. It would take him forever to get there. By then, the strangers could be gone. By then, they might have hurt Russy. They might—

His mind seemed to freeze up. And his body moved

kind of all by itself. His foot just stepped out and he turned around. All of a sudden, he was standing right in the open doorway to Russy's room.

He saw the two strangers. They both wore clothes as black as night, clothes that covered them all over, so hardly any skin was showing. And black stocking hats, the kind Jonas's mother had made him wear last winter when they went to the snow, the kind that pulled down all the way over their faces and had cutout places for their mouths and their eyes.

One of the strangers had Russy. It was a lady, that stranger. He knew that. She was shaped like a lady— and the man with the snake-hiss voice had called her a lady's name: Lorraine.

The other one, the man, saw him first. The man had scary eyes. He looked at Jonas and Jonas looked at him.

And Jonas wanted, again, more than just about anything, to turn and run away.

In order not to do that, he ran forward—he ran straight at the man with the terrible eyes. He jumped on him, he shouted, ''No!'' He would have shouted a lot more, but the scary-eyed man clamped a hand over his mouth.

''My God, Blake…'' whispered the woman.

''Shut up,'' the man hissed.

Jonas kicked and tried to hit and even bite the bad man who was holding him. But the bad man had gloves on his hands and he cupped his palm in such a way that Jonas couldn't get his teeth in it. And he was strong, the bad man.

''We'll have to take them both,'' the bad man whispered, as Jonas continued to kick and wiggle and squirm.

''No way,'' whispered the lady. ''A baby's one thing, but a kid…''

''Then what do you suggest?''

"I don't... Oh, God. I don't know..."

"If we don't take him..." The bad man got Jonas around the throat. He started squeezing. Jonas sucked for air, he grabbed the bad man's gloved fingers, tried to pull them free.

The lady went on whispering, a whisper so scared it was like someone screaming, "No! Don't. You can't. He's a child...."

Little lights seemed to dance and pop inside Jonas's head. He couldn't get any breath in his mouth and his throat was shut off, closed tight by the squeezing hands of the bad man. He was dizzy and he wanted to keep fighting, but his body was getting strange and heavy and Russy's room was starting to go away.

Now the man was holding him with just one hand, holding him around the neck, off the ground. And he felt so limp and weak. He was supposed to help his brother. But he wasn't helping. He wasn't helping at all.

The bad man reached behind him, pulled out something he'd had tucked in the back of his belt. Jonas stared. A gun. A black gun. The bad man was going to shoot him. Jonas looked right in the bad man's terrible eyes—and remembered.

The pictures. The pictures on the table in the front room downstairs, and the ones on the piano in the music room. The man in the pictures who had the bad man's eyes.

"Who is that, Mommy?"

And Mommy's voice, sad and serious, "That's your uncle Blake, my darling. He passed away a while ago...."

Passed away. Jonas knew what that meant. His uncle Blake was dead.

Or he was supposed to be dead.

Passed away. Gone to heaven—or maybe, if he'd been as bad as the look in his eyes, to the other place.

So why was he here in Russy's room? Why was he stealing Russy? Strangling Jonas? Going to shoot him with a big black gun?

Jonas hung there in that powerful gloved hand, held by his neck, waiting for the shot. It never came. His dead uncle only brought the gun down hard on the side of Jonas's head. Little stars seemed to wink bright and burst all around him.

And then there was nothing.

It was dark when he opened his eyes. The room was very quiet. He wasn't sure where he was.

But then he recognized the legs of his brother's crib. And a shadow beneath it, a shadow of red.

"My red truck…" he whispered to the silent room. It hurt, doing that. Whispering.

What was he doing here, in Russy's room? He didn't remember. His head was hurting and his throat was very sore.

He put his hands flat on the floor, to push himself up. But it was no good. His hands wouldn't push.

He laid his head down with a sigh and the world went away again.

He woke seconds later—in the bed in his cousin's house in Norman, Oklahoma, the sweet warmth that was Emma close at his side.

For a time, he didn't move. He lay there on his back, staring into the darkness at the shadowed shape of the ceiling fan overhead. His headache was gone.

Emma sighed and snuggled closer, her arm sliding

over to wrap around his chest. He should probably let her sleep.

But then again, he would go stark, raving mad if he didn't tell her everything immediately.

"Emma?" He turned on his side, cupped her nape and nuzzled his nose against hers.

"Umm? Jonas?" She smiled and she yawned.

He waited, watching her, as she came fully awake. Those green eyes met his. "What?" She blinked. "Somethin' has happened…"

"Damn right it has."

Her eyes widened.

He said it. "I had the dream."

Her smooth brows drew together.

He insisted, "I did."

"But you're…"

"Not standing in the middle of the room trying my damnedest to suck in air? Not falling over, passing out?"

She nodded, slowly, her eyes full of wonder, of growing hope. "That's right. You're not."

"I remember it all. Everything. About the night Russell was kidnapped. I remember what happened in Russell's room, I remember the kidnappers."

"Kidnappers?"

"That's what I said."

"There was more than one, then?"

He nodded. "My uncle Blake. And a woman. A woman named Lorraine."

Chapter 20

In the morning, as soon as Kimberly left for school, Jonas told Marsh and Tory everything he'd told Emma the night before.

"I'm so glad you finally remember what happened that night," Tory said sincerely, when Jonas had finished telling the tale.

"But?" Jonas prompted, already knowing what she was going to say next.

"Well, I just wish you had more to go on than the woman's first name."

"So do I," he said. "But we'll go back to Blake's house this morning, look through his files again, this time with the name Lorraine in mind." It didn't sound all that promising, really. And they all knew it. He shrugged. "It's worth a try."

"We have a computer here, in the other room," Marsh reminded him. "And it does have a Zip drive.

We could look through everything without having to go out to that shack, if you want to.''

Jonas vetoed that suggestion. "We should check for a Lorraine in the file cabinet, too. And then we did mean to look through the rest of the house. We might as well just go on out there."

Tory left for her shop at nine-thirty. Marsh got a call from his manager at the new Oklahoma City branch of his limousine service a few minutes later. There was some crisis that just couldn't wait. So Marsh gave Jonas a garage-door remote and a key to his and Tory's house, along with more keys to the shack where Blake Bravo had lived.

"I'll join you there as soon as I can get away," he promised.

"No," Jonas said. "Go on and take care of your business. Emma and I can handle things for today. We'll meet back here this evening. You'll get a full report on what we found." Assuming, he couldn't help adding silently, that we find anything at all.

"You're sure?"

"Go to work. We'll be fine. You're only a phone call away if something comes up that we can't handle without you."

At a little after ten, Jonas and Emma turned into the dusty driveway that led to Blake Bravo's house. They parked the rental car behind the ancient pickup and headed for the house. Once inside, they went straight to the office, where Jonas booted up the computer and began scanning files and running searches.

Emma checked through the tall file cabinet behind the desk. She started with the A's, reading the label on each manila folder, seeking one with the magic first name, Lorraine, on it. She reached the Z's a half an hour later.

He heard her close the bottom drawer and heave a long sigh. "Nothing in here that I can find." She came up behind him, put her hands on his shoulders. "Sorry."

"As if it's your fault," he teased, but he didn't take his eyes off the screen.

She brushed a kiss on the top of his head. "I'll just go on and start looking around the rest of the house."

He patted her hand. "Good idea."

She slipped out the door and into the hall. He could hear her, faintly, in the kitchen—the rattle of flatware as she opened a drawer, the clatter of pots and pans, the sharp click as a cabinet door anchored shut.

She returned to the office maybe twenty minutes after she had left it. He became aware of her presence before he looked up and saw her hovering in the doorway.

He shut down the file he'd been scanning and glanced her way. "What?"

She was holding what looked like an old address book, a black one, dog-eared and worn. She had a smudge of dirt on the end of her nose and she was smiling so broadly, the little beauty mark on her cheek had slipped completely into hiding. "I found this in the junk drawer in the kitchen. You know, in with the box knives and scissors and screwdrivers and rusty nails, under a stack of maps and grocery store coupons that expired months ago."

"And?"

She came toward him, flipping the book open to the page she had marked with her thumb. She held it out and pointed. "Look."

He read the name she pointed to aloud. "Smith, Lorraine." He met her shining eyes again, watched a shiver of excitement go through her. He understood that shiver. He felt just the same way—though he knew he probably shouldn't allow himself to get too worked up. At this point, it was nothing more than a first name that matched the name in his dream. It was more than possible that Blake had known more than one Lorraine in his life.

"Well?" She let out a nervous, thoroughly charming little giggle. "What do you think?"

He looked at the book again. "It's an Oklahoma City address. No area code on the phone number, so that's probably local, as well."

"That's good. Isn't it?"

"Emma. How the hell would I know?"

"It's *something,* anyway."

He reached out, rubbed his thumb over the smudge on her nose, once and then once more, until it was gone. "Yes," he said. "It is certainly something."

"I think we should give Lorraine Smith a call."

"So do I." He got his cell phone from the inside pocket of his jacket, then realized he'd need an area code, after all, since his phone had a California number. "Do you remember the area code here?"

She did, and she told him. He punched it up, followed by the number in the old address book.

After three rings a woman answered.

"Hello."

Jonas hit her with the name. "Lorraine?"

"I'm sorry," said the woman. "There's no one here by that name."

"Is this the Smith residence?"

"No, we are the Bradleys."

He reeled off Lorraine Smith's address, asked the woman if hers was the same.

"No, it is not." Impatience now threaded her voice. "Is there anything else?"

"Yes. I wonder. How long have you had had this number?"

"I don't know. A couple of years. Who *is* this?"

"Sorry to bother you." He disconnected the call, dropped the phone on the desk. "Looks like Lorraine Smith doesn't have this number anymore."

"Who was it? What did they say?"

He repeated the information the woman had given him.

"Did you believe her?"

"She seemed straightforward enough. I don't know. She could have been lying, I guess. No way to tell."

Emma was staring at him. A look that said she had plans.

He muttered suspiciously, "What?"

"Let's go to Oklahoma City. Let's see what we find at Lorraine Smith's address."

"There's more we could do here. Now that we have a possible address and a last name, we could—"

"We can do it later." She gestured at the bleak room around them. "None of this is going anywhere. And I am sick of all this brown. It's enough to suck all the enthusiasm right out of a person. I need a little change of scenery."

"Emma…"

She grabbed his arm, yanked on it playfully. "Come on. Let's get out of here. Let's see what's happenin' at Lorraine's house."

"Emma, if the woman doesn't have the same phone number, it's doubtful that she even lives there anymore."

"You don't know that—yet. But you will. As soon as we go there."

"I don't think—"

She put a finger against his lips. "You said it. Don't think. Act. Do what I say. And do it now." She yanked on his arm again.

"Wait. Let me check for an Internet connection."

"Why?"

"We can look up the address on Maphunt." He punched the right commands. But no luck. No doubt the phone and the service were both disconnected by now.

"Jonas, will you shut that thing down and let's go?"

He did as she ordered, then let her pull him from the chair.

They stopped at a convenience store for a map. As it turned out, Lorraine Smith lived, or had lived, or *might* live in an area called Mesta Park, near the heart of Oklahoma City, not far from the state capitol. It took them thirty-five minutes to get there from Blake's house.

The neighborhood was an old one, with houses of all sizes, many of them in prairie-cottage style. Jonas guessed that the majority of the houses would have been built in the first two decades of the twentieth century. Some cried out for care, others had either been kept up or lovingly restored. Mature trees, mostly sweet gums and oaks, lined the streets and grew in front of the houses, providing generous patches of cool shade, their leaves just beginning to show the first hints of autumn's gold.

Lorraine Smith's address was four doors in from the corner, a small one-story cottage, green clapboard with white trim and a red-shingle roof. Jonas pulled in at the curb and turned off the engine.

"Looks friendly," Emma said.

And it did. Plants hung in pots from the porch eaves. Lace curtains decked the windows. There was a swing

painted a whimsical shade of pink. A cheery fall wreath
of bright-colored leaves decorated with small orange and
yellow gourds hung on the front door, which had glass
panels in the center of it and more glass flanking it on
either side.

Emma was watching him.

"Say it," he recommended grimly.

"Well, now. It doesn't look the home of a kidnapper,
does it?"

"And what, exactly, does the home of a kidnapper
look like, Emma?"

She wrinkled her nose at him. "Always so logical."
She leaned on her door. "Ready?"

He wasn't. He would never be. So he didn't bother to
answer, just opened his own door and got out of the car.

They went up the walk to the front porch side by side.
Jonas rang the bell. In less than a minute, a woman was
peeking out at them through the lace curtains on the
inside of the door. She smiled pleasantly, opened the
door and then pushed the glass storm door wide as well.

"Yes?" She looked like anyone's favorite grandmother, with a strong, stocky body, friendly wrinkles
that fanned out from her eyes and gray hair pulled back
into a nice, tidy bun.

Jonas quelled the urge to introduce himself. If this
woman was his brother's kidnapper, uttering the name
Bravo would be sure to put her on her guard.

He manufactured a smile. "Hello, Lorraine."

The wrinkles in the woman's forehead deepened as
she frowned. "I'm afraid my name is Dotty." Her face
relaxed again. "Oh, I know. You must be looking for
Mrs. Smith."

"Yes," said Jonas. "Lorraine Smith."

Dotty sighed. "She passed—oh, three years ago now,

I believe. I never knew her, sad to say. I'm just the one who bought the house."

"Oh, bless her heart," Emma said. Jonas shot her a look. Her face wore the sweetest expression of honest concern. "I am sorry to hear about Mrs. Smith."

"Yes," agreed Dotty, and shook her head.

"Well, look at us," declared Emma. "Where are our manners? I'm Emma." Emma reached for Dotty's hand—the free one that wasn't holding open the storm door. Dotty let her have it. "And this is Jonas."

"Very pleased to meet you both," Dotty said, and seemed to mean it.

"Jonas has been…lookin' for Mrs. Smith for a real long time." Emma patted the back of the older woman's hand, and then gently released it.

Dotty said, "Oh. Well. As I said, she is gone now."

"We're hopin' that maybe you can tell us a little about her."

"I am sorry. I never knew her. You might try the Tillys next door, though." She gestured toward the house on the east side, a two-storey gray Colonial Revival with a broad stone porch and leaded windows in the upper story. "Camilla told me that she and Lorraine were great friends."

"Camilla Tilly," Jonas clarified.

"That's it."

"Thank you so much, Dotty," Emma said.

"You are more than welcome." With one last sweet and grandmotherly smile, Dotty pulled her storm door shut and then closed the inner door after it.

Jonas and Emma turned from the cheery fall wreath.

"Well," Jonas said as they went past the pink swing, down the steps, and out to the sidewalk, "*if* this Lorraine is the Lorraine who helped to kidnap my brother, I can

understand now why we didn't find her in any of those
files in Blake's computer. No point in keeping track of
a dead woman.''

He thought he heard Emma make a small noise of
agreement in her throat as they turned onto the walk that
led up to the house next door.

A stunning dark-eyed blond woman who might have
been anywhere from thirty-five to a decade older than
that answered when Jonas rang the bell. The woman's
mouth bloomed in the kind of siren's smile that had
probably been dropping men in their tracks for decades
now. ''Well, hello.''

Jonas smiled back. ''Hello, I'm Jonas Bravo. And this
is my wife, Emma.''

''Very pleased to meet you,'' said Emma.

The woman confirmed what Jonas had already assumed. ''I'm Camilla. Camilla Tilly.''

Jonas nodded. ''Mrs. Tilly—''

''You call me Camilla.''

''I'll do that. Camilla, we're looking for information
about Lorraine Smith, who used to live next door. Dotty
told us that maybe you could—''

''Mama, who is it?'' Another woman appeared behind
the first, a brunette. This one was definitely younger,
perhaps Emma's age. She had the same big brown eyes
as the older one. But where Camilla came across as relaxed and unhurried, this one wore a harried expression
on her pretty heart-shaped face. She carried a little boy
in her arms, one who looked maybe a few months
younger than Mandy.

''Jonas. Emma.'' Camilla continued to smile her thoroughly gorgeous smile. ''This is Joleen. She is the oldest
of my babies.''

Joleen granted them each a nod, then spoke to her

mother again. "Mama, we have to get going. Right now."

Camilla turned to Jonas. "You will have to excuse us. It is go, go, go around here lately. My middle baby is gettin' married a week from this Saturday. Joleen is plannin' everything and we are knee-deep in florists and bakers and caterin' help."

The little boy had started squirming. "Mama, dow."

"Hush, now Sammy…"

"Dow, Mama. Dow."

"Oh, all right." Joleen bent and set the child on the floor. "Stay close," she warned. "We are leaving soon."

He toddled off chanting a string of nonsense syllables.

Camilla said, "Joly, honey, these folks want to know about Lorraine."

Apparently, Joleen wasn't as trusting as Camilla and the woman next door. That pretty mouth flattened to a thin line as she flicked a wary glance from Jonas to Emma and back again. "What about Lorraine—and why?"

Jonas hesitated, wondering how much to reveal.

Emma stepped in. "A long time ago, Jonas's baby brother was kidnapped. They never found that baby. And recently, well, some information has come to light that has led us to hope that your friend Lorraine might have known somethin' about what happened way back then."

"Well." Camilla was wide-eyed at the news. "What can I say? Lorraine never mentioned a kidnapped child to me, not in all the years that we were friends."

"Lorraine died three years ago," Joleen said flatly. "So there is no way that she can help you now."

"We know that," Emma pressed on gingerly, "but

we were hopin' that, just maybe, you all might be able to tell us a little bit about her.''

"We don't have time for this. We are late as it is and we—''

Camilla touched her daughter's arm. "Joly, now, please…'' She shook her head.

Joleen sighed. "Oh, all right.'' She turned a sheepish look on Jonas and Emma. "I'm sorry. Things are just crazy around here. Sometimes it seems like I'm runnin' as fast as I can to stay in one place. I get a little cranky.''

Jonas said, "We understand.''

"Let's try again,'' Joleen suggested.

Emma beamed. "Good idea.''

Camilla suggested, "Would you like to come in?''

Joleen winced. "Mama…''

Emma answered for both of them. "No, that's all right. We can see you're in a hurry. If you could just tell us—''

"I'm sorry. Excuse me. Sammy!'' Joleen called. "Sammy, get back here…'' She vanished from the doorway in pursuit of the little boy.

Camilla was frowning. "Jonas, there is somethin'…familiar about you. Are you sure we haven't met before?''

"No, I don't believe so—just a question or two?''

The frown vanished. "Ask.''

"How did you meet Lorraine?''

Camilla thought for a moment. "Hmm. It was some time after she moved in next door. She kept to herself at first, but eventually…you know how it is. You live next door to a person and one day you get to talking and then, before you know it, there you are. Friends.''

"And when did she move in, how long ago?''

"Not long after we did.''

"You and…?"

"Samuel." The big brown eyes turned sad, suddenly. "Samuel was my husband. He's been gone for ten years now."

"I'm sorry to hear that. And you and your husband moved in…?"

"Thirty years ago," said Camilla wistfully. "And Lorraine moved in the year right after. That was before Joly was even born. Dekker was only a year old."

"Dekker? That would be your…?"

"Oh, no. Not mine. Lorraine's. Her only son."

Jonas's heart seemed to rise up and flip over in his chest. Lorraine had moved in twenty-nine years ago, along with her son. A son who was a year old at the time.

The very same age Russell would have been.

Jonas could feel Emma's eyes on him. He didn't dare turn to her. If they shared a look right then, they might give themselves away. Camilla would start asking the questions. And if Camilla started asking the questions, he'd end up having to explain a lot more than Camilla needed to know.

And besides, he reminded himself, this could all just be coincidence. They didn't even know if they had the right Lorraine, for pity's sake.

Camilla chattered on. "Lorraine raised Dekker all on her own. Her husband had left her. I think he must have been a real loser, that husband of hers. Abusive, you know? Though she would never talk about him. She'd just say, 'Milla'—that's what she always called me, Milla—she'd say, 'Milla, I have had all I ever need or want to have of men.'"

Joleen reappeared in the doorway, the little boy in her

arms again. "Mama," she said, "we have got to get movin'."

"Yes, yes. I know. In a minute—where was I? Ah. Lorraine and men. Now and then, I'd try to set her up with someone nice? But she would never agree to go out with anyone. She'd just say that all she wanted was to get by from day to day, to raise her little boy the best she could."

Jonas said casually, "Do you think you could give us Dekker's phone number?"

Joleen caught her mother's eye and gave a quick negative shake of her head.

But Camilla only waved a slender, beautifully manicured hand. "Honestly, Joly. Our Dekker is a grown-up man. He can take care of himself." Camilla turned to him again and confided, "He's like one of the family. We all love him madly."

"Of course," repeated Jonas. It seemed the appropriate response.

"The last few years, he and Joly are like *that*." Camilla held up two fingers, crossed. "Best friends. Thick as thieves."

"I understand."

"She's too protective of him."

"Mama. Dekker is a very private man. And we are gettin' later by the second. We are due at the florists ten minutes ago. And I've got one of my best customers scheduled for a weave, shampoo, cut and blow-dry in—"

"Settle down, sugar." Camilla patted her daughter's arm. "You'll have yourself a heart attack sure as you're standing here."

"Mama—"

"Try the phone book." Camilla winked at Jonas. "Dekker has a detective agency. A-1 Investigations."

They found a phone book in a kiosk at a gas station not far from Camilla Tilly's house. Dekker Smith's place of business was the third listing under "Investigators" in the Yellow Pages directory.

A-1 Investigations even had an ad: Surveillance. Background Checks. Missing Persons. Civil. Criminal. Domestic.

The address was just a few blocks away.

Emma said, "Do you think we should call first?"

"Why? To give him a chance to tell us he doesn't want to talk to us? No. I think we're better off just trying it face-to-face right up front."

A-1 Investigations was up a dim flight of stairs over a coin laundry. The sound of spinning dryers hummed through the wall as Jonas and Emma climbed to the second floor. At the top, a narrow hall confronted them, the walls slathered with gray enamel paint so thick it gave the impression of melting. The floor was speckled green linoleum. Dekker Smith had Suite 202, the second door on the right.

"Do we knock, or just go on in?" Emma asked when they stood before the door.

As if he knew. "When all else fails, fake it." He tapped his knuckles twice against the pebbled glass in the top of the door.

A man's voice called from the other side. "It's open."

Jonas gestured Emma in ahead of him.

They entered a large room with a desk, a row of four-drawer file cabinets and some chairs. Along one wall, Jonas spotted a copy machine and a fax machine, a water

cooler and a coatrack. A computer sat on the desk. There
was an inner door to the left of the desk, one that probably led to a bathroom or possibly a closet. The desk
faced the entrance door, with the room's single broad
window behind it, a window that fronted the street below. Sounds of traffic leached in through the window: a
horn honking, a bus braking—that long hydraulic squeal.
Under the traffic noise, the dryers on the first floor kept
up their soft and steady roar.

Beside him, Jonas heard Emma gasp. He ignored the
sound. Just as, at first, he refused to look at the man who
sat behind the desk.

Jonas studied the room instead, taking it all in. It was
functional. A base of operations. A place to keep records
and take care of whatever bookkeeping A-1 Investigations required. Personal touches were minimal. A couple
of framed certificates on the wall—no plants, no photos
of friends and family.

The man behind the desk rose from his chair. "I'm
Dekker Smith. How can I help you?"

Jonas looked at him then, saw a man of about his own
height, with dark hair much like his. A man with blue
eyes and a cleft in his chin. A man who bore a powerful
resemblance to himself. No wonder Camilla Tilly had
asked him if they'd met before.

But more than the resemblance to himself, Jonas saw
a man who was the mirror image of his father. As he
shook Dekker Smith's hand, Jonas had to fight the dis-
orienting sensation that he was reaching down three decades to clasp hands with a dead man.

Images of his father flooded his brain. Harry Bravo,
laughing, swinging a very young Jonas off the floor.
Harry frowning, not pleased with something Jonas had

done. Harry solemn and serious, imparting some small bit of wisdom to his oldest son...

It was one coincidence too many. It was the final co-incidence. The one that turned all the other coincidences inside out and revealed them for what they actually were.

Not coincidence at all. But an answer to the question that had haunted Jonas for three decades now, the question that had killed his father and helped to send his mother over the emotional edge.

Jonas knew at last what had happened to his vanished brother. Russell Bravo had survived to grow to man-hood, after all. One of his kidnappers had renamed him Dekker Smith and raised him as her own.

Chapter 21

Beside him, Emma was way too quiet.

Jonas glanced at her. She looked a little pale, but she forced a smile for him.

Dekker Smith said, "You are...?"

He made himself speak to the man who looked so eerily like his father come back to life. "Jonas Bravo— and this is my wife, Emma."

Emma and Dekker Smith exchanged greetings, then Dekker said, "Have a seat." He led them toward the desk and gestured at the two molded plastic chairs facing it.

Jonas and Emma sat. Their host went back around and reclaimed his seat behind the desk.

There was a silence, an extremely awkward one. Jonas realized he didn't have a clue where to begin. For some reason, he found himself thinking of Marsh, that first day—was it only two days ago? It seemed like a year— or two. Or a hundred.

Marsh, sitting in the wing chair in Jonas's office at Bravo, Incorporated, muttering, "Damn. I can't believe it. I'm here. And now I don't know where to begin...."

At the moment, Jonas found it easy to understand exactly how Marsh must have felt.

Emma seemed equally at a loss. She sat to his left in the hard plastic chair, looking down at her hands—which were folded demurely in her lap. Even her short, curve-hugging, fire-engine-red dress looked somehow subdued right then.

Dekker Smith granted them a patient smile. "I know how it is. When you need a private detective, it's usually something serious. Something it's hard to discuss with a stranger. But the problem is, if you don't tell me what you want me to do, I can't help you much, now, can I?"

Damn. The man thought they were here to hire a detective. Apparently, he hadn't picked up on the resemblance. But then, he had no reason to be looking for one.

"This is...a personal matter," Jonas said.

"I understand," said Dekker Smith. "And you have my word. Everything you tell me will be kept strictly confidential."

"I'm sorry. I guess I'm not making myself clear. I don't need a detective."

Dekker Smith frowned. "Then fill me in. What are you doing here?"

Jonas swore. "There is just no easy way to do this."

Dekker Smith said nothing.

So Jonas said it straight out. "I have reason to believe that you and I are brothers."

Dekker Smith didn't move—except for his right eyebrow. It inched toward his hairline. "I don't have a brother."

"May I...tell you a story?"

"I think maybe you'd better."

* * *

Jonas told it all. From the events of thirty years ago that had been public knowledge from the first, to the dream that had haunted him ever since, the dream he'd finally remembered just the night before. He told the parts of the story that Marsh had filled in for him. And also what they'd found in the ramshackle house where Blake Bravo had lived.

When he was done, another silence ensued.

At last, Dekker Smith said, "So. Lorraine is the name of the woman you believe was your uncle's accomplice in the kidnapping of your brother—the name you remember because you *dreamed* it."

"That's right," Jonas replied flatly.

Dekker picked up a pencil, turned it in his fingers, then dropped it to the desk again. It rolled toward Jonas and stopped just short of falling to the floor. "You found my mother's name in some old address book of your uncle's. Since her name was Lorraine, you naturally assumed the two Lorraines were the same."

"It was a lead. We followed it, that's all."

"A damn weak lead, if you ask me."

For the first time since they'd exchanged introductions, Emma spoke. "You know, Mr. Smith. Jonas is only tryin' to get to the truth here."

Dekker Smith turned his hard blue gaze on Emma. "Maybe that's so." He looked at Jonas again and said quietly, "My mother raised me on her own. She was a good woman and she did the best she could. She was not a criminal."

Emma leaned forward in her chair. "Look, I know this must be hard for you, but—"

Dekker Smith cut her off. "I have a birth certificate. It's authentic, complete with the seal of the state of

Oklahoma. I was born in Tulsa. My father's name was Smith. Dekker Smith, same as mine. And yeah, a name was all that he gave me. My mother picked up and left the bastard a few months after I was born. But make no mistake. Dekker Smith was my father. And Lorraine Kelsey Smith *was* my mother. I am sorry for what you've lost, but I'm not it. I'm not your brother. And that is all the truth I can give you.''

"Maybe you ought to go look in a mirror, Mr. Smith," Emma suggested way too sweetly. "Go look in a mirror and then come back and look at Jonas, and then maybe you'll understand what we're talkin' about here."

Dekker Smith didn't even blink. "Is there anything else?"

Emma started to speak again. Jonas beat her to it. "No," he said firmly. "I guess that's about it."

Beside him, Emma shifted tightly in her chair—but she said no more.

Jonas took out a business card and picked up the pencil that had rolled to the edge of Dekker's desk. Quickly, he wrote down the main number at Angel's Crest, as well as the number to his cell phone. Then he set both the card and the pencil back on the desk.

As if on cue, the phone rang. Dekker picked it up. "A-1 Investigations. Can you hold? Thanks." He put his hand over the receiver and looked straight at Jonas. "Goodbye," he said.

Jonas and Emma rose together and turned for the door.

They rode most of the way back to Marsh and Tory's house in silence. Then, just as Jonas turned on his blinker to get off the interstate, Emma asked softly, "What now?"

He shrugged. "We have a nice evening with Marsh and Tory and little Kimmy. And tomorrow, we go home."

"But—"

"But nothing. I've found my brother. Do you realize that I never expected that would happen? Deep down, I always believed he was dead. Now I know he's not. He's not dead. And that is a fine thing. Not dead..." He let the words trail off, then added, "But he's also not really Russell anymore. He's someone named Dekker Smith now. He grew up next door to Joleen Tilly. And the woman he truly believes was his mom was Joleen's mom's best friend. He has a whole damn history, and that history is not the history of Russell Bravo. It's the life of Dekker Smith."

"You're saying we should have expected him to deny what we told him?"

"Hell. I don't know if we should have expected it. We did what we did and he...well, his response was understandable. Imagine it from his point of view. After all these years, to be told he's not who he thinks he is, that his 'mother' was really a kidnapper's accomplice, that he was the pawn in a sick psychopath's disgustingly effective revenge scheme. I can see why he chose to simply reject it all outright."

"Maybe he will call you."

"Maybe. And maybe he's already torn up that card and tossed it into the trash."

The next morning before Kimberly went to school, Jonas and Emma said goodbye to Marsh and his family. Marsh promised that as soon as he and Tory could swing it, they'd come to L.A. for a visit. The two men embraced.

Jonas said, "You're welcome at Angel's Crest. Any time. The door is always open."

Emma and Tory were whispering to each other. The women hugged and then Kimberly had to hug both Jonas and Emma.

"Don't forget those bodyguards," Tory teased.

"They're meeting us at the airport," Jonas told his cousin's wife as he and Emma got into the car.

"Tory's having a baby," Emma told him once they'd pulled out of the driveway and headed toward the interstate.

"Is that what you were whispering about?"

"Uh-huh."

"When is this baby due?"

"In the summer."

Something in her voice alerted him. He glanced at her, but she had turned away. She was staring out her side window. "Emma?"

"Hmm?"

"Are you okay?"

"Fine." She looked at him then. He saw the sheen of tears in her eyes.

"What? What's wrong?"

"Jonas, you have come a very long way. Do you know that?"

He couldn't read her, so he asked, cautiously, "That's a compliment?"

"It sure is. I am so proud of you. When I saw you hugging your cousin back there, it hit me. You're not the man I married."

She was looking at him so tenderly—but still he sensed that something wasn't quite right. "That's good?"

"It is wonderful. I believe you could raise Mandy all on your own now and do a bang-up job of it."

"Well. Thank you."

"You're welcome."

He found he was absurdly pleased by her praise. And he decided that he'd read her wrong. Nothing else was going on. She'd been moved by the news of Tory's coming baby, and touched by the change in him.

And he *had* changed. He could feel it, the difference inside himself. He had gotten to the root of the dream at last. Found his brother, as well as a cousin he hadn't even known existed.

Both of the kidnappers were beyond the reach of human judgment—which meant they wouldn't be doing anyone else any harm. And his brother was alive and well, whether the man his brother had become chose to acknowledge him or not.

The past had truly been put to rest at last. His only real regret was that neither of his parents had lived to see it happen.

Jonas turned his full attention to the road ahead, his suspicion that something was bothering Emma already forgotten.

Home at Angel's Crest, Jonas and Emma went together to check on Mandy. They stayed in the nursery for over an hour. Mandy was irritated with them at first.

"Where have you been, Jonah? I have been waiting and waiting and you didn't come. And you, too, Emma. You didn't come, too."

They reminded her that they'd told her they were going on a little trip.

"I like trips, too. I go with you."

"We already went," Jonas explained.

"You went on the trip and now you comed back?"

"That's right."

"Next time, I go."

"We'll talk about that next time."

"No. Next time, I go."

Emma laughed then, and grabbed Mandy up in her arms. "We're here now, honey. And we're so glad to see you...."

"You better give me a big kiss," Mandy said in a warning tone.

"Good idea. Here it is, one giant-sized smackeroo comin' right at you...."

After the visit to the nursery, they both went to work. There was a lot to catch up on. Jonas was in meetings until after six, then he had a dinner appointment he couldn't get out of. That lasted until nine.

It was a quarter of ten by the time he finally climbed the stairs again at Angel's Crest. He went straight to Emma's rooms.

She was waiting for him in the sitting area, perched on the black and gold sofa, fully dressed in the same clothes she'd worn earlier in the day—a clingy purple skirt and skimpy silk top.

The Yorkies and the cat had claimed the bed. The dogs sat up when they saw him and perked up their ears. He went over and gave them each a scratch under their whiskery chins.

"Did you eat?" He left the dogs and approached her.

She nodded. "Palmer sent up a tray a couple of hours ago."

"Good." He stopped across the ebony coffee table from her and studied her face. She seemed...subdued, somehow. Too self-contained.

What had happened that morning came back to him.

How she had praised him for the way he'd changed, and shared the news that Tory was expecting another child. How he had wondered then what was on her mind that she wasn't telling him.

He found he was wondering the same thing now.

He unhooked his cuff links, bent and set them in a small Limoges dish on the coffee table. He began to unbutton his shirt. "I could use a good, hot shower."

"Jonas…"

He froze, his fingers at the second button of his shirt. He let a second or two elapse before he gave in and responded. "What?"

She surged up, reached across the coffee table and put her hands over his hands, as if to stop him from undoing even one more button. "We have to talk."

He didn't like the way she said that. "We do?"

"Yes."

"About what?"

"Come over here. Sit down…" She tugged on his hands.

He allowed her to guide him around to her side of the coffee table. They sat on the sofa, side by side. He waited. Whatever had to be said, he knew very well that he wouldn't be the one saying it.

She cleared her throat. And then she confessed bleakly, "I love you, Jonas. I think I fell in love with you on our weddin' night. And it seems to me like, every day, I keep lovin' you more."

He reached out, hooked his hand around her neck and brought her sweet face close to his. A single tear slid down her soft cheek. He rubbed it away with his thumb. "This is a problem?"

She sniffed. "I didn't think so at first, but now…"

"What? I don't get this." He felt more than a little insulted. "You actually see loving me as a problem?"

"Let me explain." Reluctantly but firmly, she pulled back.

He let her go. "That sounds like a good idea."

She folded her hands in her lap and looked down at them. "Well, it's just that, this marriage of ours, it was for a purpose. And I realized this morning…" Her head came up and she met his eyes. "That purpose is served. You are the man you need to be, for yourself, and for Mandy's sake."

"So?"

"So, you don't need me anymore."

Damn. He did not like this. He did not like it at all. "What, exactly, are you telling me?"

"Well, Jonas. It's just that I think it's time I set you free."

He regarded her for a moment. She looked so earnest, so distressed. He said with great care, "Let me make this very clear. I have no desire to be set free."

Her lower lip was trembling. "You…" She swallowed, convulsively. "You don't?"

"No. I don't. I…damn it, Emma." It wasn't easy, saying what he knew he must say next. It was something he had said to only one other woman in his life. That woman had been Blythe, and he had been a very young child at the time. "I love you, too."

"Oh, Jonas…" Another tear fell. She swiped it away with the heel of her hand.

He dared to smile. "So you see? We have no problem at all." He leaned closer.

She sighed. He almost let himself believe everything would be all right.

But then just before he could capture her lips, she

turned her head away. "I'm sorry." She drew herself up. "But I have to disagree with you."

"No, you don't." The words slipped out before he could stop them. They were something the new, improved Jonas should have had the grace not to say.

But then again, it probably didn't matter what he said. She wasn't listening anyway.

She insisted, miserably, "We do have a problem."

He raked both hands back through his hair. "Fine. All right. And that problem is?"

"Oh, Jonas…" She seemed unable to find the right words.

He waited some more, telling himself to be patient, to give her time to frame her thoughts. There was a box of tissues on the side table. She yanked one out and blew her nose. Then she wadded the tissue in her fist and said, "I think you *think* you love me. We're good together…in bed. And you're…grateful to me. For the way I helped you, for everything that's happened, from at last bein' able to remember your dream, to findin' your brother and Marsh. Sometimes, a person can confuse gratitude with love."

Irritation had begun to crackle through him. He tried to quell it. But no matter how changed he was in some ways, he remained the same man essentially. And that man hardly appreciated being told that he didn't know the difference between gratitude and love.

She began twisting her wedding ring around and around on her finger. "And in a way, I've been kind of like your therapist, now, haven't I? And it is just…well, it's a natural part of healin', for the patient to think he's in love with his doctor."

Jonas reminded himself that he was not going to begin shouting at her. "Emma, this is ridiculous. Doctors—at least doctors with even a scintilla of integrity—don't sleep with their patients. And they sure as hell don't marry them.''

''Yes, that's right. And maybe I shouldn't have—''

''The point being, you are not my doctor, damn it. And we both know it.''

''Yes, but I *have* helped you. And you are grateful.''

''And it follows, for those reasons, that I don't know love when I'm in it? Is that really what you're trying to tell me?''

''Jonas. I just think you at least need a little time. I think if I really love you—which I do—I won't take advantage of—''

''That's enough.'' He stood. ''This conversation is going nowhere at an alarming speed.''

She looked at him reproachfully. ''I am sorry you feel that way. I think what I'm doing is a wise thing. I think it's the *right* thing.''

''You love me so you're leaving me? What the hell is wise and right about that?''

''You are twisting what I've said.''

''Damn it, Emma. Listen. *I don't want you to go.*''

She shook her head. With a grim sort of fury, he recognized the look in her eye. She was certain she was right.

And there was no budging Emma Lynn Hewitt Bravo when she was certain she was right.

She said, ''I am setting you free, Jonas. I am giving you Mandy to raise. You have my word that I'll never contest your right to custody.''

He shrugged. He believed her. She was messing up royally, walking out on him like this. But she didn't tell lies. She invariably stood by her word. He would have what he'd wanted in the first place—the right to guide his little sister to adulthood.

Too bad that now he wanted so much more.

She said, "I imagine there will be papers you'll want me to sign. You know, something that says I promise I'll never sue you for custody."

He just looked at her.

She stammered on. "You could...I mean, well, as soon as Mr. McAllister has those papers ready, he can just give me a call and—"

"Enough."

She gulped—and she kept her mouth shut.

He asked, "How long am I supposed to stay away from you?"

She looked stricken. "I don't...how can we know that, right now? I just want you to have time, to be certain that this marriage, which was forced on you, is really what you want."

He decided against reiterating for the—what? Fourth or fifth time?—that he already knew what he wanted and her walking out on him was not it. "When are you leaving?"

"Right away."

"You're already packed?"

"Yes. I've taken everything out to my SUV. I was just waitin', for you to come home. So we could talk."

"I see." And he did. He saw that he'd never had a chance. She'd been ready to go before he walked in the room—and he should have known, should have taken a look around, noticed that, like that time before, when she'd packed up Mandy and run off to her own house, all the little things that made this room Emma's were gone.

"Jonas, I hope you'll let me visit Mandy. I don't want to just disappear from her life."

He had to get out of there. If he stayed, he might start throwing things. And if not that, he might actually beg her to stay. He'd never forgive himself for the former—and he'd never forgive *her* if he ended up descending to the latter.

"Come any time. I'll tell Palmer you are always welcome."

"Thank you."

He turned and left her, shutting the door quietly behind him.

Chapter 22

Palmer brought him her wedding ring the next day. She had left it with his cuff links, in the china dish on the coffee table.

Within two days, the tabloids had the story. Some smart reporter must have put two and two together and discovered that Emma had moved back to her own North Hollywood duplex.

"Trouble in Paradise," "Billionaire Dumps Dog Groomer" and "Splitsville for the Blonde and the Billionaire" were just a few of the headlines. Jonas read a couple of the stories. They were all fabrications, the only real fact involved being that Emma had been spotted apparently living at her own house. After he'd assured himself that no one was talking who shouldn't be, Jonas went back to his usual method of dealing with the press: he ignored it.

The Santa Anas came up, hot winds racing down from the northeast, roaring through the canyons, bringing on the season of fire. Blazes raged in Riverside County and near San Diego. A firefighter in Calimesa suffered a heart attack while hosing down a flaming roof. People prayed for rain. For the winds to die down.

Jonas worked and he worked hard. He ate right and made good use of the private gym at Angel's Crest. He took care of himself. Frustration and anger with Emma preyed on him. He was determined that they wouldn't bring him down.

He spent time with Mandy, and he signed her up to go three days a week to a certain excellent day care/preschool he'd learned about. It was important, he realized now, for her to get out and mix with other children. Security didn't seem quite so big an issue, now that he understood what had happened all those years ago, now that his brother's kidnapper had a face.

He decided to cut back on his security force, to relax his precautions a little. Somehow, that seemed the right thing to do. Yes, there was always danger. Random acts of cruelty and violence did occur. But he didn't want Mandy growing up thinking she had to live her life in fear.

On Saturday and again on Monday of the first week after Emma left him, he came home to find that red SUV of hers parked in the wide court in front of the house. He went straight to his private rooms when he saw she was visiting. He didn't want to run into her, didn't want to see her face or hear her voice.

He did understand that she believed she was doing him some kind of favor by leaving him. Intellectually, he understood, anyway. But in his heart and his gut something more basic was going on. It was not pretty, what he felt for her lately.

He knew that at some point, he'd be driven to go after her.

He hoped that by the time that happened, he'd have forgiven her, at least partially, for treating him like some sort of emotional idiot, for refusing to believe that he might actually know what he wanted and that what he wanted was to spend the rest of his life with her.

On Tuesday, the fifth day after Emma walked out on him, he called Ledger DelVecchio and asked him to dinner. They drank too much and they discussed, in depth, the supposed emotional superiority of women.

"They think they know it all when it comes to matters of the heart," Ledger intoned at some point well along in the evening. "But most of the time, they're just like the rest of us. Stumbling around blindfolded, in the dark without a clue…"

Jonas put Ledger in a car and sent him home at a little after two. Ledger rolled down his window to impart one last word of advice. "Give it another week or two," he said. "Then go get her."

"Drag her home by the hair, you mean?"

Ledger laughed. "No. The caveman approach is definitely passé."

"Then?"

"Tell her that she was *right*. That you really did need that time apart from her. Women love that more than anything, to be told that they're right."

"But she's not right. Not about this, anyway."

Ledger raised both hands, palms up. "Hey, what do you want from me, man? I can't help you if you insist on approaching this rationally."

Jonas grunted. "Thanks for trying."

"Well and what the hell is a friend for?" Ledger

pushed the button and his window slid up again. Jonas stepped back and the car rolled off down the drive.

Jonas woke Wednesday morning with something of a hangover. He reminded himself that he was going to have to give up trying to match Ledger drink for drink. He had a full day of meetings and important appointments. And now he would be handicapped by a headache and a queasy stomach caused by his own overindulgence.

He managed. He got through the day. It wasn't pleasant or particularly easy. But he did it.

He was able to cancel his dinner meeting, which meant he was ready to go home at a little after six. He had the evening all planned. A long, hot shower, a couple of aspirin, a little time with Mandy and a nice, leisurely meal. A little CNN in bed, and he'd call it a night. By tomorrow, he'd be feeling fine again.

He got a call on his cell phone as he was riding home. It was Dekker Smith.

Chapter 23

"I'd like to meet with you," Dekker said. "Is that possible?"

Jonas gripped the phone a little tighter than he needed to. "Of course. When?"

"Now?"

"You're here. In Los Angeles?"

"As a matter of fact, I'm outside the gates to your house."

Jonas had dinner with his brother, in the small dining room. After the meal, they retired to Jonas's study, where Dekker pulled a wallet-sized book from the inside pocket of his leather bomber jacket.

"Before she died, my mother gave this to me." He set the book on Jonas's desk. It was pink.

Jonas read the words embossed in gold letters on the front. "Every Day Diary."

A sad smile curved Dekker's mouth. "Yeah. Like

omething a teenaged girl would buy, isn't it? To write
down all her secrets in." The smile vanished. "I...lost
my wife, a few years ago. My mother died not long after.
It was a rough period for me. You could say I wasn't
exactly on the ball. When she was so sick, right at the
end, my mother gave me this book. She said she wanted
me to read it—but not until after she was gone. She said
omething about how wrong she'd been. And how much
of a coward. But she wanted me to remember that I was
the best and most important thing that had ever happened
to her."

Jonas said, "You never did read this, right?"

Dekker shrugged. "I put it away in a box, with the
rest of her treasures—with the locks of my baby hair
and my old report cards, her favorite red scarf and the
amethyst earrings she used to wear when she got dressed
up. I, well, I wasn't up to dealing with it right then. The
truth is, I had made a mess of my marriage, and the
circumstances under which my wife died were... Let's
just say things weren't going real well for me. And then
my mother died. It was all too much. I just wanted to
put it all out of my mind."

"But then, last week, *I* showed up at your door..."

"That's right. And my knee-jerk reaction was to deny
what you told me."

"But you couldn't stop thinking about it."

"Right again." Dekker reached out, brushed his hand
across the gold lettering on the front of the little pink
book. "Yesterday, I dug this out of that box. And I read
it." He looked up. "I took the first flight I could get out
here, because I think that you should to read it, too."

"Right now?"

Dekker nodded. "It shouldn't take you all that long.
She didn't fill the whole thing up, just wrote down what

she wanted me to know. It's really only one long letter
Once you've read it, we can talk—I mean, if you think
there's anything that needs saying. It's all pretty much
explained, between the covers of this little book."

Dekker left him.

Jonas sat at his desk and began to read.

My dearest Dekker,

What you need to know first is that I could not
have children. Because of an infection when I was
eighteen, both ovaries had to be removed. Until
then, I hadn't even really thought about having
kids. It was just something I knew would happen
for me someday, like it does for most of the women
in the world.

Dekker, I grew up in Oxnard, in southern California. A nice, ordinary house on an ordinary street.
My parents were divorced when I was ten, but my
mother remarried and I liked my stepfather well
enough. I had two sisters. They are probably still
alive, my sisters. But I wouldn't know.

From the time I learned I would have no babies,
a baby was all that I wanted. I felt that I had been
cheated, that what mattered most in life had been
stolen away from me. I began to do the kinds of
things I never would have done before that. Drugs.
Sneaking out at night to be with the wrong kinds
of boys. Wild things. Things that were bound to get
me in trouble.

My mother got fed up with me. She ended up
kicking me out of the house. I lived on the streets
for a while. It was rough.

And then, when I was twenty, I met Blake Bravo.
Well, he didn't go by that name when I first met

him. He went by a lot of names, he changed his names like he changed where he lived. All the time. He scared me, just looking in those crazy eyes of his would set me to trembling. I thought he might hurt me. He did hurt me. And deep down, that was fine with me. Getting hurt was what I wanted then. I wanted to destroy myself. And I was doing just that.

I had been with him for a few months when Blake told me his plan. He wanted revenge on his family. They were very rich, the Bravos, and they had cut him out of their lives and stolen his inheritance. He was going to get even and I was going to help him to do it. He had grown up in the mansion where they lived, so he knew how to get in there without being caught. He was going to kidnap a baby—his brother's baby. And I was going to take care of the baby while we waited for the huge ransom to be paid. It was all supposed to go like clockwork. And it did.

Except that his brother's older child, *your* brother, came in on us while we were taking you. I thought Blake was going to kill that poor little boy. And God forgive me, I did not stop him. I had you in my arms. And I was already thinking that I was never going to let you go. Blake hit the child with the barrel of his gun and dropped his limp body on the floor. And we ran. No one stopped us. We got out and we went to our hiding place.

Blake got the ransom. In diamonds. He had never planned to return you to your family. That was part of his revenge, that his brother would never see his child again. I don't know what he planned to do with you, at first. Maybe it's better that we'll never

know. I told him I was going to keep you. And I
meant it. He didn't argue with me. He seemed to
know you were the one thing I wouldn't back down
about. So I kept you.

We went on the move. I didn't care, where we
went, how many different names we lived under.
What we did. As long as I had you in my arms, the
baby I'd thought I would never have.

A year after we took you, I told Blake that I had
to settle down. I wanted to make a life for you. We
were in Oklahoma City by then, and he had something going with a woman who lived in Norman.
He stayed with her more and more and left us alone
a lot. I was glad. It was over between him and me.
By then, all I wanted was to be a mother to you.
And he...well, I think he was looking for a way to
get rid of us, too.

We struck a deal, Blake and me. He sold off a
few of those precious diamonds of his. He bought
me a house and a new identity. And he got you a
birth certificate. I think it must have been the birth
certificate of a baby who died. But then again, how
did he manage to get my real first name in the place
for the mother? I don't know. To this day I don't
know how he did any of that. But he was a very
clever man when he wanted to be. And so you became Dekker Smith, the child of Lorraine and Dekker Smith, Sr.

I made up the story about your bad daddy, about
how he'd ruined me for ever being with a man
again. It was easy to make people believe that I'd
really had a husband, an awful man who had abused
me. I would just think of Blake whenever I spoke
of Dekker, Sr., and everybody got the message real

clear that I couldn't bear to talk much about my past and I truly didn't want a thing to do with men ever again.

Blake left us alone, after he set us up. I am sure he kept tabs on us. He was that way. He kept track of people, he wanted to know what they were up to. If he's still alive, I'm sure he's still that way.

But he never bothered us. The last news I had of him was a few months after he got you and me our house. He said he was getting married, to that woman from Norman. I never heard from him after that. I certainly didn't go looking for him. And he left us to live our lives.

Dekker, I go to my grave a bad sinner. Sometimes I think of your real mother and father, of that little boy that Blake almost killed. I did read, in the paper, a few days after we took you, that the boy had survived what Blake did to him. But after that, I don't know what happened to him. Blake told me that your father died, some time in that first year after we took you. And that your mother had been locked up in a mental hospital. He laughed over that, the death of his own brother, his brother's wife going crazy. I tried not to listen to him. I did not want to know what had happened to your real family. More sins. Sins piled on top of sins. I am a sinner, through and through, my dearest Dekker. A cowardly sinner who never would face paying for the evil that she did.

And the most terrible sin, the worst sin of all, is that I would do it all over again. Steal you. From your real family. To have what you gave me. To see again your baby smile. To be there when you took your first step, to walk you to school that very first day, to feel your little hand holding so tight to mine.

Right now, I want only to burn this book. To destroy it, so that you will never know what I really was. But I will not destroy it. And someday soon, you will know the truth about me. Coward to the end, though, I will ask you not to read it until I am gone.

And I know that you will do what I ask. You had your hell-raiser days, and I know that lately, things have been real tough for you. But to me, you have always been a good son. The best son. So much more than I ever deserved.

And please. Do not go looking for Blake. Only bad things happen where Blake Bravo is. Go to your real family. In Los Angeles. I think it will be easy to find them. They were rich, as I already mentioned, rich and well-known in southern California. Your father was Harry Bravo. Your mother was Blythe. Your brother, that little boy who almost died trying to save you, was Jonas. They lived in Bel Air. In a beautiful house on a hill. A house they called Angel's Crest.

Go to them, Dekker. Show them this book. Tell them who you are. You are Russell Bravo, the one the newspapers called The Bravo Baby all those years ago.

Chapter 24

Dekker remained in Los Angeles until Friday. Jonas rearranged his work schedule as much as possible in order to spend all the time he could with his brother. They stayed up late into the night both Wednesday and Thursday, trying their level best to fill each other in on the last thirty years.

Dekker met Mandy. And he asked where Emma was.

"Emma has decided that I need some time away from her."

"Why?"

"That was *my* question."

"And?"

"It's a very long story."

"I've got the time—if you're willing to tell it."

So Jonas told Dekker about Blythe's will, about the marriage that had been undertaken, in the first place, for Mandy's sake. "Emma was determined to make me a better man."

"And did she?"

"Damn right. She made me a better man and then decided I couldn't possibly know my own mind when it came to our marriage."

Dekker asked, "So what are you going to do?"

"As of now, I'm in a holding pattern."

"Waiting for…?"

"I don't know. Some new approach to come to me. So far, I can think of two. One entails force, the other calls for begging."

"Not great options."

"That's why I'm in a holding pattern."

Jonas heard all about the Tilly girls, how DeDe, the middle sister, had been a rebellious teenager, but had really settled down the past year or two. Now, she was in love and getting married that very Saturday. He said that thirteen-year-old Niki had caused her share of trouble, too. And that Joleen, the oldest of the three, was the best friend a man could ever have, the solid, dependable sister who'd only made one mistake—falling for a rich SOB who knocked her up and left her flat.

Jonas said, "I think I saw her little boy."

"Sam?"

"That's the name. Looks like a great kid."

"He is. The best."

Dekker wanted to hear about Blythe. Jonas told him. About her breakdown, her recovery, her big heart and her determination to save the world.

"She sounds like a damn saint," Dekker said.

"Far from it—though the tabloids sometimes called her the Angel of Angel's Crest. Did I mention her passion for decorating?"

"No, you left that out."

"She'd no sooner get one room completely redone

than she'd start on another one. I think she changed everything in this house at least four times over before I was twenty. It drove me nuts. It seemed as if we spent our lives tripping over painters and paperhangers.''

"But you miss her, now she's gone.''

"Yes. I do. More than I can tell you.''

"I wish...I had known her.''

"And she would have given anything, to have found you before she died.''

Thursday night, Dekker said he'd decided he would change his last name to Bravo. "What is 'Smith' to me? It's just a name on a forged—or possibly stolen—birth certificate. I'm keeping Dekker, though. I'm just plain too used to it, if you want to know the truth.''

Friday afternoon, Jonas and Dekker paid a visit to McAllister, Quinn and Associates. Their meeting with Ambrose McAllister took three and a half hours. They turned over the diamonds, Blake's trophy book and Lorraine's diary. Ambrose would be contacting the authorities. As the family lawyer, it fell to him to explain how, after three decades, The Bravo Baby had come home at last.

There was also the little matter of Russell's inheritance. Blythe had never let go of the hope that someday her younger son might be found. Arrangements had been made for him. Dekker Smith was now a multimillionaire.

"I think I need a beer,'' Dekker said when they got out to the street again and were ducking into the waiting car.

They went back to Angel's Crest together and raised a couple of tall ones. After that, there was time for a meal, and then Dekker wanted to leave for the airport. He had to get back to Oklahoma City. He'd promised to be at DeDe's wedding the next day. In fact, he'd agreed to give the bride away. Jonas had already tried to talk him into taking one of the Bravo jets. But Dekker insisted that a commercial flight would do just fine.

After they'd eaten, Jonas walked Dekker out to his rental car, which one of the drivers had brought around and parked in front.

"We still have a lot to talk about," Jonas advised. "Come back as soon as you can swing it."

Dekker said that he would.

"And give Marsh a call when you get a chance." Jonas had already provided his brother with their cousin's address and phone number. "It would mean the world to him, to hear from you."

"I'll do that," Dekker promised. "And listen. Tell that wife of yours that your brother says hi. That day at my office, she seemed more determined to get through to me than you were. So I want her to know that I came to my senses."

Jonas nodded, hoping that would be the end of that particular subject.

But Dekker had no intention of stopping there. "I think, as a matter of fact, that you ought to tell her right away."

"Oh, do you?"

"Yeah. I do."

"Is that some kind of challenge?"

"You bet it is. Go get her, big brother."

"I thought I explained—"

"Forget what you explained. You love the woman, right?"

Jonas fell back a step, then shrugged. "Right."

"And she loves you?"

"That's what she says."

"Do you *believe* that she loves you?" Dekker asked with great patience.

"Yes. All right. I believe that she loves me."

"Then go get her, damn it. Right now. Tonight. Give her my message. Make her understand that you know your own damn mind and you *are* in love with her. Beg if you have to." He chuckled. "I'd skip using force, though."

"Get in the car. You'll be late for your flight."

"Do it, big brother."

"All right, damn it. I will."

Chapter 25

Twilight had spun out banners of purple across the darkening sky when Jonas reached Emma's North Hollywood duplex. The Santa Anas had died down, though the acrid smell of fire lingered, faint, but recognizable, on the evening air.

Light bled through the bedroom window he strode past on the way to her door. He took that as a sign that she would be home. When he rang the bell, he heard the Yorkies barking. They were pacing around her ankles when she answered.

He glanced down at the dogs and saw that she was wearing polka-dot polish on her toes—red with little dots of white. His gaze moved upward, over long naked legs, red shorts and about a half of a T-shirt—the thing ended underneath her breasts, leaving a smooth expanse of stomach for him to admire.

"Jonas." His name on her lips was a plea.

He looked in her eyes, then. Saw it all. Right there.

In her beautiful face. How much she had missed him. How bad it had been for her. And how damn glad she was to find him at her door.

He said, "You were right about a lot things. But you were wrong about leaving me."

She caught her lower lip between her pretty white not-quite-perfect teeth. "Oh, Jonas. I just wanted...I needed...for you to be sure."

"I *am* sure. Let me in."

She gripped the edge of the door. "Well, I don't know if—"

"Let me in, Emma. Let me in, now."

Her smooth throat moved as she swallowed. For one bleak and awful second, he thought she might refuse.

But then she stepped back. And he stepped forward. He pushed the door shut behind him.

"My brother said to tell you hi."

"You mean...?"

"Yes. He came to see me. He knows now that he's a Bravo."

"Oh, Jonas. I am so glad. It's all worked out, hasn't it? Just perfectly."

"Not quite, it hasn't."

Right then, one of the Yorkies whined in happiness. He knelt and greeted them, then snapped his fingers. They trotted off.

He stood again. "They missed me."

He watched those full breasts move beneath that little bit of shirt as she sucked in a deep breath. "Uh. Yes. It looks like they did. They missed you...."

"Did *you* miss me, Emma?"

"Oh, Jonas..."

He repeated the question, with tenderness. "Emma. Did you miss me?"

She seemed to be having trouble looking at him. She looked at the wall over his right shoulder, at the ceiling, the curtains across the room and finally down at her feet, where she appeared to be studying those polka-dot toes.

"Uh-uh." He put his finger under her chin and made her meet his eyes. "I already know the answer. But I want to hear you say it, anyway."

"Oh. Well, I…"

He rubbed his thumb over her smooth and only slightly stubborn chin. She trembled. That pleased him.

He offered, "I'll even go first. I missed you. So much. You ripped my heart out, Emma, and you took it with you when you left."

She gave a small cry. "No. Jonas. That wasn't what I wanted."

"It was what you did. Now, did you miss me?"

"Oh, please! You know that I missed you. Every day without you has been—"

"Empty?" he suggested. "Gray? Ugly? Sad?"

"Yes," she said angrily. "That's right. All those words. Exactly right."

"Then why the hell did you leave?"

She put up both hands, then dropped them to her sides again. "Because I really thought it was the right thing. To set you free. Aunt Cass used to say, 'If you love somebody, you have to be able to set them free.'" She must have read the look on his face. She scowled. "Well, all right. Maybe Sting said it first, but Aunt Cass said it, too."

"I don't give a damn who said it. It doesn't apply when the somebody you love has no desire to get away from you."

"But I thought—"

"Don't say it. I know what you thought. And you were wrong."

"But—"

"Emma. In this, you were very, very wrong."

She said nothing. Her sweet mouth was quivering.

He said, "I love you, Emma Lynn Hewitt Bravo. I love you and I miss you and I want you home with me. I want you to put your wedding ring back on and I want to tear up that damn prenuptial agreement I made you sign and I want us to spend the rest of our lives side by side."

She let out another cry.

He elaborated. "If I die, I want you to have everything that was mine. Understand? I want us to have kids, Emma. Nieces and nephews for Mandy to grow up with. I want—"

"Stop." She threw her arms around him. "It's enough. You got me." She rained kisses on his jaw, his neck, his chin. "And no more talk about dyin', Jonas Bravo. I want you alive."

He put his hands on her waist and slid them down, until he had a good grip on her round bottom. He lifted her. She jumped up to him eagerly, wrapping those gorgeous legs around him. He started walking toward the hallway, turning down it once he reached it. "Which one is your bedroom?"

She laughed. "I thought you said we were going home."

"We are. In a few minutes. This won't take long. Which way?"

He went where she pointed. Into a yellow room with a white bed and white curtains on the windows. He laid her down and quickly dispensed with her clothes.

She held out her arms to him.

But before he went into them, he reached in a pocket and took out her wedding ring. He slipped it back on her hand where it belonged.

"Never leave me again."

"Never," she vowed, and lifted her soft lips to receive his kiss.

Sometimes, in the years to come, Jonas would wake in the night and turn his head and see his wife sleeping at his side. He would remember the dream that had haunted him for thirty years, the dream that had carried the clue that had led him to find his lost brother at last. He would remember the man he had been before he knew Emma, and he would feel pride at what he had become, through her guidance and her wisdom and her love.

And he would know gratitude.

Not only to his wife, but to the women who had shaped her. To a west Texas waitress named Cassandra Hewitt. And to Blythe, who on her deathbed had seen to it that he got his chance with Emma, whether he thought that he wanted that chance or not.

He was a fortunate man. And not because of his billions. Because when he woke in the morning, he did not wake alone. When he climbed the stairs at night, it was with Emma at his side. Her love was his fortune.

He was the richest man alive.

SILHOUETTE *Romance*™

Escape to a place where a kiss is still a kiss...
Feel the breathless connection...
Fall in love as though it were
the very first time...
Experience the power of love!

Come to where favorite authors——such as
Diana Palmer, Stella Bagwell,
Marie Ferrarella and many more——
deliver heart-warming romance and genuine
emotion, time after time after time....

Silhouette Romance——
stories straight from the heart!

Silhouette®
Where love comes alive™

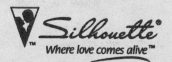

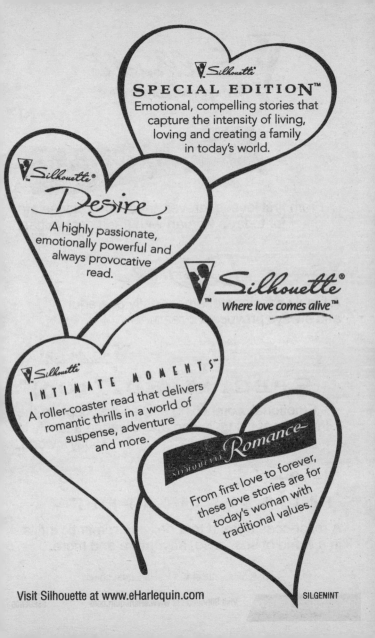

Silhouette

SPECIAL EDITION™
Emotional, compelling stories that capture the intensity of living, loving and creating a family in today's world.

Silhouette®

Desire
A highly passionate, emotionally powerful and always provocative read.

Silhouette®
Where love comes alive™

Silhouette

INTIMATE MOMENTS™
A roller-coaster read that delivers romantic thrills in a world of suspense, adventure and more.

Silhouette Romance
From first love to forever, these love stories are for today's woman with traditional values.

SILGENINT

Where love comes alive™

From first love to forever, these love stories are
for today's woman with traditional values.

A highly passionate, emotionally powerful
and always provocative read.

SPECIAL EDITION™

Emotional, compelling stories that capture the
intensity of living, loving and creating a family in
today's world.

INTIMATE MOMENTS™

A roller-coaster read that delivers romantic thrills
in a world of suspense, adventure and more.

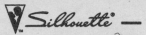